CATHERINE CAVENDISH

THE GARDEN OF BEWITCHMENT

This is a **FLAME TREE PRESS** book

Text copyright © 2020 Catherine Cavendish

FLAME TREE PRESS
6 Melbray Mews, London, SW6 3NS, UK
flametreepress.com

Distribution and warehouse:
Baker & Taylor Publisher Services (BTPS)
30 Amberwood Parkway, Ashland, OH 44805
btpubservices.com

Thanks to the Flame Tree Press team, including:
Taylor Bentley, Frances Bodiam, Federica Ciaravella, Don D'Auria, Chris Herbert, Josie Karani, Molly Rosevear, Will Rough, Mike Spender, Cat Taylor, Maria Tissot, Nick Wells, Gillian Whitaker.

The cover is created by Flame Tree Studio with thanks to Nik Keevil and Shutterstock.com.
The font families used are Avenir and Bembo.

Flame Tree Press is an imprint of Flame Tree Publishing Ltd
flametreepublishing.com

A copy of the CIP data for this book is available from the British Library and the Library of Congress.

HB ISBN: 978-1-78758-341-2
PB ISBN: 978-1-78758-339-9
ebook ISBN: 978-1-78758-342-9

Printed in the UK at Clays, Suffolk

CATHERINE CAVENDISH

THE GARDEN OF BEWITCHMENT

FLAME TREE PRESS
London & New York

For Colin, without whom…

CHAPTER ONE

1893

Lady Mandolyne saw it first.

She heard it on the breeze that fluttered the leaves. Saw it in the clouds, ghosted silver by the full moon. The change bringing whispering and a taste of danger. It came to her in the gathering storm as the clouds faded to gray black and rain fell in an icy shower that chilled and stung her face and arms.

On a cold November night.

When she went mad.

Evelyn Wainwright tapped her teeth with the wire-framed reading spectacles she habitually wore on a thin gold chain around her neck. Sitting opposite her, Claire, her twin sister, fidgeted nervously.

"Well?" she asked. "What do you think of it?"

Evelyn liked keeping her sister waiting. Not that she used it to exert her authority over her shy sibling. Naturally, no such thought ever crossed her mind. Not even for a moment. She counted the seconds as the clock ticked them away on the mantelpiece. Eleven... twelve...thirteen...

"I think it has possibilities, Claire. Of course we can't put our *Chronicles of Calladocia* in the same category as the Brontës' sagas of Northangerland and Glass Town, but then, who could rival them? Their spark, their creativity—"

"But, Ev—"

A flash from Evelyn's dark brown eyes chastened Claire. She lowered her head and mumbled into her lap. "Sorry. I didn't mean to interrupt."

Evelyn folded the neatly written pages of their combined work and pushed her chair back from the table. She stood, smoothing out imaginary wrinkles in her dress. She simply could not abide untidiness, whether of person or home. Evelyn's clothes were always neatly pressed; creases would not dare make an appearance. Claire on the other hand…

Evelyn leaned on the table. "Now your task for today is to decide what – or who – it is that scares Lady Mandolyne so much."

Claire's face broke into a broad smile. "Oh, but I already know. I wonder if you can guess."

Evelyn bit back the annoyance that always rose within her when her sister tried to be enigmatic. It never worked. She hadn't the cunning for it.

"If I knew, Claire, I wouldn't be asking you, would I? So tell me, what is this creeping menace?"

"The ghost of Branwell Brontë."

Evelyn slammed her fist down on the table so hard the top of the inkwell flew open and the pen fell out, splattering her writing tablet with a spreading violet-blue puddle.

Claire jumped up. "Oh, Ev. It's going to leave a terrible stain."

"Never mind that now. How many times have we had this same conversation, Claire? You cannot put real people into the story. Branwell Brontë – may his poor tortured soul rest in peace – is lying peacefully in his grave in Haworth. You cannot resurrect his ghost and have it wandering all over Calladocia. Fact and fiction do not mix. Now let this be an end of it. Come up with another menace but leave poor Mr. Brontë out of it. Now let's get this mess cleaned up. Go and fetch a cloth."

Evelyn couldn't look at Claire's face. She knew it would be screwed up, all ready to erupt in floods of tears.

"Oh, Ev." Claire ran out of the room, sobbing.

Evelyn raised her eyes to heaven. "Lord, give me strength to deal with my sister. What am I to do with her? Sometimes I think she was born simple, but she can write so well when the fancy takes her. If only she would stop this futile obsession with Branwell Brontë. Thank goodness she was too young ever to have met him, else goodness alone knows what trouble she would have found herself in at his hands." She didn't add 'if she had met him'. Evelyn knew only too well that their close proximity to Haworth and Branwell's well-documented habit of frequenting every hostelry in every town and village between Halifax and his home there meant her besotted twin would have ensured a meeting took place. She would even have overcome her chronic shyness.

But Branwell was in his grave before the sisters were even conceived. In 1848 he had succumbed to the excesses of opiates and alcohol at the tender age of thirty one – four years younger than Evelyn and Claire were today. That was forty-five years ago, and now none of the prodigiously talented Brontë family remained.

Evelyn sighed and strolled over to the window. Outside, the usual bustle of the busy street rushed by her gaze. Horses and carts, the occasional fancy carriage and pair. Neighbors walking by, some catching her gaze and quickly averting their eyes.

Neighbors. That was why they had to leave this place. So many prying eyes. So many people who thought the sisters' own private business was theirs to gawp and gossip over. Jealousy. That was all it was. All it ever had been. Their father had been a canny businessman. He had made a lot of money selling off fields for property development to feed the ever-expanding needs of the prosperous town of Sugden Heath in the West Riding of Yorkshire. He had no sons, so it stood to reason he would leave all his land and wealth to his twin daughters. Evelyn permitted herself a little smile, just as old Mrs. Entwhistle waddled past. The woman scowled at her and shook her head so vigorously her hat was in danger of blowing off. She crammed it on her head, and a surge of giggles left Evelyn helpless. So what if the woman saw her? Evelyn reckoned the old biddy and she held mutual levels of dislike for each other.

In Sugden Heath, a woman's role was to be a traditional wife and mother, subservient to her husband in all things, and certainly, if the woman found herself to be unmarried at the age of thirty-five, there should be nothing to laugh about. She should be pitied for the poor old spinster she had become. She should dress in black, with lace shawls, and sit and crochet. On Sundays she should make her way meekly to church, clutching her prayer book and, for the rest of the week, should busy herself with good works.

Evelyn didn't fit the mold – and neither did her sister.

She turned away from the window as Claire entered the room, cloth in hand. She began to dab at the ink stain to no great effect.

"I'm sorry, Ev," she said.

Evelyn waved her hand in a dismissive gesture. She sat back down at the table, positioned her spectacles carefully on her nose, tucking the wire behind her ears. Giving up on the stain, Claire resumed her seat opposite her. She placed her writing tablet over it. Out of sight, out of mind.

"Mrs. Entwhistle was out and about again," Evelyn said, picking up the current day's edition of the *Yorkshire Post*.

"Did she see you?"

Evelyn smiled. "Oh, yes. I got the disapproving look."

"The one where her face screws up and her chins wobble?"

Evelyn laughed. "That's the one. I shan't be sad to see the last of her."

"In a way, I'll be sad to leave here, though. It's been our home all our lives."

Evelyn laid her hand over Claire's. "But you do see it's the right thing to do, don't you? You know we can't stay here. Not after...after Father's death. They'll never leave us alone. You do understand, don't you, Claire? I wouldn't uproot us if there wasn't a good reason."

Claire shook her head, a tear at the corner of her eye. *Oh, please, God, not the waterworks again,* Evelyn thought. "No, I do understand, honestly, I do. I just wish it wasn't necessary and that if we have to go we could move to Haworth."

Evelyn retrieved her hand and sighed. Yet another subject as worn out as their old servant's knees. "Claire. You know how you shrink away from the window every time anyone walks by. You keep your bedroom curtains closed all day, as well as all night, and you won't go out unless I virtually throw you out of the door. You saw how busy Haworth was when we last visited there. The Brontë Society will be establishing their museum in the center of the village as soon as they find suitable premises, and the place is already brimful of visitors gawping through windows and pestering any resident they think might be old enough to have actually met one of the family. You wouldn't last a week there. All those people trampling over the flower beds and peering through at you. No, Claire. We'll find a nice cottage. Somewhere secluded. Not too far from Haworth and right on the moors. Then we'll have our privacy and the countryside we both love so much."

Claire managed the faintest of smiles, barely raising the corners of her lips.

Evelyn resumed her reading of the property advertisements. She tapped the page. "Here's one. It sounds perfect. Thornton Wensley, on a private lane leading to moorland. Two bedrooms, pleasant aspects to front and rear. Better still, it's in our price range. What do you think?"

Claire hesitated. "It sounds fine. I'm sure it will be...fine."

"That's settled then. I will call the property agents in the morning and arrange for us to visit it. If it's suitable, you'll be close to Haworth but without its disadvantages."

"Yes, I can see that."

"There's a station at Thornton Wensley, and it's on the track to Haworth. We can visit whenever you want."

At last, Evelyn was rewarded by a smile that actually looked as if some effort had been expended. She might as well mention the one drawback now. It seemed as good a time as any. "Of course, Nancy won't be able to come with us. There'll be no room, and it's too far for her to travel every day. I'm quite sure we'll be able to find a daily woman from the village to cook and clean for us."

To Evelyn's surprise, Claire shrugged. "I don't like Nancy very much. She can be very cruel when you're not around."

"This is the first I've heard of it. What has she done to you?"

A frown passed over Claire's face. "Oh, it doesn't matter now. If she won't be staying with us, I would rather forget about it."

"You can tell me, you know. If she has laid a finger on you to harm you in any way—"

"Oh, no. It's nothing like that. I meant sometimes she says some hurtful things."

"Nancy is getting on in years. I have noticed she has become a little forgetful of late. Perhaps it's time she retired anyway."

"Yes," Claire said, and Evelyn wondered why she sounded so emphatic.

★   ★   ★

"I am quite sure you would be very happy here. Heather Cottage, as you can see, is built of local millstone grit, and the walls are a good eighteen inches thick, so no need to worry about those fierce moorland gales getting in through the cracks. There aren't any." The estate agent smiled and unlocked the door to the cottage. Gesturing for Evelyn to enter, he stood back, enabling her to pass him. As she crossed the threshold, she had the strangest feeling of having been there before. She hesitated.

"Are you all right, Miss Wainwright? You have turned a little pale."

She shrugged the odd sensation off. "I am perfectly well, thank you. Just a little…indigestion…I think."

The smell of fresh paint wafted under her nostrils. "Someone has been busy, I see." She indicated the newly decorated walls and skirting boards.

"Yes, the owner was most concerned that everything should be pristine."

"Precisely how I like it." She smiled, masking another odd fluttering feeling in her stomach. She wished Claire had come with her. It felt wrong not to have her sister along when such an important decision needed to be made. Maybe she could make another appointment to view? But Claire would probably back out of that one at the last moment, as she had on this occasion.

A movement outside the window attracted her attention.

A tall man, dressed in a Norfolk jacket, trousers and sturdy walking boots, was making his way up the lane toward the moor. He took his time and progressed with a slight but noticeable limp. Judging by his tight-lipped expression, the effort pained him more than a little. He moved slowly, enough for Evelyn to take in his features. A flat cap shielded his eyes but revealed dark brown hair. The man was clean-shaven and, from the cut of his clothes, not short of money. As he went by, he caught her watching him and tipped his hat to her. His smile showed even, white teeth. Evelyn acknowledged his gesture with a slight nod, and the moment had passed. The man continued on his labored way, although she was certain he limped less. He probably did not want her to think him crippled. Although why should it matter to him? Something niggled her about the man. Did she know him? If so, she couldn't think from where. But still, there was something…

"Miss Wainwright?" The estate agent had been speaking to her, and she hadn't registered a word of what he'd said.

"We'll take it. The cottage. *This* cottage. We'll buy it."

The agent looked as if he couldn't believe his luck. He recovered himself, determined, no doubt, to get her out of here and ready to sign all the necessary papers before she had a chance to change her mind. On the way back to Sugden Heath, she remembered she hadn't even seen the upstairs rooms. And Claire had seen none of it.

★ ★ ★

Evelyn shielded her eyes from the sun as she stared up at the cottage. Next to her, Claire seemed jumpy. She kept glancing this way and that as if scared someone might see her.

"Oh, come on, Ev, open the door."

"All right, Claire. Give me a chance." Evelyn fumbled in her purse and found her key. She unlocked the door. "See how pretty it is inside. You're going to love it."

Claire took a few uncertain steps before joining her sister in the house. Evelyn led her down the short hall and opened the door of the living room. Sunlight streamed through the mullioned windows with their small, square panes. The polished wooden floor gleamed, and a smell of beeswax and lavender hung in the air, replacing the paint smell of a few weeks earlier and filling the area with a welcoming, homely aroma.

Claire circumnavigated the room, touching the substantial fabric of the green velvet curtains. Her eyes met Evelyn's. Full of uncertainty. "Are you sure this is right for us?"

"Quite sure. Oh, I know it looks a bit bare now," Evelyn said, "but just imagine how it will be when we have our own pretty things in here. The table can go here." Evelyn stood in the center of the room. "And over there," she said, pointing to the wall behind Claire, "our bookcases. It will be perfect. Now, let me show you the dining room."

With a swish of her skirt, Evelyn left the room and crossed the hall. More sunlight cast rays of brilliant light over a room emptier than the one they had just left. This one had no curtains. "I thought Mama's red taffeta with the ivory valances would fit nicely in here, and the dining room table will look lovely. The cherrywood will blend perfectly. What do you think?"

Claire stared all around her, eyes wide. She sighed. "I suppose we can make it our own."

Evelyn put her hands on her sister's shoulders. "There, you see, Claire? I told you everything would be fine. Just the two of us. Away from prying eyes and nosy servants."

"I thought we were getting a daily woman from the village."

"Do you really think we need one? I feel we could manage perfectly well by ourselves."

Claire looked as if her sister had threatened her with a bullet. "But we've never managed on our own. I wouldn't have the first idea how to lay up a fire or use a cooking range, would you?"

"No, not yet. But we are young enough to learn these things. And won't it be so much better than having to watch what we say in front of servants?"

"It never bothered you with Nancy."

"We inherited her from Mama and Father. She was always... well...there."

"No escaping her." Claire's mouth curled in an ugly grimace.

Why did she hate Nancy so?

"Let's get back. We have packing to do, and, of course, I have yet to tell Nancy her services will no longer be required. Where will she go, do you think?"

"Why would I care?" Claire turned her back and left Evelyn wondering.

★   ★   ★

Back at the house in Sugden Heath, Evelyn summoned Nancy to the drawing room. As the elderly woman shuffled in, Evelyn wondered when she had grown so old. Nancy had always been Nancy. Ageless and as much a part of the fixtures and fittings of the place as the chaise longue Evelyn sat on now.

Nancy raised pale blue eyes to her mistress.

"You sent for me, miss?"

"Yes, Nancy. I'm afraid I have some bad news for you."

The woman blinked, and for the first time, Evelyn caught a glimpse of something unpleasant behind those eyes. Something Claire must have sensed or witnessed.

The woman folded her arms. "Bad news, miss? What sort of bad news?"

Evelyn swallowed. "Since our father died, my sister and I have become increasingly uncomfortable in this house. It's too large for the two of us, and the upkeep is expensive."

"Is it, miss? I understood the master had left you comfortably provided for."

Impertinent. Servants weren't supposed to challenge their employers, and her tone and demeanor screamed just that, while her expression had transformed into a look of defiance.

"Nancy, I know you have been with this family for many years."

"More than forty. Since the master and mistress were first married."

Did she honestly think this gave her more right to be here than she and Claire? Evelyn moved on swiftly. "You have given valiant service through all those years, but now, I'm afraid, it is time to go our separate ways. I would imagine you have a little put by for your retirement?" Her father had never been a stingy employer, and all Nancy's needs had been provided for as part of her room and board, which left the wages she earned mostly for herself.

Nancy nodded. She seemed to have been expecting this conversation. Certainly she showed no sign of shock. No quiet resignation to her inevitable fate either.

Evelyn took a deep breath. "Is there something you would like to say to me, Nancy?"

"Not particularly, miss. I do, as you say, have a little put by, and I have a sister in Bradford who has always said she will take me in if I was left in this situation."

Evelyn realized she had never even known Nancy had a sister. She knew nothing about this woman who had lived with them all her life. How old was this sister? Nancy must be getting on for eighty if she was a day. She dismissed the thought. None of her business, after all.

"Then it is time for you to take a well-earned rest, Nancy. Miss Claire and I will be moving to a cottage in Thornton Wensley in a few weeks' time. Hopefully this will give you enough time to sort out things with your sister."

"Oh, I don't need weeks, miss. I can leave tomorrow. Today, if you prefer."

"What? No. No, there's no need."

"I would prefer it, miss. If you don't mind."

"But why, Nancy? Have you not been happy here?"

"Not really, miss. Not for a long time, if I'm being truthful."

"When did that happen?"

"After the mistress died, it became more…difficult. The master didn't want to have anything to do with the domestic side of things.

Then one by one the staff left and weren't replaced, until it was just me doing everything. Oh, I didn't mind that so much. I've always been a hard worker, but I found it difficult to…to…"

For the first time in this awkward interview, Nancy was clearly nonplussed. The feeling was infectious. Evelyn fought to retain her composure. She had not expected this reaction at all.

"Please help me understand, Nancy. Has there been some friction between you and my sister, perhaps?"

Nancy flashed her a look Evelyn struggled to comprehend. The older woman stared down at her hands and clasped them, as if taking comfort in the physical contact.

"I would really rather not say," she said at last.

"I don't understand. Why not? Nancy, if something has been troubling you, I need to know. Have I done something to upset you?"

Nancy continued to inspect her folded hands. Evelyn waited, her impatience mounting. What on earth was the matter with the woman? The cook didn't usually find herself lost for words.

She would wait no longer. "Nancy?"

The woman met her gaze. "I would rather not go into it, if you don't mind. I'm sure everything will work itself out now. I shall be happy with my sister and you… Thornton Wensley, you said?"

"Yes." Why wouldn't the cook tell her what was on her mind? She couldn't force it out of her, although, right now, Evelyn wished she could. "I am most concerned. Something has clearly troubled you, and I can't help feeling it is connected in some way with either myself or my sister. Why won't you tell me?"

Nancy shrugged and shook her head. "I'm sorry, miss. I would rather not say any more. I'll pack my bags and be gone in the morning. I'll make sure everything is tidy, clean and all the laundry's up to date. The baking is all done, and there's plenty of food in the pantry to keep you going."

Without waiting to be dismissed, Nancy turned on her heel and limped out of the room, leaving Evelyn too stunned to protest.

At dinner, Evelyn waited until the cook had left them alone with the main course before she challenged her sister. "Has something happened between you and Nancy? The woman can hardly leave here fast enough."

Claire shrugged and concentrated on her steak and kidney pudding.

"Really, Claire, you can do better than that. Have you had a falling-out? An argument?"

Claire shook her head, indicating her mouth was too full to speak.

Evelyn waited until she swallowed. Claire loaded up her fork, ready to take another mouthful. "No, Claire, please answer me."

Claire put her fork down and studied it for a moment. She looked up. "I have never said a cross word to Nancy. She just hates me for some reason. I don't understand it, and I don't like it, but what can I do? I am always civil to her, and she repays me with hostility and rudeness. Sometimes she simply ignores me. Other times she looks at me as if I'm... oh, I don't know...something she would like to scrape off her shoe."

"*Claire!*" Evelyn had never heard her sister speak so disrespectfully of anyone before.

"I'm sorry, Ev, but it's how she makes me feel. I'm glad she's going. When will we be rid of her?"

"By her own request, she leaves tomorrow after breakfast. She'll be staying with her sister in Bradford."

"What sister?"

"Ah, so I'm not the only one who has been so neglectful as to not know a simple fact like that about a servant of such long standing."

"I didn't know she had any family."

"Nor did I, but apparently she has, so that's a good thing."

"You don't need to feel guilty, Ev, and I certainly shan't." Claire resumed her meal by devouring the contents of her fork.

Evelyn didn't reply but watched as her sister stabbed one small new potato after another, for all the world as if she were stabbing Nancy herself. Goosebumps rose on her neck. At this moment, she was relieved she wasn't the one being targeted by her sister's wrath.

CHAPTER TWO

"Come and see my room, Ev. I've done it up now and it looks so pretty."

Evelyn followed Claire at the gallop, from the newly rechristened drawing room, up a flight of stairs to her sister's bedroom. Situated at the back of the cottage, the bedrooms looked directly out over the heather-clad moors, rising up ahead of them and stretching, on a clear day such as this, as far as the horizon. In late summer, these would blossom into a purple carpet, covering the land as far as the eye could see. Sweet, fresh air drifted in through the partially open window, ruffling the floral-patterned curtains. The single bed was covered in a chintzy-looking bedspread embroidered by Claire herself over many winter nights, and the plain oak wardrobe and dressing table, with its long mirror and padded stool, completed the simple but charming effect.

"Such a comfortable room, and what a view," Evelyn said, smiling in admiration.

"Your room looks lovely too. A bit more formal than mine, but lovely just the same."

Evelyn knew Claire's tastes didn't extend to deep-blue velvet in the bedroom, but Evelyn preferred to sleep in a dark room, whereas her sister liked to be woken by the first rays of a new dawn stroking her forehead. Dear Claire, so passionate and romantic. Evelyn glanced up at the wall. A framed print hung over the small mantel. A familiar figure. Branwell Brontë.

"I couldn't leave him behind, could I? Besides, the new owners wouldn't have wanted him. They probably didn't even know who he was."

"Probably. They didn't strike me as great readers." Evelyn strolled over to take a closer look. The familiar profile, etched in black. A deprecating self-portrait where the artist had deliberately exaggerated his long nose and unkempt hair. Not the most flattering of pictures, but, if Claire wanted it in her room, why not? What was the harm?

"He will inspire me to write more adventures of Calladocia," Claire said.

"Good. I've been thinking it's about time we resumed our tales. Poor Lady Mandolyne has been waiting to find out what threatens her in the mist for quite long enough."

Claire laughed. "I'm quite sure I know just what it is, and before you say anything, no, it's not Branwell, but I have him to thank for it."

"How?"

"He told me, but I'm sworn to secrecy until I get it all down on paper. You'll have to wait."

Evelyn tried to read what was in her sister's eyes and failed. "Claire, you do realize Branwell Brontë is long dead and buried. He can't tell you anything. Besides, you never met him."

Claire gave a light laugh and put her finger to her lips. "I told you, I'm sworn to secrecy. You'll simply have to contain your curiosity until we reveal all."

"We?"

But Claire hadn't heard her, or chose not to. She had skipped out of the room like a young girl, excited to be playing with her next new toy.

Evelyn followed at a distance and watched her sister hitch up her skirt and trot down the stairs, humming to herself. What did go on in the girl's head sometimes? Evelyn shrugged and slowly descended, one measured step at a time.

★   ★   ★

Evelyn laid down her pen and read through her work. Seated at the opposite side of the table, Claire worked on, head lowered, pen scratching furiously for a minute or so, followed by a brief pause while she filled up its reservoir with ink.

"You look very thoughtful, Ev," she said. "Is something troubling you?"

Evelyn shook her head. "No. I wondered what you were writing. Are you ready to share it with me yet?" She almost added, "Or won't Branwell let you?" but bit her tongue instead.

Claire smiled. "Nearly. About another half hour or so and then all will be revealed."

Evelyn returned the smile and resumed her reading. She gave up after a couple of minutes. The sound of Claire's scratching pen seemed to grow louder until it overwhelmed every other sound in the room. The steadily ticking wall clock, its rhythmic pendulum that usually calmed and soothed her, but not today. Her work was no good. The story made no sense. Evelyn hoped Lady Mandolyne was faring better in Claire's hands than Sir Dreyfus Monroe in her own. Poor Sir Dreyfus, back from fighting in darkest Africa only to find his sweetheart married to the bounder, Lord Estival Drew-Cunningfort. Evelyn had seen him challenge the cad to a duel only for the little worm to wriggle out of it by pleading a prior engagement. The man had no honor and deserved all the insults Sir Dreyfus poured over him, but the fact remained – her hero had been cuckolded and must now try to rebuild his reputation and his life. The only problem was, Evelyn hadn't a clue how to set about it.

Unable to stand the sound of Claire's furious scribbling any longer, Evelyn pushed her chair back and stood. Claire had become so engrossed in her work she apparently didn't notice her sister staring at her. A stray lock of hair escaped its clip yet again, only to be tucked hurriedly and none too successfully behind her ear.

Evelyn sauntered over to the window. The lane – quiet, as usual. In the couple of weeks they had lived there, she had only ever seen a handful of people go past each day. Usually the same ones. There was no reason to go up this lane unless you inhabited one of the half dozen cottages. Granted the lane led up to the moors, but there were more obvious pathways to attract those wishing to take a stroll among the heather. So peaceful. So tranquil. Heather Cottage had to be the most perfect place she could have chosen. But then her stomach gave a strange flutter again. She hadn't felt it since the day she first set eyes on the house, but now it came back. Stronger than before and, with it, the strong sensation that maybe she hadn't chosen Heather Cottage at all.

Maybe it had chosen her.

Someone moved into her field of vision. That man. The one she had seen before. Dressed the same in his well-tailored Norfolk jacket. Once again, he caught her eye and tipped his hat to her, and she was struck by the recognition in his look. Yet, try as she might, she could think of no occasion when their paths might have crossed, apart from the last time he had walked past her cottage.

"There. It's done." Claire's sudden exclamation made Evelyn jump.

"You've finished the scene?"

"I have indeed. Listen. You'll like this. Maybe you will even love it."

Evelyn seated herself back at the table as Claire shuffled her papers. "Ready?" she asked, her eyes shining.

"Ready," Evelyn said, folding her hands on the table in front of her.

"Now you remember Lady Mandolyne had seen and heard something on the night she went mad? Well, here it is." Claire coughed.

She rose from her slumbers, her black hair flowing behind her in a wave. She stretched long, tapering fingers up to the moon, and her voice cried out to the creatures that stirred in the night. One by one they returned her call, until the one she had sensed emerged. The forest fell silent, save for one long, low howl that rose to a crescendo. Lady Mandolyne waited. Her heart beat wildly. He must come now, she begged.

Slowly the trees parted, revealing their secret. The howling died away. A figure emerged. Large, looming, its gray-black fur gleaming in the moonlight. Its eyes burned into her with orange fire.

Lady Mandolyne sighed, her voice no more than a breath. 'You have come at last.'

The creature bared its fangs, but Lady Mandolyne knew she had nothing to fear. The beast of the night was of her own creation. How could it possibly do her harm?

As if on cue, the animal padded towards her on soft paws. It stopped mere inches away from her flowing skirt. Slowly she bent and caressed the thick fur of its neck.

'Tonight, I shall run with you, Sir Aedwulf. We will take to the hills, cross the Titanium River, and we shall not stop until we reach Arcadia, or else die in the attempt.'

Claire stopped reading and laid her papers down.

"But there is more, surely?" Evelyn said. "You've been writing for hours."

"Oh, yes, there's more, but I thought I would share the part that really matters. The reason for Lady Mandolyne's madness. What do you think of it?"

Evelyn considered her words carefully. "I certainly like it. It will need a little…polishing…I think, but, on the whole, it's quite good. It doesn't tell us the reason for her madness, though. It gives us an example of it. An extreme example certainly. But we still don't know what turned her from a mild-mannered yet free spirit, into the madwoman she became. I think we need to discuss it and decide together."

Claire's face crumpled. "But Lady Mandolyne has always been my creation, Ev. You have Sir Dreyfus and his family, fellow soldiers and the like. I never tell you how to write *them*, do I?"

"No, that's true, you don't, but it doesn't stop me seeking your advice when I am getting stuck. In fact I need your help now. Poor Sir Dreyfus—"

"Oh, damn Sir Dreyfus." Claire clapped her hand to her mouth, her eyes wide in shock.

"*Claire!*" Evelyn slapped the table. "I never heard you use such language before."

Claire lowered her hand. "I am sorry, Ev. It slipped out. I felt so proud of that scene, and you obviously don't like it. You've dismissed it entirely."

"I have done no such thing. It's a fine scene. In its way. But we need a proper reason for Lady Mandolyne's insanity." Evelyn stood, her hands on her hips. "I think I need a break from Calladocia. I'm going for a walk."

"I think I shall remain here. Perhaps I too need a break. I shall read for a little."

"Very well."

⋆   ⋆   ⋆

As she closed the front door behind her, a little thrill shot up Evelyn's spine. What if she should encounter the stranger who had passed the cottage earlier? So, what if she did? She shook her head, annoyed with herself, then pulled her gloves a little farther up her arms and started up the lane.

"Good afternoon, Miss Wainwright." The elderly neighbors Evelyn knew as Mr. and Mrs. Skelton greeted her.

"Good afternoon. Pleasant weather." At least Mr. Skelton seemed calm today. When she had first met him, on the day she and Claire moved in, he had looked as if she had shot him. Extraordinary reaction.

"Indeed. A beautiful afternoon, especially up there." Mrs. Skelton pointed back at the moors. "We have had a lovely walk. The gorse is truly beautiful now."

"I shall look forward to seeing it."

"You can't miss it," Mr. Skelton said as he and his wife moved on, bound for home and a nice cup of tea, no doubt.

Her neighbor proved as good as his word. The golden gorse shrouded the moorland. Evelyn made steady progress in her stout walking shoes. Claire said they made her feet look huge, but Evelyn found them far more practical than the wooden pattens her sister wore over her shoes to keep her feet dry.

The breeze rustled the grasses and formed the only sound, save for a solitary curlew circling overhead, calling, maybe warning its young, nesting on the ground, not that they had anything to fear from her.

The sun warmed her face. Late spring. Evelyn's favorite time of the year. Claire preferred summer. But to Evelyn, the sight of fresh leaves, newly unfurled, the vibrant blossom after months of winter, filled her heart with happiness. Now, wandering alone on Wensley Moor, she felt alive, newly awakened, refreshed.

She climbed steadily, following the narrow footpath worn down by generations of people who had trodden this way before her. Within a few minutes, she had made it almost to the top of the hill, gazing down at the valley beneath. In the distance, Sugden Heath's mill chimneys belched thick gray smoke, fortunately far enough away that she could not smell it and, in turn, it couldn't leave its coat of grime over the heath. Directly below her lay farm cottages, rolling fields, some cultivating crops, others home to hardy sheep, their lambs already growing up.

It's so peaceful here.

She looked around her. Ahead, crags, like jagged teeth, rose up from the ground. Behind her, the path she had just climbed. She decided to ascend a little farther. The crags might provide somewhere she could sit and contemplate for a while.

Evelyn hauled herself up by holding on to a massive rock, its stone cold to her touch. All around it lay others, randomly scattered as if some giant had tossed them in the air like pebbles and then left them to lie where they fell.

She selected a flat-topped stone and sat down. Her resting place provided an excellent view of the surrounding countryside, this time unfettered by the mill town. She relaxed, in pleasant silence, watching the fluffy white clouds in the brilliant blue sky, hearing the curlew and smelling the fresh grass.

"Good afternoon, madam."

Startled, Evelyn put her hand to her throat. Her cheeks burned as she recognized the man from earlier. He tipped his cap to her and smiled. Now she could see his eyes, she saw they were deep brown. Kind eyes.

When he spoke, his voice held warmth and strength. She noted the walking stick. Surely he hadn't had that before.

"I am so sorry. I didn't mean to scare you, but I think I may have seen you earlier?"

"You walked past my cottage."

"I thought so. My name is Matthew Dixon." He held out his hand.

She touched it lightly with her gloved hand. "Evelyn Wainwright. Miss," she added.

"A pleasure to meet you, Miss Wainwright. Such a glorious day."

"It is indeed."

"My doctor tells me I must take exercise, and what better exercise is there than walking on these moors at this time of the year?"

"I quite agree." Could her responses be more stilted? She, who was never tongue-tied, now sounded like her sister, whose lack of social skills had long been a constant source of regret to Evelyn. She moistened her lips and tried. "Your doctor? You have been unwell, Mr. Dixon?"

"A skiing accident in Switzerland. Entirely my own fault. I managed to fall halfway down a mountain and injured several vertebrae. Put me completely out of action for three months, but I am recovering now. I had to learn to walk again. Hence this." He tapped the stick. "Although I hope to be rid of it soon. I started out this afternoon without it, but I had barely gone past your cottage when I realized what a mistake I had made, so I returned home and got it. With any luck before the autumn or, if I have my way, next week, I shall be able to consign it to the back of a cupboard for good." He grinned, and Evelyn smiled. "May I join you for a few minutes? I think I need a short rest before going back."

"By all means," Evelyn said, and her companion selected a flat stone opposite her. He eased himself down onto it. "That's better. Added to an excursion into Halifax this morning, I think I may have done a little too much walking today."

"Have you lived in Thornton Wensley long, Mr. Dixon?"

"I don't really live here at all. I am staying in my cousin's cottage for a few months to recuperate. My home is in Bradford, but my doctors agreed some fresh moorland air would be just the thing to get me back on my feet. I have only been here a short time, but I'm already feeling much stronger, so they're probably right. How about you, Miss Wainwright?"

"My sister and I moved here a few weeks ago. We lived in Sugden Heath but, following my father's death, decided the time had come for a change."

"So here we are."

"It would appear so, Mr. Dixon." His easy manner and ability to make her feel at ease in his company made her warm to this man. She liked the way he gazed out over the landscape, clearly appreciating the stunning scenery.

"God's own country, Yorkshire," he said at last. "My cousin who owns the cottage prefers the green rolling countryside of Wiltshire, but I find it altogether too pretty. Give me the raw, jagged crags, the marshes and the heather any day."

Evelyn smiled. Her thoughts exactly. "I love the way the wind whistles over the moor. Like someone sighing." Her companion nodded, and, out of the corner of her eye, she became aware of him gazing at her intently, as if he was trying to call on some distant memory that remained tantalizingly out of reach.

The sun disappeared behind a cloud, and a chill passed through her. "I think I will have to start back, Mr. Dixon," she said, getting to her feet. In an instant, he was there with a steadying hand, his leg apparently not troubling him as much after his rest. "Thank you," she said as she straightened. "It has been a pleasure to chat with you. I hope we may meet again." Her mother would not have approved of her being so forward. So what? He did not seem to mind.

"Undoubtedly we shall, Miss Wainwright. I am only a few doors away from you. Please don't hesitate to call on me if I can be of any help to you or your sister."

"Thank you. I shall remember that. Good day, Mr. Dixon."

He tipped his cap to her, and his smile sent a little thrill of excitement up her spine.

Was he watching her as she descended the steep footpath? She could feel someone's eyes on her. She mustn't turn around or give any indication she was aware of it. A scuffling sound. Someone walking close up behind her. She quickened her pace. Still she heard the footsteps growing ever closer. Getting louder and more urgent as she stumbled over loose stones and gravel. Her pace had quickened to a run, and breathing was becoming more difficult in her tight corset. Her heart beat faster too. She still had some distance to cover before she reached the lane and the safety of home.

Oh, this is ridiculous.

Evelyn stopped and spun around.

No one there. No sign of Matthew Dixon or anyone else. No footsteps. Only the sighing wind and the solitary curlew circling overhead. She wished with all her heart it could speak.

My imagination running away with me again. Yes, that was all. Altogether too much time spent on living with fictional characters in Calladocia. She smiled at herself and resumed her walk, at a much steadier pace. No more footsteps dogged her, and a few minutes later she arrived back at the cottage.

Claire looked up from the chaise longue and laid her book down. "Enjoy your walk?"

"Yes. I met one of our neighbors – a Mr. Matthew Dixon. He is staying here for a few months while he recuperates from a nasty accident."

"Oh? Is that why your cheeks are so pink?"

"Are they? I expect it's the sun. It was quite glorious up there on the moors until it clouded over. Still, it is quite early in the year, isn't it?"

"I suppose so." Claire picked up her book and flicked through a few pages.

Evelyn looked at her reflection in the mirror as she removed her hat, smoothing her hair. Claire was right. Her cheeks were pleasantly flushed, and as for her eyes... Weren't they a little brighter than usual? Good country air. Healthy. "You should get out more, Claire. You always stay inside. It's not good for you."

"I'm perfectly fine with my books and my writing. You're the outdoors, gregarious type. Not me."

"I'm not particularly gregarious."

"Really? You're out for half an hour and come back with a man in tow."

"Oh, nonsense, Claire. I was out for over an hour, and Mr. Dixon is not 'in tow'."

Claire made a harrumphing noise.

"If you weren't so obsessed with a dead wastrel, you might actually find the real world has something to offer you."

Claire threw down her book. "That's too much, Ev. Branwell was not a wastrel. None of his family understood him and expected far too much. Imagine growing up in a house full of women – none of whom were expecting to be married – and you knew your role was to fulfill everyone's expectations, be brilliantly successful and able to afford to keep the lot of them, as well as an aging father and yourself? The prospect's enough to drive anyone to drink."

Her sister's voice had been rising hysterically. "Calm down, Claire." Evelyn made a move toward her sister.

"I will *not* calm down. I am fed up with your snide remarks about Branwell. If you knew him as I do..." Her voice trailed off, and a horrified look spread across her face, matched, Evelyn knew, by her own.

"Claire, can't you see what's happening to you? This obsession of yours is out of hand. You don't know Branwell. You never met him. He was dead long before you were born. You must take hold of yourself. This is the real world, and the late Branwell Brontë has no place in it."

Claire's eyes stared at her out of her pinched white face. "You never understood and you never will. Oh, what's the point?" Claire charged out of the room, slammed the drawing room door so hard the pictures shook, and then stamped up the stairs. Another door slam told Evelyn her sister had closeted herself up in her bedroom. No doubt that would be it for the rest of the day.

★ ★ ★

Evelyn couldn't even tempt Claire downstairs to eat her favorite cottage pie, usually a meal Claire would never miss, even if she felt ill. Evelyn covered the pie dish with muslin and laid her sister's portion away in the cool of the pantry. She could eat it tomorrow.

She spent a quiet evening by the fire in a room that had turned chilly as the sun set. The glow of the oil lamps gave the room a cozy feel, and Evelyn exhaled as she put her feet up on her mother's velvet-covered footstool. Her earlier exertions had tired her more than she realized, and in a few minutes her eyes grew heavy and she dozed.

When she awoke, the fire had grown cold. She checked the time. Five minutes past midnight. With a massive yawn, she stood and picked up an oil lamp to light her way to bed.

At the foot of the stairs, her skin prickled. Voices. Coming from upstairs. One unmistakably Claire's. The other? Was Claire talking to herself? They both did on occasions, but something about this seemed different. Evelyn mounted the staircase. The voices grew louder. At the top of the stairs, she paused outside her sister's door. The voices had gone quiet now. She must have been imagining it. Or maybe the voices had drifted in from outside in the lane. Passersby on their way home from a visit to the public house perhaps.

Satisfied there was no one but her sister in her room, Evelyn took a step toward her own door, directly opposite.

She froze. That sound. A deep, resonant laugh.

A man's laugh. And it had come from Claire's room.

CHAPTER THREE

Claire loved her twin dearly, even if there were times she could cheerfully throttle her. And today had been one of those. So Ev had met a man she had taken a shine to. Maybe the man in question…what was his name? Matthew Dixon. Yes. A good, solid name. Nothing fancy. Perhaps her instant attraction to him had been reciprocated. Claire would have to get a look at him and make sure her sister wasn't going to make a fool out of herself. After all, she had no one, whereas Claire had…

Claire studied the print of Branwell in silhouette, which took pride of place on her wall. Life had been pretty dull until he had come into her life, and to think she just sort of stumbled over him. Riveted by Emily Brontë's *Wuthering Heights*, she had decided to find out all she could about the family. Mrs. Gaskell's detailed biography of Charlotte had provided an excellent starting point, although the author had been scathing about the only Brontë brother. Claire, ever the supporter of the underdog, had felt sorry for him at first, but, after that wonderful night…

She hugged the memory to her. If she closed her eyes she could see him, standing in her room at Sugden Heath, a glass of brandy in one hand and a cigar in the other. She could even smell the delicious aroma now. If she concentrated…

And then he had smiled at her, taken her hand. Music played from somewhere, and they danced. He held her closer than he should for a couple who had only just met and hadn't even been formally introduced. But it didn't matter. What did she and Branwell care for formality and outdated customs?

"Oh, Branwell," she breathed. "I wish you were here now. I hope you can find me."

"I would never lose you." His voice startled her. She peered around the room, which had grown quite dark. She must light a candle. There was one by her bed.

"Branwell?" She fumbled for the small vesta box, flipped it open and extracted a match, which she then struck. The phosphorous blazed brilliantly for a moment, illuminating his face, only for a second. Maybe not so long, but it was enough. Branwell. He had come back. Everything would be fine in her world now.

The candle flickered with every breath she took. "Branwell, are you still here?"

"I'm still here, my love."

She held the candle at arm's length, but she couldn't see him. "Where are you?"

A breath, like a kiss, caressed her cheek. "I am right here. Beside you."

She touched her cheek, feeling the cool spot. "I have missed you so much, Branwell."

"And I you, but I am here now."

"My sister doesn't believe me."

"Your sister has other matters in mind. She worries about you."

"She has met someone today. Maybe he'll be the one she marries."

"But not you, my little rose. You are mine."

"I know, Branwell. Aren't we lucky?"

"Yes."

Claire heard the creak of the stairs. "Ev's coming up. We'd better be quiet until she's safely tucked up in bed."

Branwell laughed.

"Shush, she'll hear you."

Claire held her breath. Her sister was outside her door. No, she had moved away. Stopped. She whispered to Branwell. "She heard you."

He whispered back. "What if she did?"

What if she did? He was right. At least she wouldn't be able to deny anymore. Maybe she should meet Branwell.

A soft click told Claire Ev had closed her bedroom door, hopefully with herself behind it.

"Branwell?"

Silence.

"Are you still there?"

Silence.

Claire lit a candle on her dressing table. It illuminated the other side of the room with a shadowy glow, but enough so she could see the empty space. Branwell had gone. A tear formed in the corner of her eye, and she brushed it away. "Oh, Branwell, why do our meetings have to be so short?"

No one answered her, but on the other side of the room, the candle flickered, sputtered and then went out. The smell of smoke drifted toward her, infused with a faint aroma of cigars.

★   ★   ★

"Who were you talking to last night?"

Claire stared past her sister, focusing on the drawing room wall behind her. She hated it when Ev questioned her like that. Her eyes bored into her, leaving nowhere to hide. She could try lying, but her sister would be on to her in an instant. Nothing else for it.

"Branwell." She held her breath, readying herself for the onslaught she felt sure would follow.

Her sister slammed down her cup so hard onto the saucer Claire braced herself for the shattering of china, but it somehow held together.

"Claire, this delusion of yours has to stop. You couldn't have been talking to Branwell. Were you talking to yourself?"

Claire bit her lip. "No. I told you. It was Branwell."

"And how did he get into your room? Did he knock at the door? I'm sure I heard no one and I would have. I sat downstairs the whole evening. Or maybe he shinned up the drainpipe."

"Now you're being ridiculous." Claire wished she could take her words back. Too late. They were out there, never to be retrieved.

"What did you say? Ridiculous, am I? May I remind you I

am not the one imagining herself to be communing with a ghost. I am not the one disguising her voice and talking to herself. And tell me, when did you take up smoking?"

"I don't smoke and I don't talk to myself. You heard Branwell last night. He smoked a cigar."

Evelyn stared at Claire as if a stranger sat there. Claire wished she could reassure her. Tell her some comforting lie, because at this moment her sister looked bewildered, as if she hadn't a clue what to do with her.

"I'm going out for a walk," Evelyn said. "Maybe some time alone will give us both a chance to think."

"Maybe you're right."

Claire washed up the breakfast dishes, her mind racing. How could she convince Ev every word was true? As she finished towel drying the crockery, she made the only possible decision she could.

Ev would have to see – or at least hear – Branwell for herself.

Claire folded the towel neatly over its rail and made her way up to her room. Once inside, she closed the door, seated herself at her dressing table and closed her eyes. She concentrated hard.

Branwell, please come to me, please. I need to talk to you.

The cottage remained silent.

Branwell, please.

Still silence.

Finally, Claire opened her eyes. He hadn't answered her summons. Her spirits low, she made to stand. Then stopped. A new scent had drifted into the room. Leather and tobacco. Instantly, her mood lightened. He hadn't ignored her call for help.

"Branwell?"

A faint knocking sound came from the wall opposite. Claire went over to it and listened. The knocking grew louder and she stepped back. This hadn't happened before. "Branwell, I don't understand. Are you trying to tell me something?"

The knocking stopped. A heavy silence made Claire hold her breath. A vein throbbed at her temple, and a feeling of trepidation took hold of her. Something about this did not feel right. He had never tried to contact her this way. A breath on her cheek, the faintest of kisses, the aroma of cigar smoke...but never this. Was it even him?

A rattling. It came from the framed self-portrait. Claire watched in horror as the picture swayed and hit the wall repeatedly as if shaken by some unseen hand. Then, without warning, it flew off the wall and crashed on the floor, shattering the frame.

Claire screamed. Outside her door, thumping noises as if someone was slamming their fist into the wall. She threw open her door. Nothing there. Still the thumping continued. It seemed to be coming from all directions at once.

"Stop it! Stop it!"

The noise grew louder. The smell of leather and tobacco evaporated, and a new, unpleasant acrid stench caught at the back of her throat and made her choke. Tears streamed down from her stinging eyes. She staggered back into her room, and the door slammed shut so hard the whole cottage shook.

Her bed creaked, then lifted itself, hovering at a crazy angle, depositing pillows and bedclothes onto the floor in an untidy heap. The deafening thumping and banging echoed all around her, and Claire clapped her hands over her ears. She half crawled to a corner of her room and curled into a ball, her head on her knees, and arms protecting herself.

This could not be Branwell. He wouldn't scare her like this. "Please go away. Whatever you are. Go away and leave me alone."

As quickly as it had started the cacophony stopped, leaving Claire alone in her wrecked room, the stench of ammonia all around her.

★   ★   ★

"Miss Wainwright. Enjoying your walk?" Matthew Dixon dropped into step next to her as Evelyn made her way up the path to the higher ground.

"Yes, indeed, Mr. Dixon. I trust you are too? How is your leg today?"

"Every day a little better, I think. Thank you for asking. We are certainly fortunate with the weather. This is the third day running we have had no rain." He smiled.

"Oh, I don't think the Yorkshire weather is as entirely inclement as some would make out," Evelyn said. Already, she felt better, lighter than she had before he joined her.

"Your sister doesn't accompany you on your walks?"

"She's more of a homebody," Evelyn said, hoping the frown she knew she had made at the mention of Claire hadn't been too obvious.

"Such a shame. She misses out on all this." He waved his stick, indicating the view.

"I have told her, but she is as stubborn as I am, I'm afraid."

"Perhaps I could persuade her. We could have a picnic."

"That would be most pleasant, but I doubt you would change her mind. She hates insects, and the thought of enticing them by providing cakes and jam would be too much for her."

"Then we shall not have cakes and jam. We shall have ham and cucumber sandwiches instead. I don't think insects are especially partial to ham and cucumber."

Evelyn laughed. She felt so relaxed in his company. She wouldn't want to share him with Claire anyway. She felt guilty for thinking such an uncharitable thought, but really her sister had become impossible.

"Miss Wainwright, I hope you won't think me too intrusive, but I couldn't help noticing you seem a little preoccupied today. I hope there is nothing troubling you?"

Evelyn sighed. She had hoped her demeanor wouldn't have made it so apparent. "My sister and I had a stupid argument at breakfast. I hate it when we fall out, and it seems to be happening more frequently recently. She has become a little distracted with…" Why was she unburdening herself like this? For heaven's sake, she hardly knew him. Now she would have to finish her sentence, but if she told him the truth, he would probably wonder if she too had been tainted by the same madness that seemed to have overtaken her sister. After all, these things ran in families, didn't they? Everyone knew that. Oh well, she had begun. Too late to stop now.

"My sister has become a little preoccupied with a story she is writing and one of the characters in particular." Well, she had only told a half lie.

"Oh, she's an author?"

"We both dabble a little. For our own amusement, although one day, if we ever finish a book, we may seek publication."

"My goodness, two more sisters to hail from the moors of the West Riding."

"I wouldn't compare our efforts to the works of the Brontë sisters."

"I am sure you find them inspiring, though, don't you?"

"Most certainly."

"What is your favorite work of theirs?"

"Mine would be *Jane Eyre*, although for my sister, it would have to be *Wuthering Heights*."

"Visions of the dastardly Heathcliff, no doubt."

"Quite. She believes his character to have been based on that of Emily Brontë's only brother. Branwell."

"Branwell. Ah yes." Mr. Dixon looked away.

"Did you know him?" Silly question. Mr. Dixon must be far too young to have met him.

"Not personally. My grandfather used to sup with him in Haworth. He said he was a fearsome drinker. He could down two pints of ale and call for a large brandy before Grandfather had taken more than a couple of sips. Amiable chap, though, Branwell. Very popular with both men and ladies."

"Yes, I heard he had quite a reputation as a ladies' man."

"He had a certain…charm." Mr. Dixon stopped. His leg must have been paining him. Certainly, his expression had grown strained.

"Shall we sit for a while?" Evelyn suggested. "I confess to feeling a little tired."

"An excellent idea." He lowered himself down onto a grass-covered stone.

Evelyn did likewise and they sat in comfortable silence for a few minutes. In a tree nearby, a blackbird sang tunefully to his lady. The tree itself had grown bent at an acute angle, no doubt battered by harsh winds and deep winter snow over many years.

Finally Evelyn sighed. "I think I should be getting back. My sister will wonder what has become of me."

"Allow me to escort you."

"Thank you, Mr. Dixon."

"And please call me Matthew. I know we haven't been acquainted for long, so this is probably a serious breach of etiquette, but I would like us to be friends, and friends have a habit of calling each other by their first names."

Evelyn hesitated, but really where did the harm lie? She could almost hear her mother reproving her. Or maybe the rattle of her bones as she turned in her grave. But Mama wasn't here anymore. Evelyn was a grown woman in her thirties. Free to make her own choices.

"I should like that very much, Matthew. I am Evelyn. My sister calls me Ev, although I rather wish she wouldn't. I think it sounds so common."

"Then Evelyn it shall be."

Together they made their way back down to the lane. Not a single soul passed them. At the door of her cottage, Matthew took Evelyn's gloved hand. "Thank you for a most enjoyable walk. I hope we will do it again very soon, and do please think about the picnic. Maybe your sister will surprise you."

Evelyn didn't tell him she had already had enough surprises from Claire to last her a long time. Instead, she smiled, nodded and wished him a good day.

★   ★   ★

She could hear Claire's sobs from the hallway. Evelyn raced up the stairs.

Nothing could have prepared her for the devastation of her sister's bedroom or the sight of Claire, distraught, trembling and curled up tightly in the corner of the room.

"Whatever happened here? It looks like an earthquake hit it."

Claire couldn't speak for the heaving sobs choking her. Evelyn cradled her head in her arms and rocked her back and forth as Mama had done all those years ago.

At last, Claire calmed herself enough to sit up. She took Evelyn's proffered handkerchief and dried her tears.

"Are you ready to tell me now?" Evelyn asked gently.

Claire nodded. "I don't know what happened. One minute I was sitting here, and the next Branwell's picture crashed to the floor, and that's when…" Her eyes welled up again.

"It's all right, Claire. Take your time. What happened then?"

"A lot of banging and thumping but no one here to make the noise. Then there was this horrible smell. Like… You remember when that tomcat used to come round, trying to get at our queen when we were children?"

Evelyn wrinkled her nose. "Only too well. A horrible smell. It used to spray everywhere, and Mama was furious. I can't smell anything now, though." She glanced over at the bed. "What happened there?"

"It rose up off the floor."

"What? But how?"

Claire shook her head. "If I hadn't seen it myself, I wouldn't have believed it, but it looked as if someone was lifting it. As if it weighed virtually nothing. It tossed around, which is why the covers are on the floor. Then it all stopped. I have been so scared, Ev. I don't know what caused all this."

"Nor do I," Evelyn said.

"I'm frightened it's something I did."

"Why? What could you possibly have done? Unless you did all this yourself, of course." Could she have? That bed was made of brass. Heavy. But then she only had Claire's word for it that events had happened the way she had related them. Why would Claire lie, though?

"I... I asked Branwell to come to me."

"Oh, Claire. Not that again."

"I don't believe it was him. Something else did this. Something intended to scare me. It succeeded. Branwell would never do such a thing."

Evelyn held Claire close to her. She would do anything to protect her sister, but, looking at the devastation all around her and feeling the woman trembling like a frightened lamb in her arms, she had no answers. Claire needed help, and right now, she had no idea how to provide it.

★   ★   ★

The following morning, Claire seemed much brighter. Her usually pale face had a tinge of color.

"Did you sleep well?" Evelyn asked.

Claire made a rocking motion with her hand. "Not too bad. At least I didn't have any nightmares."

"That's good at least. Claire, why don't we go out together today? Up on the moors where you can breathe the fresh air and get some color in your cheeks."

Claire smiled. "And you might just catch a glimpse of Mr. Dixon."

"It's true Matthew might be there."

"Oh, first-name terms. Very cozy."

There had been no hint of jealousy. Claire was teasing her. "He is a charming gentleman, and he has invited us both to have a picnic with him."

"Don't you think I would be a little in the way? I don't want to play gooseberry."

"Oh, nothing of the sort. Mr. Dixon wouldn't have asked if he hadn't meant it."

Claire frowned briefly, and then the moment passed. "No, I

would rather not. Really, Ev. You go and enjoy yourself, and I will stay here with my book."

"You're not worried about being alone…after yesterday?"

Claire shook her head. "I'm made of sterner stuff than you think I am. I shall stay downstairs, and at the first sign of trouble I promise I will come and find you."

"Only if you're sure."

"I'm sure."

"I would like to go."

"Then what are you waiting for? Tell Mr. Dixon you accept his kind invitation but unfortunately your sister feels a little indisposed and is unable to accept. Go and enjoy yourself. You're not my nursemaid."

Had she behaved like a nanny?

A sharp knock at the door gave her a start. "Whoever can that be?"

Claire shook her head and stood. "You answer it. I don't feel in the mood for seeing anyone today. I'll wait in my room until they've gone."

A typical response. Claire's shyness wouldn't allow her to say as much as "hello" to a stranger if she could help it.

Matthew Dixon removed his cap and smiled at her as he stood in the doorway, the sun at his back. "I do hope you will forgive this intrusion, but the weather is beautiful today. I wondered if you had made any decision about my invitation."

"I have. My sister is a little unwell, so she has decided to remain at home for the day, but I would be delighted to accept."

"I'm so relieved. You see…" He reached to the side of him and produced a covered basket. "I came prepared just in case. Ham and cucumber sandwiches as promised, chicken, chilled white wine, fruit. I hope everything will be to your liking."

"It sounds like a feast. Please come in, Matthew, while I get my coat."

He stepped over the threshold and immediately drew a sharp breath.

"Is something wrong?" Evelyn asked. The color had drained from his face, and for a second, he looked as if he might pass out.

He put his hand to his head. "Sorry. I don't know what happened. I had the strangest feeling as I stepped into your cottage."

Memories of yesterday flooded back to Evelyn. "What sort of feeling?"

"I can't explain it really. First I was sure I had been here before, even though I know I have never once set foot here. Then I had the strongest urge to get out of here as fast as I could. I must apologize, Evelyn. That sounds awfully rude of me and has nothing to do with you, I can assure you. It felt as if the house... Oh, this sounds too ridiculous."

"No, please go on. I want to hear it, and I promise I shall not take offense."

He hesitated for a moment before continuing. "I felt as if the house was trying to get rid of me. Or warn me. I'm afraid none of this makes sense."

"What if I told you my sister had an unexplained occurrence here yesterday when I went out? I came home to find her room in ruins and her distraught, huddled in a corner. She swore she had done nothing, but something had entered her room and deliberately wrecked it. Naturally I felt reluctant to believe her at the time, but now you've told me this, I begin to wonder. I know so little about this cottage. We bought it in something of a hurry."

"But you have not experienced anything untoward yourself?"

Evelyn shook her head. "Not yet, but we have only lived here for a few weeks."

Matthew rubbed his forehead.

"Do you feel any better now?" Evelyn asked. At least he looked less pale.

"Better, but still not comfortable being here. Shall we go? Maybe if we talk about it on our picnic?"

"That sounds like a good idea." Evelyn grabbed a light summer coat, struggled into her walking shoes and crammed a hat on her head, securing it firmly with a hatpin decorated with a silver thistle. "Oh, my gloves. I mustn't go without my gloves. Mama would come back and haunt me."

Matthew flinched. He held the door open for her, and then they were out in the brilliant sunshine with a mere hint of a breeze.

They spoke little on their climb, but once they reached the crags, Evelyn laid out the red check cloth Matthew had brought, anchoring it at four corners with stones.

The roast chicken tasted delicious, and the little sandwiches accompanied the wine perfectly. Matthew stretched his legs out and leaned back against a rock, its surface smooth from many centuries of weathering.

"That's better. I hadn't realized how hungry I was. How good it is to eat simple fare in charming company." He clinked his glass with Evelyn's.

She smiled. "I was thinking much the same." If only every day could be like this and if only she didn't have this nagging worry over Claire. How were things at the cottage now? But Claire had promised she would get out of there if anything took a threatening turn.

"It's such a shame about the cottage," she said and realized she had spoken her thoughts out loud, ruining the peaceful ambience.

"Was it the house you had always dreamed of?"

"Not entirely. You see, Sugden Heath, for all it's a bustling mill town, can be a very small place indeed if your father happens to have been one of the area's largest employers and he chose to sell up his land for property. A lot of people lost their jobs either directly or indirectly because of it, while the decision made him a great deal of money. Money that he subsequently left to us. That created more disquiet. Many in the community did not agree with leaving so much to daughters, but my father had no sons; who else should he leave it to?"

"So I am dining on cold chicken and ham sandwiches with a wealthy heiress?" Matthew winked at her, and Evelyn felt her cheeks burn.

"A lot of the money is held in trust until such time as my sister or I marry. Not that either of us are looking to do so anytime soon. Even then there are a lot of stipulations. Father did his best to protect us against fortune hunters, but he could do nothing to still the gossiping tongues of Sugden Heath. Every time one of us stepped out into town, we could see the turned faces, the whispers behind hands. They called us unnatural, and worse. Jealousy does terrible things to some people. The situation became so bad my sister refused to go out. She is still inclined towards reclusiveness. It's going to take a long time for her to gain her confidence back."

"I can see that. I'm lucky to have independent means, courtesy of my father, who made a lot of money mining copper in Africa. He died there a few years ago in a shocking accident. They had no warning, and the roof caved in, crushing sixty men, including himself. His brother runs the mine now. I was schooled in England and have lived here most of my life. I can't see me following in my father's footsteps, but once I am fully mobile again, I want to do something with my life. I'm afraid I have rather wasted it up until now. The skiing accident brought me to my senses. I could have died. Almost did, in fact. If I hadn't been in a party, I could have perished where I fell on the mountain."

"That must have been a frightful experience."

"Not one I would care to repeat. Suffice it to say my skiing days are behind me. I'm thinking of taking up golf." He smiled and Evelyn laughed. "As for your cottage, though, there's a lot of history in those walls."

"Yes, I believe the cottages were built in the early eighteenth century. Of course, it's never been a grand house. Far from it. But my sister and I needed somewhere small and quiet where we could look after ourselves. There have been sacrifices, but we believed they were worth it. We had to leave most of our furniture behind in our old home. It simply wouldn't fit. But we like it. Maybe I should say, 'liked'. I am having serious doubts now."

"My cousin knows a little of the history of his cottage, and I believe all six were built at the same time. They used to be owned by the Monkton family, whose eldest sons each served as the local squire. The dwellings were built for some of the family's senior staff, but when the last squire died without issue, they were sold separately. That would be about twenty-five years ago. Gerald bought his off the first owner. There are some stories about the squires, though. They each had a reputation with the young women of the village, and it is said you can see a lot of similar features on the faces of the local inhabitants."

"Oh dear!" Evelyn said, covering her mouth with her hand.

"I think there is some truth in it. Have you seen the baker's wife? And the owner of the haberdashery shop? Not to mention the local butcher and the postman."

"No, I have never noticed, but I shall make a special note to look out for it in future."

"You'll see I'm right. There are the usual crop of ghosts – both likely and unlikely – ranging from an imp who can change form and become a butterfly, a snake or a beautiful young woman with flowing raven hair, depending on what time of the year it is and who sees it. Whichever version you see is guaranteed to be the last thing you witness."

"Sounds a bit gruesome."

"All true. Allegedly. Then there's old Aloysius Monkton. The last squire of Thornton Wensley. He is supposed to walk up our lane after dark on fine summer evenings. He enjoyed hiking on the moors, and you can often hear his dogs barking, as he loved to take them with him. Gerald told me they sound like wolves. There are no reports of actual wolves in this area, of course, but you never know..."

"It all sounds far more exciting than I thought. Or maybe daunting is a better word."

"Oh, it's all a lot of hokum, but around the fire on long winter's evenings, what else are you going to do but see who can come up with the most outlandish ghost story?"

"Where our cottage is concerned, I don't think you need to use too much imagination. Do you think there is really something wrong with it, Matthew?"

Matthew gave her a long, studied look. "Let me put it this way. I have seen enough in my life to make me believe there are some things best left alone and some things we will never explain, for all our science and evolution. Our ancestors knew more about these elemental spirits than we do. It seems the more advanced and civilized we have become, the more we have lost touch with nature and the forces surrounding us. Now I have thoroughly bored you."

"No, no. You haven't, I assure you. I find this fascinating. What have you seen that has led you to this conclusion? Has anything happened in your cousin's cottage?"

"Not since I have been living there, but, like you, I have only been here a short time. Gerald told me shortly before he and his family moved to Wiltshire, he heard noises at night. At first he thought nothing of it. Old houses make all sorts of creaking and groaning noises as the timbers settle and so on, but one night, he awoke to hear someone coughing downstairs. Thinking there might be an intruder, he moved as quietly as possible out of the room and down the stairs. His wife and two young boys slept on, apparently oblivious to everything. The more he descended the stairs, the louder the coughing grew. It sounded like someone in real pain. A consumptive perhaps. The curtains were open, and a full moon lit up the backyard and the moors beyond. Gerald tiptoed into the living room, and there, surrounded by an aura of silver moonbeams, stood a female figure. Gerald couldn't stop a cry escaping him at the unexpected sight, and the apparition vanished."

Goosebumps broke out on Evelyn's arms, and the hairs on the back of her neck prickled. "What a terrifying experience. And his wife and children knew nothing of this?"

Matthew shook his head. "The next morning Gerald asked them if they had heard any noises in the night, and each said they hadn't. In fact his wife said she had experienced the best night's sleep she could remember for months. The boys, too, said they had slept soundly."

"How strange. It's almost as if that's too much of a coincidence."

"Which is what Gerald thought."

"And he told you about this before you moved in?"

"Yes. It didn't worry me unduly, because I'm prepared for it. If indeed it happened at all. And clearly the ghost meant him no harm. As for my own experiences, I had occasion to stay with an uncle and aunt in Harrogate. I would have been about ten years old, recovering from chicken pox. The house was older than ours. Built in the reign of Charles II, I believe. My elder brother was away at boarding school, and my parents were in Africa, so I was pretty much left to my own devices. I no longer felt poorly, the spots weren't troubling me as badly, and I had grown bored of my own company. The house had an extensive attic running the full length and breadth of the building, and I had been expressly forbidden from going up there. Telling that to a ten-year-old boy – especially one with too much time on his hands – is a recipe for disaster. The weather had been consistently poor, with showers and storms practically every day. On yet another rainy day, my aunt and uncle were out, the servants were all occupied with their tasks, so I crept up there. Usually, they kept the door locked. The housekeeper kept the key in her pantry, but today, for some reason, it was open. I made my way up the stairs and entered a world that would have kept any child engrossed for hours if not days. Old rocking horses, a massive dolls' house, armies of tin soldiers, every toy you can imagine lay up there, long discarded and dusty. Cobwebs brushed my face, and soon I must have been coated in a layer of dust myself.

"I discovered a box. Brightly colored. It was called The Garden of Bewitchment, and I opened it to find a board and all manner of items to decorate it with. A small wooden manor house with windows made of magnifying glass so when you looked through them you could see an entire room, exquisitely furnished with characters that seemed to move with your eyes. Trees made of some unusual, springy material. You used these to build the perimeter of your garden. A rockery, a pool so lifelike you felt your fingers would get wet if you touched it. The surface looked like it had been made of glass or crystal, and it sparkled in the light coming in through the attic windows. There were so many parts. Soon, my garden began to take shape with the manor house in its designated spot at the heart of it. I placed a bird's nest in one of the taller trees and fancied I could hear the birds chirruping. I put delicate, exquisite butterflies on the leaves of sunflowers and hollyhocks, and my nose detected the perfume of sweet peas, which I had planted next to a wall. A greenhouse contained so many pots of tomatoes, aromatic herbs and scarlet geraniums, and a box hedge gave off the scent of summer. Oh, yes, Evelyn, I believed I could smell all these things, that it wasn't called The Garden of Bewitchment for nothing. Time flew by, and I lost all track of it. The light began to fade, and I realized my aunt and uncle would be back at any moment. I left the garden where it lay and hurried to greet them."

"What a wonderful toy. Did you ever go back up there?"

Matthew's face darkened. "Oh, yes. The very next day. Yet again the weather was inclement and my aunt and uncle were visiting friends in York. When I had made sure I wouldn't be spotted, I raced up to the attic and negotiated my way back to where I had left the garden. The sight that met me will stay with me for the rest of my life."

"Oh, my heavens, what was it?"

"The garden had died. The pool had dried up. There was no sign of the glassy surface that looked so much like water. The trees were withered, and the birds lay dead on the ground. I picked up the house and peered through. Or tried to peer through. Every window had been blacked out somehow. I could see nothing. As if the house had died too. When I went to replace it on the board, it crumbled in my hands until only dust remained. Weeds grew where the flowers had bloomed. Ground elder had choked every last one of them, but this too withered as soon as I touched it. The beautiful, enchanted garden had died."

"How extraordinary. What did you do then?"

"I picked up the pieces as best I could to put them back in the box, but each one met the fate of the house, until the box was full of dust and ash. Even the bright colors of the box itself had faded to a muddy brown. I sat and cried. Yes, a ten-year-old boy, brought up never to blub. I sobbed my heart out for the destruction of so much beauty."

"Did you ever find out what caused it?"

Matthew shook his head. "Maybe exposure to the air had destroyed it. I asked a science teacher once a few years later, and he didn't even believe me about the garden in all its glory. He told me to be careful to draw the line between fact and fantasy. But the story doesn't end there."

Evelyn, by now riveted, sat further forward.

"When I had pulled myself together and dried my tears, I remained kneeling on the floor, the box in front of me. I think by that time I had prepared myself for almost anything, but even in my tormented state I couldn't believe my eyes when one of the edges of the box lifted, followed by another and another until it became obvious that something inside the thing wanted to push the lid off, although for what purpose I could only wait and see. I watched in increasing horror as something curled its way out and upward. Tentacles, shaped like a climbing plant. Convolvulus maybe, or ivy. But not green – jet black. It stank like sour milk. The sourest you can imagine. It grew and grew upward so fast, and the nursery story of 'Jack and the Beanstalk' flashed into my mind. Only this was no beanstalk. Not unless the Devil has one in Hell. I saw and heard a black vulture issue a raspy, hissing cry, sprang to my feet and raced out of there as if Lucifer himself was behind me. At the foot of the stairs, I turned the handle, but the door wouldn't open. Maybe the housekeeper had remembered she had left it unlocked the day before and had come to rectify her error. I yelled, no longer caring if anyone heard me. I could hear the beating of wings. At any second the vulture would attack me. Then the door flew open, I fell out, and it slammed hard behind me. That's the last time I ever ventured into the attic."

Evelyn sat in stunned silence as Matthew, seemingly relieved to have divested himself of this fantastic story, leaned back against the rock.

Evelyn recovered herself sufficiently to speak. "That is some story."

"And I will gladly swear on a stack of Bibles it is as true as the air we are breathing."

"And you never told anyone? Your aunt and uncle?"

"Apart from the skeptical science teacher, you are the first person I have ever told. But I think you can see now why I retain such an open mind, and am cautious in dealing with anything of a… supernatural nature."

"This all makes my experience, and Claire's, tame by comparison." Evelyn felt ashamed as if she had made a huge fuss about nothing.

"No, no, Evelyn. Yours was as real and terrifying for you as mine was for me. Over the years I have ventured into many toy shops and asked the shopkeeper if he stocked The Garden of Bewitchment, and no one has ever heard of it. I have been anxious to trace any others so they can be destroyed. Where it came from I have no idea, and I certainly didn't want to talk to my relations about it. That may even have been the reason they didn't want me to go to the attic in the first place. They were certainly adamant about it. They would not have appreciated such a breach of trust on my part, and I would probably have been sent packing, never to return. I liked them, and the house, for all it contained something evil in the attic, held a constant source of fascination for me."

"So did the…thing…ever come down into the main house?"

"Not that I know of. For all I know it's still there, festering away. I visited on a number of occasions over the following years until my uncle died and my aunt went to live with my cousin Adele. The house was sold and I lost touch. Whether the new owners ever experienced anything or even went up there, I have no idea, and now my aunt is dead too, so the story is over as far as I am concerned. As to the vulture, well, I have learned black vultures do indeed emit a raspy, hissing cry and are indigenous to parts of the United States and South America. Certainly such a creature does not belong in the West Riding of Yorkshire. The plant, on the other hand, is a complete mystery, and, in the absence of evidence to the contrary, I am forced to concede its origins are supernatural."

Sitting here, in brilliant sunshine with a moorland breeze keeping the temperature at a pleasant level, Evelyn contemplated what she had just heard. A few days ago, she wouldn't have given the supernatural a second thought. She would have dismissed it as impossible. Preposterous even.

Now the impossible had become the likeliest explanation.

CHAPTER FOUR

Ev thinks I'm going mad, and maybe I am, but I know Branwell has visited me as much as I know whatever tore my room apart was not him, nor anything to do with him. She, who has never had a young man in her life, never enjoyed the attentions of someone who truly cares for her... until now, that is. Who is Matthew Dixon, and why is he here? When we were growing up, there were plenty of eligible suitors beating a path to our door, but she would entertain none of them. Now, he only has to walk past the cottage and she is all of aflutter. What curious set of circumstances has brought him here to cross our path in this manner? I am not at all sure I like it, or him. As for Branwell, he has told me not to trust him. Ev and I have always had to be wary of gold diggers, and, for all Mr. Dixon's protestations of inherited wealth, I see no sign of it. He lives alone in a cottage belonging to his cousin. A 'grace and favor' arrangement if ever I saw one. Perhaps I should engineer a meeting with him. Alone. Gauge for myself what his intentions are towards my sister. For what affects her must certainly affect me too.

Claire set down her pen and closed her diary, taking care to lock it before tucking it into the little secret drawer of the bureau. Ev must never read that. These were her private thoughts, ones she shared with no one. Ones she would *never* share with anyone.

She glanced at the clock. Five past three. If he was as much a creature of habit as he appeared to be, he would be passing their door within the next fifteen minutes or so. With Ev out buying groceries, Claire would have just enough time to get herself ready and go out.

She tried to tidy her hair, but, as usual, it refused to stay pinned no matter how many clips she used. Her dress had creased too. Never mind, her light summer coat would cover it. One look confirmed her fears. She would merely be swapping one set of creases for another. Did men even notice such things? How did Evelyn always manage to look immaculate, whereas the best *she* could manage was to resemble a sloppily made bed? Thank goodness Branwell didn't seem to mind. Claire's cheeks burned as she remembered that he normally saw her in her nightdress anyway, and it didn't matter if that was a little crumpled.

Hurriedly she pushed the thought aside and secured the straps of her pattens over her shoes. Who knew how marshy the moors would be? Even after a few days of sunshine and no rain.

With one last adjustment – this time of a wayward hat seemingly hell-bent on falling off – Claire opened the front door. Matthew Dixon had already passed and was making his way up the lane. Claire quickened her step until, slightly breathless, she caught up with him.

"Mr. Dixon," she called, trying not to breathe heavily. He stopped and turned, recognition dying in his eyes as he focused on her. "Evelyn?" he asked uncertainly.

"Oh, no, dear me, no. But a lot of people confuse us. We are identical. At least we were born identical. Ev is my sister. I am Claire Wainwright." She stuck out a slightly grubby gloved hand, which he took gently in his.

"A pleasure to meet you," he said, his eyes not leaving her for one second. "Please forgive me. I don't mean to stare, but I haven't met identical twins before, and the likeness is truly remarkable."

"I quite understand. It happens a great deal. Well, when I go out, that is. I expect Ev told you I tend to stay at home a lot, and I am intensely shy."

He looked as if he didn't know whether, or how, to answer.

"It's quite all right, Mr. Dixon. I know my sister is overprotective of me. As a child, I often took sick, and she is more like an older sister than a twin. She used to nursemaid me, you see. Just the two of us in our room, day after day, while I recovered from my latest ailment."

"But you are quite well now?"

"Oh, yes, strong as a horse. Much stronger than Ev thinks I am anyway." Claire warmed to him. He had a kind smile and deep-set eyes radiating warmth. No wonder her sister was so smitten. Not that Claire would be jealous of anyone her sister took a liking to, unless they happened to look anything like Branwell, of course.

But Mr. Dixon *did* look a little like Branwell. Or Claire's version of him anyway.

"Is your sister not accompanying you today, Miss Wainwright?"

"Oh, please, call me Claire. No, she is out buying provisions. If you like, I would be happy to accompany you on your walk." Did he just hesitate? Why did he keep staring at her in such a fashion? A wave of uncertainty spread over Claire. He seemed charming enough, but could it all be an act? He smiled and the moment passed.

"I should be delighted. I had hoped you would join your sister and me for our picnic yesterday, but she informed me you were indisposed."

"Not really indisposed, just a little... Oh, nothing really, but I didn't really feel up to being sociable."

"Your sister told me of the unnerving experience you had."

"Did she?" *Ev had no right!* Claire fought to retain her composure.

"I do hope I haven't spoken out of turn. She is very concerned about you."

Claire swallowed acid. "As I mentioned, she is overprotective of me. It *was* a peculiar experience, but I am quite over it now."

An awkward silence followed. Claire wondered whether she should apologize for taking offence so easily. After all, it wasn't Mr. Dixon's fault if Ev betrayed a confidence. But Claire didn't feel sorry. The thought of these two gossiping about her behind her back filled her with righteous anger and fueled her rapidly cooling feelings toward Mr. Dixon.

They walked on, without speaking, for a few minutes until they crested the hill and reached some crags that looked almost as if someone had fashioned them into stone chairs.

"Let's rest here awhile," Mr. Dixon suggested.

Claire nodded and arranged herself untidily on a crag.

"I do feel we have started off on a bad note," he said, flashing her a smile. "May we start again?"

Claire laughed, her apprehension diminishing. "I love my sister very much, but we don't always agree. I am sorry you have been caught up in one of our...moments."

"I can assure you your sister had nothing but your interests at heart. She merely sought my opinion, and I gave it, as best I could."

"And what opinion would that be, Mr. Dixon?"

"Oh, please, call me Matthew, Claire. I do want us to be friends. I told her I believed there were unearthly manifestations, whatever you choose to call them. The cottages have their share of ghost stories, true or imaginary."

"I know what I saw, Matthew. And what I saw couldn't have been of this earth. My room had been upturned. A picture smashed, the bed raised, sheets thrown on the floor, books torn from their bookcase and flung across from one side to the other."

"It must have been terrifying."

"At least you don't disbelieve me."

"How could I? You witnessed it. Your sister witnessed the aftermath. From what she described, I cannot see how you could have been responsible. If you will forgive me for saying this, I doubt you would have had the strength to raise a heavy brass bed in the manner she described. You told her it had been upended as if someone had lifted it at one end?"

"Yes. It would take a person of great strength to do that."

"Truly shocking."

"If I could understand why it happened, I might find it easier to understand. Is it a demon? An angry spirit? A ghost?"

"I wish I could give you an answer, Claire. I truly do. I know such manifestations are not rare. And they occur all over the world. Most often they start and then continue for a little while before stopping, never to be heard from again. All I can advise is to try to put it out of your mind as much as possible. If you dwell on it, you could find it takes over your life and robs you of your sleep."

"I didn't sleep well last night. Every little creak brought me awake."

"But every house creaks. Especially old ones such as those we are living in."

"Yes, you are right. But..."

"I'm sure it will get easier as the days go by and nothing else untoward happens."

"I hope so, Matthew."

★   ★   ★

"What were your impressions of Matthew, Claire?"

"A charming gentleman. At least on the surface. But I do wonder if his motives are entirely...honorable."

"Whatever do you mean?"

"I don't know. Maybe I am imagining it, but there is a look in his eyes sometimes, and I can't read it. His mouth says one thing, and his eyes... They seem to search. As if he has a question he can't bring himself to ask." Ev's look of bewilderment, mixed with skepticism, unsettled Claire. "I'm probably reading too much into it."

Evelyn paused in the act of placing a bag of flour and some eggs into the pantry. "Yes, I rather think you are. He is an easy person to be with, and I find his company congenial and entertaining. He is also a great help in this strange situation in which we find ourselves. Maybe the discomfort you feel is simply because he, like us, is trying to fathom out why these unnerving things are happening." Ev sighed. "Anyway, I'm glad you went out today. I know it's difficult for you to meet strangers."

"Oh, Ev, I'm not nearly as helpless as you think I am."

"Nevertheless—"

Claire stood up, knocking her chair off-balance. "I'm going to my room."

Ev's look of horror made her want to smack her. "Are you sure you'll be—"

"I shall do precisely as Matthew advised. I shall not think about it. I will go to my room, pick up my book, sit in my chair by the window and read." Ev didn't need to know what else she would be doing.

She heard her sister come out into the hall as she flounced up the stairs, conscious of Ev's eyes burning into her back.

With her door closed and a pleasant smell of lavender coming from the bowl on her dressing table, Claire inhaled deeply and picked up her worn copy of *The Tenant of Wildfell Hall*. She sat down with the book in her lap and closed her eyes.

Branwell. Are you there?

Behind closed lids, she sensed the room grow darker. A momentary panic set in. What if the...she didn't even have a name for it...was back? Then came the reassuring aroma of leather and cigars.

Branwell.

Unseen lips caressed hers with the lightest of touches. A featherlight stroke of her hand. She opened her eyes, praying she would see him. A glimpse, a shadow. Anything to let her know he was truly there.

But it did not come. She remained alone. And then something caught her eye. Something on the floor in front of the wardrobe.

Something that didn't belong there.

She set her book down, stood and made her way across the room. A box. Quite a sizeable and colorful one too. Bending down, she picked it up and examined it. Where had it come from? They didn't possess such a thing.

"How extraordinary."

She sat on the edge of her bed and prized off the cardboard lid. The board looked brand new. She unfolded it and laid it on the bed. She stared at the contents of the box that had been hidden underneath it. There lay all manner of miniature garden trees, plants, a splendid manor house, crystal pool. So lifelike. Even birds and butterflies to adorn the scenery.

Claire picked up a tree. It felt like no other toy she had ever handled. The branches, twigs and leaves seemed almost alive in her hand. They sprang back and emitted a heady smell like a perfect May day.

"Ev?" she called, and then remembered. Ev had planned to go straight out again as soon as she had put the provisions away. Maybe she had been cleaning in Claire's room earlier...or she had put something away in the wardrobe. Perhaps this game, or whatever it was, had fallen out. It wasn't theirs, so it must have been there since the previous owners had lived here.

Claire picked up the box lid. The illustration showed an exquisite landscape. Apart from that and the title of the toy, nothing else. Her creative gene sparked. She cleared a couple of ornaments off the top of her small chest of drawers and set the board down. It covered every inch of its new home. Using the box illustration as a guide, Claire picked up the house, ready to place it in the center, when the windows caught her eye. She peered closely through one on the ground floor and marveled at the detail. The image was three-dimensional. The figure of a woman sat at a piano, in full evening dress, flanked by two men equally well attired. A small group of adults sat in Regency-style chairs, clearly listening intently to the performance. The whole scene struck her as so realistic Claire could almost hear the tinkling of the piano keys. She peered into an upstairs room where an elderly lady lay in bed, her white hair mostly covered by a nightcap and her wrinkled face peaceful in slumber.

In the next room, a man stood in front of a mirror, adjusting his bow tie. Another man, presumably his valet, stood observing him. Claire was just about to leave the scene when she stopped and peered in again. Unable to believe what she saw, she blinked rapidly and looked closer. No, she wasn't seeing things. There stood the mirror. And the valet, just as before.

But the man had been frozen in the act of smoothing his hair.

Claire tossed the house onto the bed. A cry emanated from it. No, *cries*.

She raced out of her room and down the stairs, meeting Ev returning from her walk.

"Whatever's happened, Claire? You're as pale as death."

"Nothing, Ev. It's all right. I... Oh, you may as well see it. I'll show you."

Claire led the way back to her room. "I found this toy. A garden you build yourself. It looked lovely, so I thought I would make it. Then—" She stopped and stared. Her bedroom was tidy, as she had left it.

But the toy garden had vanished.

"I don't understand. I left it here." She touched the top of the chest of drawers, its ornaments replaced as before.

"Claire. You said it was a toy garden. Did it have a name?"

"Yes. The Garden of Bewitchment."

"Oh no." Evelyn sank down on Claire's bed.

"What do you mean? Have you heard of it? I wondered where it had come from."

"I couldn't tell you. I have no idea, but Matthew played with a Garden of Bewitchment. It turned out to be dangerous. Very dangerous. It might have even killed him if he hadn't left it alone. Even then..." Evelyn shuddered.

"So, you didn't put it in my room?"

Evelyn shook her head. "Matthew said he had tried to find another one like it, and no toy shop owner had ever heard of it."

"So what is it doing here, then?"

"I should very much like to know."

"It has to be Matthew, doesn't it? He's the only one who knows of this toy's existence."

"Oh come on, Claire. Why on earth would Matthew sneak into your room and deposit a toy there, only to snatch it back again? How would he have gained access to your room in the first place?"

Claire opened her window and peered out. "You suggested it once yourself. Maybe Matthew could have shinned up the drainpipe, or even up the Russian vine."

Evelyn joined her. "I wasn't being serious about the drainpipe then as you well know. The fastenings are far too rusted to hold any adult's weight. As for the Russian vine...a squirrel would have problems clinging on to it."

Claire withdrew back into the room. "You explain it then because I'm sure I can't. Maybe he hid in the attic and came down to put the toy there. He might still be in the cottage."

"Firstly, we don't have an attic, and secondly, the whole idea is preposterous. I am going to tell him about it, though. It's such a strange coincidence. He only told me about it a day or two ago, and then it turns up here."

"You're not suggesting it's the same one as his? Well, that settles it then. It *must* be his doing."

"I shall ask him about it, and we shall see his reaction. I will be accompanying him on his walk tomorrow afternoon. You can come too if you like."

"No thanks, I'll leave you two lovebirds to your own devices if you don't mind. But please be careful, Ev. He's charming, and I like him, but I still don't fully trust him. Especially after this."

"I promise, I'll take care, but you must promise not to jump to conclusions simply because they provide an apparently quick and easy answer."

Claire nodded, but her doubts remained.

"I'm going to get changed, and, as it's my turn to prepare dinner for us, I thought a nice piece of poached salmon might be in order."

"Sounds perfect," Claire said, and watched as her sister left the room, her skirt swishing.

After she had gone, Claire looked around the room. She opened her wardrobe, half expecting the toy to be there, but only her clothes greeted her.

She turned back to the bed, and something on the floor caught her eye. She bent to pick it up, turning it over in her hand.

A piece of greenery, soft and realistic.

A piece of The Garden of Bewitchment lay in the palm of her hand.

CHAPTER FIVE

Matthew shielded his eyes from the sun that showed increased strength today. "I always find coincidences difficult to believe."

"Claire wondered if it could be the same toy you spoke to me about. That somehow it had manifested itself here."

"Not guilty. Oh, it sounds like the same model, but certainly not mine."

"I am so sorry, I didn't mean to imply—"

"Of course not, but you are bound to wonder. I tell you about a macabre experience, and then the self-same Garden of Bewitchment appears mysteriously in your sister's bedroom, after I had told you no toy maker I have spoken to has ever heard of it. I would feel the same way. Too much of a coincidence."

"But that is what it has to be, doesn't it?"

Matthew didn't answer, and Evelyn felt increasingly anxious. What if Claire had been right and he couldn't altogether be trusted? What if he did know all about them and was simply after their money? He didn't fit the image of a typical gold digger. *But what is a typical gold digger?* She shook her head, hoping he hadn't noticed.

"Evelyn, I want you to promise me something."

"Yes?"

"I want you to promise me if that toy turns up again you will burn it until not one trace of it remains. Do you understand? It's terribly important. Not one leaf, butterfly...nothing must remain."

"Is there something you know about it that you're not telling me?"

"No, just a hunch, I suppose. I have always felt something evil about that thing, and now I'm convinced there is more to it than even I imagined. None of it will come to any good, and you would be putting your lives in danger if you went anywhere near it. So, promise me you'll tell Claire, and if either of you stumble over it again, throw it into the nearest fireplace and set a match to it. A whole box of matches if necessary."

"I promise, and I'll tell Claire the moment I return home."

"Then I will rest much easier knowing that."

"Thank you, Matthew."

"You're thanking me? I can't help feeling responsible for that dreadful monstrosity entering your life. I don't know how, but there has to be a link."

"You haven't seen it in years. You left it at your aunt's house. In the attic. Shut away where no one would have any cause to find it."

"Evidently someone did, and don't forget, the evil mess was growing, maybe... Oh, I don't know. All we can do is speculate. But I can't believe there is more than one of those things in this world."

"I have never seen it, but my sister described the box to me, and it sounded as you had described yours. Surely toys are produced to be sold in their hundreds, if not thousands."

"Not this one. I am convinced this was either unique or there were very few made. This is no ordinary toy, as you now know for yourself. Toys don't appear and disappear, and they certainly don't behave as this one did for me. Thank goodness your sister never built the garden."

"Maybe that's why it disappeared."

Matthew looked at her questioningly.

"Perhaps it had been found by the wrong person. It wasn't meant for her at all. A mistake of some kind."

"Possibly. You told me it scared her. Something about the house."

"She swore she saw a figure had changed position the second time she looked at it. It scared her, and she threw the house down onto the bed and ran out of her room. When she returned, with me in tow, the whole thing had vanished."

"Let's hope you're right. Maybe, like us, the Devil isn't infallible. He makes mistakes too."

"The Devil? You really believe this toy is the work of the Devil?"

"Ask your sister what she thinks. I wouldn't be surprised if she agreed with me."

*   *   *

"I have looked for it, Ev. I searched my wardrobe, yours, all the cupboards upstairs and down. It's gone."

Evelyn sighed. "What a relief. Matthew is most concerned about it. I'm certain he hasn't had anything to do with its appearance, but he was adamant. Should it show up again, it must be destroyed."

"I won't argue with that. You really like him, don't you, Ev?"

Evelyn felt her cheeks burn. "I find him a most amiable companion."

"Oh, Ev, now you sound like Aunt Susan. 'Amiable companion' indeed. I think you're sweet on him."

"Oh, stop it, Claire."

"I think he looks a little like Branwell, don't you?"

"Branwell? Not a bit of it. Branwell was shorter, and he had a longer nose and... He doesn't look a bit like Branwell."

"In my mind, he does."

Evelyn didn't appreciate her tone. When she became petulant, Claire's lip would curl ever so slightly. Like now. Any second and she would be arguing for the sake of it. Evelyn felt in no mood for one of Claire's tantrums. She changed the subject.

"I think a day out in Leeds would do us both good. We haven't been for so long."

"I knew you would miss the bookshops and the hat shops. Oh, and let's not forget, the gown shops."

"Living in the country, I have no need of fancy gowns or hats and, as for books... Well, all right then, I will admit I have grown tired of the ones we have. I've read them all at least five times. Oh, I could read *Jane Eyre* a hundred times and not grow bored of it. In fact, I probably have. But a few new titles would be stimulating."

"Yes, I agree. And we need some new stories for our *Chronicles of Calladocia*."

"Tomorrow, then. If we catch the eight o'clock train, we can be in Leeds nice and early."

"It will make a change to do something together," Claire said.

"It will indeed." A momentary fear clutched her. *What if it happens again?* She reminded herself that there was no reason it should. Not really. Not if they kept to the plan.

CHAPTER SIX

"Oh, for heaven's sake, Ev. I'm not a child, you know. You're not my mother. I hate clothes shopping. It's of no interest to me whatsoever. If I want to go off on my own for half an hour, then so be it." Claire spun on her heel and raced out of the store. Evelyn watched her, dismayed, dangling a smart fashionable hat from her fingers.

"Are you quite well, madam?"

Evelyn balked at the patronizing tone of the sales assistant. "Perfectly well, thank you," she lied. "I was merely consulting my sister on whether this hat would go well with my navy blue coat. She didn't appear to think so."

It had happened again. The same as the time in that fancy store in Bradford. A look, composed partly of pity and partly of confusion. But they were doing nothing out of the ordinary. Claire and Evelyn, two identical sisters out on a shopping spree. If you could call buying three books and a possible hat a spree. And now, Claire had thrown a tantrum...again.

Evelyn turned her back on the interfering shop assistant, hoping she would take the obvious hint and move away to someone who might appreciate her condescension.

But this woman was made of sterner stuff. "I am sure this hat would complement navy, black or gray. It is such a lovely shade of gray, don't you think?"

Without a word, Evelyn slammed the hat back on its display stand and strode out of the store, her head held high, not catching the eye of any of the startled assistants and customers who had witnessed her less than careful handling of the expensive piece of millinery.

Once out among the anonymous crowds of the busy street,

Evelyn spotted Claire peering into a bookshop window. She caught up with her. "Why did you do that, Claire? Everything had been going perfectly well. We were having a pleasant day out."

"I told you. I hate clothes shopping. And I don't like the way everyone stares at us. I feel like a performer in Buffalo Bill's Wild West show."

Evelyn's temper had cooled. She hated to see Claire upset. "It's because we look so alike. People don't see too many identical twins, especially not of our age. Normally we would not be seen out together. We would be out with our own children, or husbands, and no one would guess either of us harbored a mirror image of ourselves."

"But do you think we look so alike? We dress differently, wear our hair...differently."

Evelyn smiled. "You could always use a few more hairclips."

"I know," Claire said. "You always look so well turned out. I don't know how you do it."

"A hot flat iron," Evelyn said and winked at her sister. "I'm tired of the city now. We have what we came for. Let's go home and read our new books."

Claire's eyes lit up. "A fine suggestion. Let's do that."

They spoke little on the train ride home, enjoying the solace of having the compartment all to themselves. Evelyn gazed out of the window at the countryside rushing by. Even though the windows were closed, she sensed the change in the air from smoky and gritty to fresh, clean and pure. Except for the steam and soot from the engine, of course.

Back home, the sisters eased off tight city boots. "Why do we do it, Claire? I, for one, would be so much more comfortable in my walking shoes."

"Convention, Ev. Mama always taught us to dress up to go into the city. 'You never know who you might meet,' she used to say. Do you remember?"

"I do. Mama said quite a lot of things I have thought better of in recent years."

"Such as?" Claire asked.

"Marry well, was one. She so wanted us to marry doctors or barristers. Someone in a profession. Never in trade."

"Oh goodness me, no. The shame of it. Do you remember how scathing she was of poor Caroline Illingworth, who married that grocer from Bingley?"

"Oh, yes. Poor Caroline. And Mama wasn't the worst of them. The biddies had a field day with her. They decided there had to be a reason she had married beneath her station."

"How disappointed they were when it took a year for Caroline to show signs of having consummated her relationship with Harry Sutcliffe."

They laughed. It felt good to have their closeness restored. Evelyn wiggled her toes, feeling the life throb back into them as her circulation returned. Her sister did the same.

"Right," Evelyn said at last. "Time for a cup of tea and then settle down with our books. I'm going to start with one of Mr. Conan Doyle's most recent – *The Firm of Girdlestone.*"

"Are there any murders in it?"

"Oh, yes, I'm sure there will be."

"Mama would not have approved."

"No. I don't suppose she would. Good job she'll never know, isn't it?"

Claire's laugh followed her into the kitchen.

As Evelyn made the tea, she reflected. Mama certainly would not have approved of her latest book, but she would have been horrified if she had seen what Claire was no doubt tucking into right now. Thomas Hardy's racy *Tess of the D'Urbervilles* had drawn raised eyebrows from the bookseller. Evelyn had felt sure he had wanted to say something – to protest this was not a suitable novel for a lady – but as that would have meant losing a sale, along with possible future custom, he had wisely kept his mouth shut, rung up the amount and accepted her sister's cash before wrapping the novel carefully in all-concealing brown paper.

Evelyn returned with a tray covered in tea things to find Claire engrossed. Without a word, she poured out the fragrant Ceylon brand they preferred and passed a cup to Claire, who accepted it without a word.

Evelyn settled herself comfortably and picked up her book, but had read no more than a few pages before her eyes grew heavy and she finally gave up the struggle to stay awake.

Claire's screaming woke her.

Evelyn jumped to her feet and raced up the stairs to the source of the commotion. In her room, Claire was tugging at something that had entangled itself around her wrists.

"Get it off me, please, Ev. Get it off me!"

For a second, Evelyn couldn't move. The sight of the blackened vine-like tendril, squeezing tighter and tighter around Claire's wrists, mesmerized her.

Another scream from Claire brought her to her senses. She grabbed hold of the squirming, rubberlike vine and tugged at it. The harder she pulled, the tighter it gripped. Claire's hands were white, numb-looking – the blood supply cut off.

"This is no good," Evelyn said. "I need scissors. A knife."

"Hurry, please, Ev! It hurts so much."

Evelyn dashed into her own room and rummaged in a small sewing workbasket. She found the little pair of silver scissors that had been her mother's. Rushing back, she grabbed the vine, now cutting into her sister's skin. Tiny rivulets of blood dripped from the wounds it inflicted.

The little scissors hacked away. Evelyn feared they were too blunt for such a job. The plant squealed. *It's in actual pain. It can feel.*

The vine gave, and Evelyn had cut through. Its screams died away as she hacked at it, flinging tendrils and leaves, which quickly withered and died on the floor.

When the last of the evil thing had been reduced to nothing more than dried leaves, Evelyn wrapped her sobbing sister in her arms. Her own body heaved with the exertion and fear. When they finally calmed down, Evelyn let Claire go. "Let me bandage those wrists for you. They look so raw."

Claire let Evelyn lead her into the bathroom, where she bathed the red and angry-looking wounds.

"I thought that dreadful toy had disappeared. Did it come back?"

Claire shook her head. "I forgot. I found a small piece. So tiny, it was. I never gave it another thought. I put it in my trinket box, and, when you were asleep, I felt so tired I thought I would take a short nap. I had just dropped off when I felt something tighten around my wrist. My trinket box had somehow fallen and upended on the floor and...you know the rest."

Evelyn poured a few drops of iodine onto a lint dressing. Its pungent aroma filled the small bathroom. "I'm afraid this is going to sting rather a lot."

She gritted her teeth and gently patted first one wrist and then, using a clean dressing, the other. Claire flinched at each initial contact and bit her lip, screwing up her eyes. A tear appeared at the corner of each one, but she didn't cry out.

Evelyn finished tying the bandages gently around Claire's wrists. "That should help ease them and stop any infection from that horrible thing."

Claire lowered her arms. "Why is it doing this? What can it possibly want from us?"

"I don't know. I really don't, but we must burn whatever's left of the vine. Now."

The withered leaves lay where they had left them. Evelyn hesitated. How were they going to scoop that thing up without touching it and risking a repeat of what had just happened to Claire? The plant looked dead enough now, but what if it was merely lying dormant? Maybe it could regenerate at the slightest contact with human flesh?

Evelyn recoiled as wild ideas crashed backward and forward through her brain. She must stop it or what little self-control she had left would evaporate. She shook herself. "I'm going down to the kitchen to fetch a shovel and an old bag. Keep an eye on it, but don't get any closer. Call me if it moves. Even an inch."

Claire nodded.

In the kitchen, Evelyn stoked up the fire in the range and extricated the smaller of the two coal shovels. She selected a sizeable paper grocery bag. It would be plenty big enough to hold the remains and ensure she didn't have to get her hands anywhere near them.

Back upstairs, she found Claire staring at the debris on her floor. "I'm as sure as I can be it's dead," she said.

"All the same, we can't be too careful. Matthew said destroy it, which is what we shall do. Now, Claire, please hold the bag open. Wider. Good. I'm going to shovel that thing in there."

Claire's hands trembled, and the bag shook.

"Keep it steady, please, Claire. I don't want to drop it and have to start again."

Claire tightened her grip, and the trembling stopped. She held the bag wide open and steady.

Taking care not to spill any, Evelyn edged the shovel under the vine and maneuvered the bits onto it. A smell of putrefaction rose up from the carpet, and Evelyn wrinkled her nose. Claire recoiled, almost losing her grip on the bag.

"Claire. Be careful. Don't drop it."

"Sorry, Ev. I hadn't expected such an awful stench."

"Neither had I. It seems our friend here may be dead, but it still has at least one more trick up its sleeve." In another context Evelyn would have laughed at the inappropriateness of this remark, but right now, laughter was the furthest thing from her mind.

"Got it." She shook the shovel gently to secure the contents as she slowly transferred them to the bag.

With a rustle, the debris slid off and into the bag. "Screw it up tightly," Evelyn said, but Claire was already doing so.

"It won't get out of there in a hurry," she said and followed Evelyn down the stairs.

Using a sturdy cloth to protect her hands from burning, Evelyn threw open the door of the kitchen range and stepped back. The fire raged within. Claire did not hesitate. She got as close as she dared, then threw the bag and its unearthly contents into the consuming flames.

"Did you hear that?" Claire asked.

Evelyn nodded, unable to comprehend. "It screamed. It wasn't dead."

The flames burned high in the range. The cries of the dying plant sounded like a tortured child.

"Look." Claire pointed a shaking finger at the smoke seeping out of the doors. "It can't do that. Ev, it can't, can it?"

Evelyn shook her head and watched. The smoke coiled upward, then dissipated, falling into nothing as the screams died down and finally stopped.

"Is it over?" Claire whispered.

"I hope so. I truly hope so." But as Evelyn tentatively opened the doors of the range and peered in, she realized. Only ashes remained of the evil plant, but it had taken all the fire's energy to kill it. The flames were extinguished. Somehow she knew this was only the beginning. But of what?

★   ★   ★

"Is there no way we can discover the nature of this plant, or whatever it is?" Evelyn asked Matthew as they sat on the crags the following afternoon.

"Believe me. I have tried. I have been in every library from here to York and back. I have written to the Museums of Natural History in the major capital cities of the world. I have described the different plants and trees in the garden – especially the one you and I both encountered. I've even drawn a fair representation of the thing. All the ones that bothered to reply have said the same thing. It is unknown to them. They have no record of any such strain of plant. One particularly unhelpful museum director suggested maybe I would be advised to consult with a doctor specializing in diseases of the mind."

"How dreadful."

"Would you have believed it if you hadn't seen it with your own eyes? Did you truly believe me when I first told you about that toy and what it did? None of these people had met me, and all they had to go on was a fantastic story plus a drawing that I could easily have made up, with a little imagination and some incredible claims."

"I suppose I would have found it difficult. But when you first told me about your experiences, I did believe you, Matthew. I could tell you weren't lying."

"You could see me. They couldn't."

★   ★   ★

Claire had become quiet and withdrawn, and, after two days of constant rain and howling gales, Evelyn felt as if the walls of the cottage were closing in on her. She hated being confined like this, and Claire's almost total silence only served to make the atmosphere more claustrophobic. Nothing more had happened. No manifestations of the deadly toy or smells of putrefaction. The place was quiet, save for the ticking of the clock, which seemed to grow louder until Evelyn wanted to shut it off altogether.

Finally she could stand it no longer.

"I'm going out, Claire."

Her sister raised shocked eyes from the book she was reading. "But the weather's terrible, Ev. You'll catch your death."

"It's only rain. I'm not a hothouse flower."

Claire shrugged and went back to her reading. Evelyn pulled on her boots and buttoned up her coat. She secured her hat with an extra hatpin and decided against the umbrella. In this wind it would only blow itself inside out and offer her no protection from the elements. No, she would simply have to brave it. Her ankle-length waterproof would keep most of the rain off.

Evelyn opened the door and stepped out at the same time that a rushing gust of wind nearly knocked her off her feet. The lane was empty. Most sensible people were staying put, but she pushed on, the wind in her face, rain lashing her cheeks and threatening to tear her hat off.

The muddy pathway up to the crags meant Evelyn had to take care not to slip. The rain got into her eyes, half blinding her, and she told herself she must be mad to venture out in this, but the thought of turning around and going back to Heather Cottage gave her the determination to keep on. Besides, up by the crags was an overhanging rock where she could shelter for a few minutes.

She scrambled up to the crags and found it. Under the rock, the earth seemed dry and the instant relief from the biting wind brought her some respite. Here she could pause a while and clear her mind.

A rain-filled mist hung low over the moor, creating poor visibility. The wind whistled and howled. Evelyn had an overwhelming urge to let her voice mingle with it, to scream out her frustration and fears. She opened her mouth, took a deep breath and yelled as hard as her lungs would allow. The wind whipped away her scream, which became one with it. It felt good to let her emotions go. She repeated her cry as the mist swirled.

A large bird – a buzzard by the looks of it – swooped low, a few feet ahead of her, and for one second she locked eyes with it before it flapped its wings and flew off. How wonderful to be able to go wherever you wanted, to soar off into the sky, free, no fears because *you* were the predator; no one would hunt you down. Her heart soared with it, and, without warning, Evelyn burst into tears.

Stupid, she told herself, but the worry over Claire and that awful toy had taken its toll.

Evelyn wiped her eyes and her tear-tracked cheeks. She took a deep, ragged breath and replaced her now sodden handkerchief in her pocket.

The rain eased off, and, as the minutes ticked by, the mist began to lift. In the sky, a pale sun seemed to be trying hard to break through the still-gray clouds.

She could now see further, and, some yards away, a figure moved, taking her by surprise. Her position, under the rock, gave her camouflage. Whoever it was would be unaware of being observed. As she continued to stare, she became aware that the figure was a man. One with a slight limp. He seemed to have no stick, but she recognized him straightaway. What was Matthew doing up here in this weather? The same as her?

The more she watched him, the more curious Evelyn became. He seemed to be searching...no, hiding something. He picked something up. A small spade. Now he was digging, having difficulty in the rocky soil.

She toyed with the idea of surprising him but decided against it. Much better to observe for now.

Matthew laid his spade against a rock and bent down. He seemed to be scrabbling in the dirt. Most odd. He straightened, picked up the spade and set it down. More scrabbling. He was *hiding* it, *burying* the spade. Why would he need to do that?

With one final look at his handiwork, he moved away from the rock, and Evelyn realized he was headed in her direction. He would be bound to see her. He would have to pass her on the way back down the hill. In an instant, she made up her mind. Bending low, she emerged from her shelter and half ran around to the back of the rock. She stood as straight as she could in the still-powerful wind and began to approach him as if she had simply been on her normal walk.

As Matthew caught her eye, she could see her presence had startled him, but his recovery was almost instantaneous. Almost.

She held on to her hat as a sudden gust of wind threatened to rip it off her head. "Matthew. It seems you and I are the only ones brave or foolhardy enough to come up here in this weather."

"Indeed, Evelyn. Have you been up here long?"

"Oh, no, I have only just got here. I set off late to avoid the worst of the rain." The lie tripped easily off her tongue. Why shouldn't it? He had something to hide. His actions and reaction to her made that perfectly clear. "How about you? Did you get caught in the worst of it?"

"Fortunately not. I can have only been moments ahead of you. I am surprised we didn't see each other walking up here."

"I expect the mist had something to do with it."

"I should imagine so."

He had lied to her. Quite blatantly. He must have been up there longer than he implied. He had already finished using his spade when Evelyn had first spotted him. She looked down at his hands. A little damp earth had stained his fingers. "Gracious, I hope you didn't fall." She nodded toward his hands. Now would he admit what he had been up to?

He seemed momentarily taken aback but quickly recovered himself. "It's nothing. Merely a slight slip. This is the first day I have tried walking any distance without my stick. It had become more of a nuisance than an aid, but I probably shouldn't have chosen a day when the path was muddy to embark on my first solo voyage."

Another blatant lie. She wanted to challenge him on it, but he would hardly be likely to confess. For some reason he thought it necessary to deliberately withhold something from her, which could only mean he had something to hide. Maybe something that could affect herself and her sister.

Suddenly Evelyn saw her new friend in a different light, and she didn't like what she saw. Claire's doubts rang in her mind. Matthew Dixon had shown himself to be a man of secrets, and she must find out what those secrets were.

CHAPTER SEVEN

Lady Mandolyne gazed out of her turret window over the sparkling waters of the Titanium River. Far in the distance lay the fabled land of Arcadia, spoken of in reverent whispers by all who knew of its legend. Cloaked in myth and mystery, it was even argued by some that it couldn't exist. That a place of such pure perfection could only be the product of verbal tradition – handed down from mother to daughter, father to son, for generations.

But Lady Mandolyne knew it existed. There could be no question. She had seen it.

"Well, what do you think?" Claire's excitement could not be contained.

Evelyn folded her spectacles and let them fall around her neck on their delicate chain. "So, are you saying Arcadia is a product of her imagination? Because if so I shall have to go back and rewrite some of Sir Dreyfus's scenes. He arrived there at the head of his army when the residents called on him for help against the marauding hordes of Devoria."

"No, no. You won't need to do that. It does exist. But Lady Mandolyne is, by now, so insane she cannot distinguish fact from fiction. She has never been to Arcadia. All she knows of it is contained in the fables she learned as a child. But she believes she has seen it with her own eyes."

Evelyn thought for a moment. A smile spread across her face. "I like it, Claire. I think it works well."

"Oh, thank goodness. I thought we were going to have another argument, and I do so hate rowing with you, Ev."

"Me too. We are both so passionate about Calladocia. I wonder if the Brontës had arguments over Northangerland and Glass Town?"

"I would be most surprised if they didn't. All siblings argue, don't they? Each one is convinced they know best."

Evelyn's face clouded over. "Claire, you remember what I told you about Matthew being up on the moors yesterday?"

"Yes. Very suspicious."

"I agree. I want to find out what he was doing up there. Will you come with me?"

"But what if we run into him?"

"He doesn't walk up there in the evening, and the nights are light enough now that we could go up there at, say, nine or ten o'clock and still be able to see what we were doing."

"The lighter nights might bring him out too."

Evelyn thought for a moment. "I shall ask him."

"What?"

"This afternoon, when I meet him on our walk, I shall ask him how he spends his evenings."

"Won't he find that a bit suspicious?"

"Not if I make it casual."

"Oh, Ev, I don't know. Please be careful. If he is up to no good, he could be dangerous."

"Don't worry, I'm no martyr. I promise I won't put myself in any danger."

Claire's frown told her she didn't believe her. Too bad. Evelyn had to do this.

★   ★   ★

"It's certainly a treat to be able to read without lamplight so late into the evening," Evelyn said as she and Matthew walked up the pathway.

"Indeed, although I must confess I tend to fall asleep by ten o'clock. I rise early, you see. I'm usually up and around by six."

"You *are* an early bird."

"Always have been. A habit I got into at school and never broke."

"There are worse habits. I find it difficult to sleep when it's still light outside, even with my dark curtains."

"I can't say it has ever bothered me. I could sleep anywhere."

They stopped to admire the view. Evelyn inhaled deeply. "Yesterday's rain has washed everything clean. You can smell the sap in the grass."

"And the earthy smell of peat," he laughed.

"You can't have our moorland without a peaty scent."

"Indeed."

They stood in silence. Evelyn's mind raced. She had managed to get the answer to her question without arousing his suspicions. Tonight, she and Claire would be able to come up to the moor, secure in the knowledge he wouldn't disturb them. Then they would discover what had required the use of a spade and needed to be hidden. Evelyn prayed she wouldn't live to regret any discovery they made. A part of her wanted to forget the whole thing. Let the man have his secrets. But a nagging doubt wouldn't let her. If his secret had something to do with Claire and herself, surely they had a right to know. More than a right. They *needed* to know.

★   ★   ★

"Are you sure we should be doing this, Ev?"

"Not entirely, but we need to know we can trust him. There is probably a perfectly simple explanation for what I saw, but until we know for certain... I have to be sure, Claire. Too much is at stake. What if he is somehow behind the manifestations?"

"How?"

"I have no idea, but you've heard of those illusionists? They can make things disappear before your eyes and reappear somewhere entirely different."

"Those are circus tricks."

"Maybe. But supposing he's learned some of them?"

Claire gave her a skeptical look. It did sound far-fetched, but then so was a bed rising, apparently all by itself, and a toy that could become so real it nearly killed Claire.

Evelyn opened the door. "Let's get this over with."

"And you're sure he won't catch us?"

"It's after nine now, and he told me he is usually in bed by ten. He still tires quite easily, so I can't see him returning to the moor after our walk this afternoon."

Claire took a step outside the door, and Evelyn closed and locked it before she could change her mind.

Up on the moor, the breeze had turned chilly and the sun was sinking, leaving the promise of a fiery sunset.

"I was standing here." She indicated the rocky outcrop. "It's well sheltered. He was over there." She pointed at the rock that had occupied Matthew's time and energy. "Come on, we don't have too much time before we lose the light."

Evelyn strode through the heather, catching her skirt on more than one occasion but failing to tear the strong fabric. A mumbled groan and the sound of a tiny rip told her Claire had not been so fortunate.

By the rock, the earth looked freshly disturbed, although patted down so in a few days no one would have been able to tell. "Whatever he was up to, he wanted to conceal it. Did you bring the trowel as I asked you to?"

Claire nodded and removed it from the folds of her coat. She handed it to Evelyn, who immediately bent down and started digging, taking care not to stab too hard at the soil. Whatever Matthew had hidden might be delicate, although why he would hide such an item up here defied her comprehension. Her first success proved short-lived. The spade lay half revealed. Evelyn quickly troweled soil over it. She started again, a foot or so away.

Claire watched patiently as Evelyn turned up each trowel-full of empty earth.

"How long did he dig for?"

Evelyn paused. "I don't really know. The mist made everything too murky at first, and I didn't see him. He had almost finished by the time it lifted."

"Try a little further on. The earth seems softer there, and it has definitely been disturbed recently."

Evelyn nodded. The exertion made her back ache.

"Do you want me to take over?" Claire asked.

"Maybe later. I'm all right at the moment."

Her trowel hit something, making a deep thud. Maybe a box.

"I've got something."

Heedless of the dirt, Claire knelt down and peered closer. Evelyn kept digging. Within seconds, a small tin box lay in front of them. It was plain and had a lock. Evelyn picked it up, noting its weight. It seemed surprisingly heavy for something so relatively small. She shook it, but nothing rattled. She tried to open it, but the lid wouldn't budge. "Locked."

"We could force it open," Claire suggested.

Tempting, but…

"How would he know it was us?" Claire asked. "Here it is, buried on common ground. Someone's dog could have dug it up, the owner could have forced the box open and then reburied it. We are going to rebury it, aren't we, Ev?"

"Of course. I only want to see what's inside." Without another thought, she grabbed the trowel and tried to force it between the lid and the box. It held firm.

"Let me try."

Evelyn handed Claire the tin, and her sister exerted all her effort trying to prize it open.

"It's no use, Ev. I can't shift it. We need a screwdriver or something with a sharp point. Or maybe we could pick the lock." She removed a hair clip and straightened it.

"What on earth do you know about picking locks? And what *are* you doing?"

"I read about it."

"Don't tell me you've been reading those penny dreadfuls again. Where do you get them from? You never go out without me."

"Ah, that's not strictly true. I do go out. Now and again. I get them in the village. It's only harmless fun."

Evelyn screwed her nose up. Nothing would ever induce her to read one of those awful rags. Fleetingly she wondered when Claire did go on these excursions alone. This was the first she had heard of them. Maybe her sister's chronic shyness was gradually wearing off. This thought should have brought her comfort, but she couldn't help worrying. Claire could be so naïve.

Claire was now hard at work, poking the lock with her hairpin. She only succeeded in bending the hairpin first this way and then that until the thing had been rendered unusable either for its original purpose or as a tool of petty crime.

"This is getting us nowhere at all," Evelyn said. "Let's bury it again and return tomorrow with more suitable implements."

She held out her hand, and, reluctantly, Claire handed back the box.

Evelyn set it back down in the soil and quickly reburied it, patting the dirt down firmly on top. "There. No one would ever know it had been disturbed."

Twilight was fast fading into darkness.

"Come on, Claire. Let's get back while we still have sufficient light to see where we're going. I don't want to fall into any potholes."

The sisters stumbled and hurried back to the cottage. They met no one along the way, for which Evelyn offered a silent prayer of thanks.

Back home, Evelyn stared in dismay at the hem of Claire's skirt. "You had better change and bring me that dress. It's torn and so filthy I can no longer tell what color it's supposed to be."

Claire nodded and hurried up the stairs.

★   ★   ★

The next day, Evelyn went out at the usual time for her afternoon walk. Today, though, Matthew didn't join her. Maybe he had other engagements. It was really none of her business. They were acquaintances and barely knew each other. Still she missed him and remonstrated with herself while a part of her prayed hard that whatever resided in the box wouldn't implicate him in some scheme designed to part Claire and her from their inheritance.

She stayed up at the crags rather longer than usual, but when, after an hour, there was still no sign of Matthew, she reluctantly turned back for home.

★   ★   ★

A little after nine that evening saw the two sisters back on the deserted moors. A curlew cried overhead.

"It's a good job that bird can't speak," Claire said. "She'd go spilling the beans to Matthew."

Evelyn forced a smile. Claire was doing her best to lighten the tension, but, armed with as many pointed tools as they could find, Evelyn's mood was hardly conducive to finding levity in anything.

Once again, she took the trowel from Claire and commenced digging in the same spot as the previous night. Soil mounted up until the area resembled a miniature grave plot.

"I don't understand it. There's nothing here."

"Are you sure you're digging in exactly the same place? Remember, you couldn't find it at first last night."

"That's why I took such great care to note the exact spot, and that's where I've been digging." Evelyn unsuccessfully tried to quash the frustration mounting inside her. She threw the trowel down and straightened, wincing at the sharp pain stabbing her lower back. "There's no point in denying it. Either he or somebody else has been here and dug it up. It's gone."

"But why? I don't understand. I can't imagine who would want to dig up Matthew's box in the first place. Apart from us, of course."

"Precisely. That leaves only one possible conclusion. Matthew is up to no good here, and he has realized someone is on to him. Maybe I didn't pat the soil down correctly. I don't know. I was as careful as I could."

"I know you were. I watched you. Oh, Ev, what shall we do now? We can't trust him, can we?"

Evelyn shook her head. "Whatever happens, both you and I must treat Matthew exactly as before. He cannot know, or even suspect, we were the ones who disinterred his precious box."

"This is like one of the stories I read."

"This is real life, Claire. It's much more sinister."

Concealing the tools they had brought within their coats, they scrambled back over the moor and onto the pathway. Once in the lane, they met Mr. Skelton coming in the opposite direction, returning from the public house, no doubt. He tipped his hat to them, and a faint smell of whisky wafted toward them as he passed. "Good evening, Miss Wainwright," he said to Evelyn.

"Good evening, Mr. Skelton," she replied, and they carried on walking in their respective directions.

Once out of earshot, Claire whispered to her sister. "How incredibly rude of him. Did you see the way he simply ignored me?"

"Oh, I'm sure he didn't, Claire. He probably meant to say 'Miss Wainwright' to you too, but he had obviously had a drink or two."

"Even so, that's no excuse for being impolite."

"Don't let it worry you, Claire."

Claire muttered something Evelyn couldn't hear. She didn't bother to ask her to repeat it.

*　*　*

Evelyn couldn't sleep. Her mind wouldn't let her. Thoughts of Matthew. Fears for his honesty. What did he keep in the box? Did Pandora feel like this before she opened hers and let out all the evils of the world? More crazy thoughts and questions. Her brain kept on feeding her information, ideas, suggestions, until she crawled out of bed, clutching her head.

The breeze had died down, leaving a sultry night, its humidity penetrating the thick stone walls of the cottage. Evelyn knew she had lost the battle for sleep. She tied her dressing gown around her and padded down the stairs in bare feet, grateful for the cool stone floor of the kitchen.

She poured milk into a small saucepan and placed it on the range. Hot milk. Her mother's remedy for almost everything when she had been a child.

While she waited for the milk to heat up, Evelyn wandered over to the window. Here, at the back of the house, a small yard led to a flight of stone steps – a shortcut to the moors, but one Evelyn had decided to ignore. The stones were worn and uneven and the steps narrow and steep.

The moon shone bright and full. Silvery-white light illuminated the yard and the steps. Evelyn could even clearly see the path that ran along the top.

And the man standing there.

Evelyn jumped back. Had he seen her? Cautiously, she bent low and peered up. A puff of smoke curled up from whatever he was smoking. He was also turned away from her.

She glanced back at the clock. Two fifteen. Who would be standing there at this time of night? She focused on his hat. A stylish bowler. His hair appeared to be a reddish brown, but it was difficult to tell from the little she could see of it.

A sudden noise behind her, a sizzling splash and the acrid smell of burned milk assailed her. She dashed to the range and, grabbing a cloth, dragged the saucepan onto the draining board. She wiped up the spillage before half filling her mug with the remainder of the milk.

By the time she could return to the window, the man had gone.

★　　★　　★

Evelyn left Claire asleep, quietly closing the door behind her. Outside, the morning air tasted fresh and dewy. She made her way up the lane, but instead of continuing onto the path leading up to the crags, she doubled back on herself in order to take the track running at the back of their cottage. When she stood directly opposite, looking down at the back door, she glanced around. Sure enough, there on the ground where the man had been standing, a fresh-looking stubbed-out cigarette butt lay on the flattened grass. But who had he been? This mysterious man wandering around in the dead of night, who happened to stop above their home? Evelyn carried on past the row of cottages and into open country. The area was mostly coarse grassland with gorse, the small yellow flowers adding color and brightness.

Ahead of her, a few people were out walking their dogs. This terrain proved easier to negotiate than her usual route. Above her, storm clouds promised heavy rain to come, and a sudden chill breeze made Evelyn shiver. She had only donned a light summer coat, totally unsuited to a torrential downpour and certainly not protective enough in a chilly wind. Time to go back.

Evelyn turned and caught her breath. Standing a few yards away, a man doffed his bowler hat to her, smiled and walked away.

★　　★　　★

"What did he look like, Ev?"

"Fairly tall, probably three inches taller than me, with reddish-brown hair, collar length. He wore a dark gray bowler and a tweed suit. The strangest thing, though…"

"What?"

"I am certain I've seen him before…late last night when I came downstairs because I couldn't sleep. He was standing on the track that runs along the top, outside the back of our cottage. There's something about him…" Evelyn shook her head. "No, you'll think I'm crazy."

"Oh, you can't stop now. What else?"

"In profile, as he turned to go, he looked so much like your print of Branwell. Quite uncanny."

Claire stared. "Branwell? Here?"

"No, obviously it couldn't be him, but maybe some relation."

"There *are* no Brontë relations. Not around here anyway. Maybe in Ireland."

"Coincidence. Nothing more, nothing less. Pure coincidence. And I did only catch a glimpse of him in profile. Full face... I'm not sure I know what Branwell Brontë looks like full face."

"There are very few pictures of him, only the odd self-portrait, and he never did himself justice. He always seemed to parody himself."

A thud sounded from upstairs.

"What on earth...?" Evelyn hitched up her skirts and took to the stairs, Claire close behind her.

In Claire's bedroom, the wardrobe door stood open. As they moved toward it, it slammed shut. Claire let out a cry.

Evelyn bit her lip, took a deep breath and wrenched the door open again.

There on the floor of the wardrobe lay the box. The Garden of Bewitchment.

"It's back."

Evelyn bent to pick it up.

"Be careful, Ev."

"I have to pick it up to take it downstairs. We must burn it. Remember what Matthew said."

"Supposing he lied to you about it?"

"It's evil, Claire. Remember how one little bit of it attacked you. Remember what it took to kill that?"

Claire touched the bandage on her right wrist. "We can't burn it in the house."

"We can hardly start a fire outside. The neighbors..."

"Oh, hang the neighbors."

"You go downstairs and open the door on the kitchen range, stoke up the fire. It will burn quicker with a good fire going. Make sure it's burning stronger than the last one. I'll follow you."

Claire looked as if she was about to challenge Evelyn but thought better of it. She left and hurried down the stairs.

Evelyn looked again at the box. The thought of touching it filled her with dread. She grabbed a long scarf and wrapped it around her hands. At least she wouldn't come into direct contact with the toy.

Gingerly she picked it up, holding it at arm's length. It seemed so innocent. A simple box illustrating a beautiful garden. Any child, or adult even, would be drawn to it.

Evelyn carried it carefully downstairs, taking care not to tilt or jar the box. The heat hit her as soon as she stepped into the kitchen. The fire blazed fiercely. Claire stepped back, wiping her sweaty brow.

Evelyn threw the box and its contents into the fire. Claire shut the door of the range.

They couldn't see anything, but the fire had to be consuming the thing. The sisters waited.

"Let's leave it for half an hour and check on it then," Evelyn said. "It should be well and truly ashes by then."

"What did it want from us?"

"We'll probably never know. The thing was pure evil, and now it's gone. We don't need to worry about it anymore."

"Will you go out this afternoon?" Claire asked as they made their way into the drawing room.

"Not if the rain carries on like this." She indicated the window, where the rain beat a tattoo.

A sharp rap at the door made them both jump.

"You see to it, Ev. I'm going upstairs for a lie down. Seeing that…thing again has worn me out."

Evelyn waited until her sister had reached the top of the stairs before answering the door.

"Matthew! Whatever has brought you out in such dreadful weather?"

"May I come in?"

"Of course." Evelyn held the door open, and the dripping and disheveled man limped in. It seemed to have worsened since she had seen him up at the crags.

"I must apologize for disturbing you and calling unannounced, but I couldn't help feeling something was terribly wrong."

Evelyn struggled to keep her composure. "Wrong?"

"Yes. Have you seen anything unusual?"

"As a matter of fact we have. A short while ago, we heard a thump and went to investigate, only to find that hideous toy had returned. It was lying in my sister's wardrobe."

"I knew it. I felt it. Don't ask me how, but I suppose I must have a connection to it in some way. Where is it now?"

"We burned it, as you advised."

"And you are sure you caught every piece?"

"As sure as I can be. It's in the kitchen range. Claire made sure the fire was good and high."

"May I see?"

"Of course. It should be burned up by now. We were going to wait half an hour or so to be certain, but the fire was so strong I'm sure it would have burned to cinders in a few minutes."

"Let's hope so."

Evelyn led the way. The kitchen felt unusually cold. "That's strange."

She picked up the cloth and was struck by the lack of warmth as she turned the lever to open the fire.

"What the…?" Evelyn stared in disbelief. The fire had gone out, as if it hadn't been lit for a day or more. Stone cold. Ashes lay at the bottom and there, neatly lying in pristine condition, the box. "But this isn't possible. I put it in there myself. The fire was raging."

"I don't doubt you, Evelyn. I am quite sure everything was exactly as you say."

"But what do we do now? Light another fire?"

"Certainly not here, and we do have to get this thing out of here now. Do you have a bag I can put it in?"

"Yes, of course."

"We'd better tie it up with string first so it doesn't fall open."

Evelyn fetched the big roll of sturdy twine, some scissors and a strong, large brown paper shopping bag with string handles.

Matthew tied up the box firmly. "We'll need matches and a little kindling to get the fire started."

"Matthew, we can't start a fire outside in this weather. It won't burn."

"There are some small caves up on the moors. The rain never gets in there."

"You seem to have discovered more of this area than I have," Evelyn said, and hoped he didn't get the catch in her voice.

Matthew gave her a slight smile and shoved the box into the bag. "Our main problem is how to keep this bag from disintegrating in the rain. Do you have something else?"

"I have a small suitcase."

"Excellent."

Evelyn went into the drawing room, opened the door of the tall cupboard and reached the little case down from the top shelf. She handed it to Matthew.

"Perfect." He unlatched it and slid the bag and its contents inside. The box fitted snugly, and Matthew closed the suitcase.

"I can do this alone. You don't have to come with me."

"No, it's very kind of you, but I would rather see the end of this thing for myself."

"Do you want to get your sister?"

"No, let's leave her sleeping. This has been a terrible ordeal for her. Especially as this thing manifested itself yet again in her room rather than mine. She naturally feels as if she is its real target."

Matthew nodded, and, suitably dressed against the elements, the two began their journey up to the crags.

⋆   ⋆   ⋆

Larger than the rock she had taken refuge under, the cave, while still small, was enclosed on three sides and big enough to provide dry shelter for them both. Matthew set about laying a small fire while Evelyn waited to hand him the matches. After placing the toy on top of the little pyre, Matthew struck a match and lit some screwed-up newspaper, which he then set under the kindling. The fire spluttered at first, then took hold.

He stood back and watched as the flames licked at the box. Soon they were surrounding it.

"I don't understand," Matthew said. "It should be burning now. It's cardboard and flimsy balsa wood."

Evelyn watched in mounting disbelief as the flames burned the kindling but left the box clean. Presently they died down. In a couple of minutes, the fire had extinguished.

"I'm glad you were with me, Evelyn. If this had happened and I had told you about it, you wouldn't have believed me."

"Yes, I would. The kitchen range, remember? This is the same thing all over again."

"I have my petrol lighter with me," Matthew said. "I filled it yesterday. I could empty it over the box directly and set fire to it."

"It's worth trying."

Matthew picked the box off the ashes and laid it on the hard, dry earth. He emptied the contents of the small lighter over the box. Barely more than a few drops of the highly flammable substance dripped out. "I only hope it's enough," he said.

"How much petrol do you need to burn a box?"

"I don't know. I've never tried." Matthew struck a match and set it to the petrol.

"Careful. You'll burn yourself."

"I shall be fine. I—"

The flames shot into the air, catching Matthew's wrist and hand. He staggered backward. Evelyn stripped off her coat and smothered his arm with it. The smell of burning flesh filled the air.

"My God, Matthew. How did that happen? There was barely any petrol in it."

Matthew managed to speak through teeth gritted against the pain. "Look...look at the...box."

Evelyn looked. "There's not a mark on it. Not one. How is it possible? Matthew? Matthew!"

He lay slumped against the back wall of the cave. Passed out.

A few seconds later, he stirred.

"Let me see your arm," Evelyn said, gently unwrapping it from the coat. The affected area had turned red and had already slightly swollen up. It looked painful. Fortunately not nearly as bad as she had feared, given the ferocity of the flame that had attacked him. "We need to get you back so I can clean this. We have some aloe vera ointment at home. It is very good for burns. I don't think you'll need to consult a doctor, but if you wish I can send Claire round to the apothecary when we return."

"No. No. It's not too bad."

"You're clearly in pain, Matthew. Come on, let's get you back."

"The box…"

"We'll have to leave it here. At least it's out of the house." Silently she prayed it wouldn't find its way back either.

Matthew looked in too much pain to protest. Evelyn helped him to his feet. The sooner she could get Matthew back to her cottage and get those burns dressed, the better. Evelyn had seen an infected burn years earlier when Ivy, the kitchen maid, had an accident with a frying pan. Nancy had cleaned the wound and wrapped a bandage around it, but a few days later the poor girl was still in agony, requiring the ministrations not only of the cook but also of Violet, the parlor maid. Ivy's screams echoed through the entire house, and Evelyn had been left unsupervised. Her curiosity took hold and she sneaked down the servants' stairs, into the kitchen. Unnoticed, she witnessed the distraught girl, little more than a child herself, as Nancy tried to change the three-day-old bandage, peeling it off skin to which it had become adhered. Violet did her best to restrain the terrified girl who thrashed around, pleading for an end to her torment.

Evelyn had been fascinated by the sight of blood and bright yellow pus, mingling together in a foulness that set the parlor maid reeling, her hand to her nose.

Then the cook noticed Evelyn. She shouted to Violet, "Get Miss Evelyn back upstairs immediately. This is not for her eyes."

She had been bundled up the stairs, where she sought out Claire, regaling the story of the unfortunate kitchen maid's woes to her in graphic detail until her sister had pleaded with her to stop. Of course, Evelyn had elaborated a little. It made for a far better story if she described the girl's hand swollen up like a carcass left to rot on the road.

She never saw the kitchen maid again, nor did she know what had happened to her. A week later, a new girl arrived and nothing more was ever said of young Ivy.

There was no sign of Claire when they returned. Perhaps she was still upstairs, or maybe she was out on one of her secret jaunts. Evelyn hadn't time to concern herself. She had more important work to do.

In the kitchen, Evelyn mixed hot water from the large copper kettle on the range with cold from the water pump. The tepid water seemed to bring some relief after the initial sting of contact. Matthew's pinched expression relaxed a little as Evelyn carefully bathed the burns.

Next she applied aloe vera ointment. "This should help the healing process," she said. "I think you've been lucky. The burns are clearly superficial, although they must hurt a great deal."

"I have known worse," Matthew said. "But I wouldn't recommend it."

"I'll put a dressing on and then bandage you up. The most important thing is to keep the area clean and also make sure the dressing doesn't stick to the wound." Again the image of poor, screaming Ivy flashed into her mind.

With Matthew suitably bandaged and nursing a strong cup of tea in her drawing room, Evelyn still couldn't make her mind up about him. He seemed genuinely pleasant and grateful for her attention. If only that locked box didn't keep bothering her...

"We will have to destroy that toy, Evelyn."

"I know. The question is, how? It seems to resist all attempts to burn it. Perhaps if we bury it?"

"It might work. Bury it deep enough and place a rock on top of it. Left on the moors like that should be sufficient to ensure no one accidentally digs it up."

"After all, who buries anything on the moors?" Evelyn asked, a smile on her face. Did he react? If he did, the moment passed in an instant. "I mean, it's not as if anyone digging for peat would go there."

"No, they would go further onto the moor itself."

"The problem is…"

He held up his bandaged hand.

"I can dig," Evelyn said. "I used to tend a patch of our garden at home. I planted all manner of flowers and herbs."

"This might require more strenuous digging."

"Don't worry, Matthew. I'm not as weak and feeble as you might think." She had kept her tone light.

"I'm sorry, Evelyn. I didn't mean to imply that."

Evelyn smiled again. "It's quite all right. Shall we return there tomorrow morning? If you feel up to it."

"Tomorrow morning will be fine." Matthew stood. "And now, it is time for me to go home. Thank you for your kindness, Evelyn."

"Not at all." Evelyn opened the door for him.

After he had gone, she went in search of her sister.

She was nowhere to be found.

CHAPTER EIGHT

Dear Diary, Ev thinks I am helpless without her, but she's wrong. I can do far more for myself than she could possibly imagine, and one thing I am determined to do is find out whether Matthew is who he claims to be.

Claire took the left-hand path, walking along past the cottage and deeper onto the moor itself, grateful that the rain had stopped at last. As she strode out, the land became softer, greener. Behind her, bleak rocks and heather-strewn marsh. In front of her, the bright yellow gorse gave way to lush grass, cowslips and tall daisies. A small copse of trees looked as if they might provide welcome cool shade from the sun, which had begun to burn down on Claire's neck. She should have worn the wide-brimmed hat she always wore in bright sunlight, but the weather had been gloomy when she set out and she had selected a summery hat offering no protection from the powerful rays.

As she approached the copse, it became clear the trees merely served as a screen for something much more interesting. All thoughts of Matthew forgotten and her curiosity thoroughly aroused, Claire pressed on.

The tall trees smelled of sap and pine, and up ahead, the bluest bird Claire had ever seen hopped from branch to branch, its beady eyes watching her. Butterflies she had never seen before fluttered their various scarlet, golden, purple and green wings. The air filled with the sweetest birdsong.

How amazing. I must tell Ev...

But why shouldn't she have her own secrets?

The copse gave way to a clearing, with all manner of brilliantly colored flowers and shrubs, planted in beds. Cobbled pathways wended their way around them. Somehow or other Claire had stumbled into a garden.

But why there in the middle of the moor? Claire hesitated. She must be trespassing, although for the life of her she couldn't remember seeing any sign indicating she had crossed into private property. No gates, no fencing, and if there was a garden, it followed there must be a house.

The path took a sudden swing to the left, and Claire followed it, then stopped. There in front of her stood a magnificent house. Verandas stretched around it on the first floor. In front of it, roses bloomed in abundance with brilliant scarlet, orange and yellow blooms. A three-tiered stone fountain, decorated with demonic-looking carved gargoyles, cascaded water into its pool through an intricately carved pineapple on the top.

The scene looked vaguely familiar.

No sign of anyone. Claire moved slowly toward the house, crunching gravel.

The faint tinkle of piano keys drifted out from a front room. Claire followed the sound. She glanced through the window and instantly stepped back. The scene. The woman playing, the people sitting around in rapt attention.

The toy.

Claire gasped. Out of the corner of her eye she caught a movement.

Someone running.

Or something.

Still running, keeping close to the trees and concealed from view.

"Oh, won't someone help me? Help me, please." The woman's voice came from the downstairs room where, only seconds before, someone was playing the piano.

"No! This isn't real. This cannot be happening." Claire stared at the face of the distraught woman who pointed at her through the window. The sun disappeared behind a cloud, and a mist descended like a blanket. It only took mere seconds before Claire felt the chill, the sense of being shrouded in dampness. Still the woman pointed at her.

No, not at her. *Behind* her.

Claire spun round. Visibility was almost nil. But scurrying noises were coming closer.

The woman cried out again. "Help me. Please. Somebody help me!"

Her voice rang clear in Claire's ear. Clear and familiar. Claire turned back. The mist was spreading. In a moment she wouldn't be able to see the house. Right before it happened, she called out to the woman. "Lady Mandolyne? What do you see?"

Something rushed up behind her. Too fast to escape from. It took her down with it, and Claire blacked out.

★   ★   ★

"Miss Wainwright, are you all right?" Claire opened her eyes and looked into the kindly face of their neighbor Mr. Skelton. She struggled to sit, and he assisted her.

"I must have fainted," she said, aware of a nagging headache behind her eyes.

"You gave me quite a stir," Mr. Skelton said, helping her to her feet.

A sudden wave of dizziness sent her staggering.

Mr. Skelton steadied her. "I think I had better escort you home."

"Thank you." Then she remembered. The house. The garden. Even the small copse of trees. "Where have they gone?"

Mr. Skelton blinked in the brilliant sunshine. "Where have what gone, my dear?"

Claire looked wildly around at the gorse-covered moorland. "What happened to me?"

"I'm afraid I can't answer that. I was taking a walk and saw you lying on the ground."

"How long? I mean, how long ago did you find me?"

"Only a few seconds before you came to. I don't think you can have been here for long. You certainly weren't here when I first came up here this morning."

"When was that, Mr. Skelton? Do you remember?"

"Certainly I do. The church clock had just struck the half hour. Half past ten."

"And what is the time now?"

Mr. Skelton looked at her curiously for a moment before taking out his pocket watch. "Eleven thirty."

"I must have been here," Claire said. "I know I left home at around ten twenty. I walked up here, found the copse and the beautiful garden—"

"I'm sorry to interrupt, but I don't know of any copse around here, and this is all wild moorland. There is no garden. Only our little cottage ones at the back of our houses."

"No, this one was magnificent. Trees, flower borders and beds, a fountain with these horrible gargoyles, just as you see carved on old churches, and a pineapple carved on the top...and a mansion with verandas all around it. And there was a woman..." *Lady Mandolyne.* "But she doesn't exist."

"My dear Miss Wainwright. We simply must get you home. I think you must have bumped your head when you fell. You did fall, didn't you? You didn't just decide to sit down and then fell asleep in the sun? It is a very warm day."

"No, no. I fell. Someone...something pushed me..." The memory of being thrown down to the ground by a powerful force returned. "Yes. Something pushed me to the ground. Something Lady Mandolyne feared." The words of the *Chronicles* came back to her. Words she herself had written. "Lady Mandolyne saw it first."

Mr. Skelton looked confused. "Didn't you just say this woman? Lady Mandolyne? That she didn't exist?"

Claire nodded, then shook her head. The throbbing upped its intensity. Nausea started to bubble up in her stomach. "It's complicated."

"Come along, then."

"Yes, my sister will wonder where I am. I didn't tell her I was going out."

"Never mind. I'm sure she'll be glad to see you."

The walk back seemed to take twice as long as when she had set out, but eventually she waved Mr. Skelton off at her door.

Inside, she leaned against the door, her head banging.

Struggling to walk without being sick, she made it into the kitchen and poured herself a long glass of water. She took a few drops of laudanum from a bottle on a shelf, added it to the glass and drank down half the water in one go.

Her stomach protested the sudden rush of liquid. Realizing her mistake almost immediately, she dashed to the outside toilet, and the remains of her breakfast followed by bile emptied into the pan. She staggered back out into the fresh air and leaned against the cold stone wall, praying for her head to stop thumping.

Finally she felt strong enough to stagger up the stairs and into her bedroom, where she collapsed on her bed and fell asleep almost instantly.

★   ★   ★

She awoke to the fragrant smells of dinner cooking. Claire glanced at her clock. She had been asleep for nearly six hours.

The remains of her headache still played around her temples, making the skin feel tender when she touched it.

Now all she had to do was tell Ev. But would her sister believe her?

★   ★   ★

"And when you came round, you saw no sign of the house or the garden with that amazing fountain? Or..." Evelyn hesitated. "Lady Mandolyne?"

"Ev, it was as if none of it had ever been there."

Evelyn set her knife and fork together on her empty plate and dabbed her lips with her napkin. If anyone else but Claire had told her that fantastic story, she would never have believed them, but she knew her sister. At worst Claire had convinced herself she had seen what she recounted. At best, she really had been there and it all happened exactly as she said.

"I think we need to go back together."

Claire's eyes opened wide. "Oh, no, Ev. I don't think so."

"I can go on my own, but I need you to show me exactly where this copse was. I could be wandering around the moor for hours and never see it."

"Even if I did come with you, who is to say it will be there? It wasn't when Mr. Skelton found me."

"Did you mention anything at all to him about it?"

Claire nodded. "He said there was no such thing. That it didn't exist. He must have thought I had gone crazy, and maybe I have." She sighed. "I felt too ill to protest. I just wanted to come home."

"You are all right now, though?"

"My head's a bit sore, but apart from that…"

"Let me see your head. You say something charged at you, knocking you unconscious."

"I don't remember anything else."

"Maybe it bruised you. Let me check."

Evelyn gently felt Claire's head. As she touched the nape of her neck, Claire flinched.

Evelyn gently moved the hair away. "You've definitely got a bruise there, and it's a bit swollen. I'll get the witch hazel. That should speed up the healing."

Claire sat patiently while Evelyn dabbed witch hazel over the affected area. "Ev, I think you're right. I think we should go back there together. I need to see it for myself. Maybe the bump on my head caused me to have some sort of delusion. For all I know, I might not be remembering it at all. My brain could be playing tricks on me."

Evelyn stopped dabbing. She picked up the bottle and cloth. "We'll go tomorrow, if you're feeling up to it. I do wonder, though… If the blow to your neck caused you to have a delusion, we are still left with the question – who, or what, hit you?"

★　　★　　★

"It was around here. I'm sure of it. The moor changed. There was grass instead of gorse, and then I saw the copse in the distance."

Evelyn looked at the gorse bushes spreading ahead and to either side of them. "Let's walk on a little further."

Claire stopped still. "No, it was definitely around here, but it's different. There should be cowslips, lush grass..."

"Maybe we veered off the path." Evelyn couldn't see how. There was one path, and they were on it.

They continued on in silence, alone on the moor. A breeze whipped up, and Ev fixed her hatpin more securely. Claire's hair managed its usual bid for escape, wild wisps of it fluttering around her face. She brushed it out of her eyes.

"It's no good, Ev. We're not going to find it. Maybe I tripped and hit my head against a stone. Perhaps this whole thing is a product of my imagination."

Evelyn pointed ahead of them. Her finger shook. "Claire?"

"Yes?"

A few yards ahead, a figure had emerged, apparently from nowhere. She moved slowly toward them. A woman dressed in a silk robe, the fabric of which floated around her. Her long, raven hair flowed around her shoulders. Behind her, a fountain Evelyn recognized from Claire's description, its distinctive gargoyles and pineapple carving unmistakable.

"Tell me you see her," Evelyn whispered.

"I see her."

"Do you know her?"

"She is exactly as I imagined her. Exactly as I saw her yesterday."

"Who is she?"

"Lady Mandolyne."

CHAPTER NINE

"Claire! Claire! I'm losing you. I can't see you anymore!" Evelyn's panic turned her blood ice cold. One moment she was staring at a beautiful woman – Claire's lovely and tragic Lady Mandolyne – and the next, she was shrouded in a dense fog that materialized from nowhere.

In the distance, Claire screamed.

"*Claire!*"

Swirling out of the fog, the beautiful face of Lady Mandolyne filled her field of vision. Her lips curled; a smile became a macabre grin. The woman became a creature. Serpentine features replaced the perfect, flawless complexion. A forked tongue flicked in and out of the scaly mouth. The creature slid to the ground, no longer supported by legs. Fear welled up inside Evelyn. *This isn't real. It isn't happening.*

The creature wrapped itself around her, its grip tightening as it flexed its muscled body, and Evelyn began to spin, slowly at first, then faster, ever faster as the creature turned her as easily as a child's spinning top.

Stop this. Stop this now!

Nothing answered. Far away, Claire's screams echoed as if from a long tunnel.

"Claire! I can't find you. I can't get to you. I'm trapped here!"

Round and round, she spun, her head reeling and her vision filled with curious shapes, mesmerizing her. *Concentrate, I must concentrate. It's all in my head. None of it is real.*

The spinning stopped as quickly as it had begun. Evelyn gave herself up to the nebulous white cloud that now enfolded her. It offered protection, softness, warmth. But in among the comfort, an unpleasant, sulfurous stench wafted into her nostrils.

No. Not safe. Not real. She must stop it. She mustn't give in to it. It meant her harm. She must rescue Claire.

She closed her eyes, trying to focus on moorland, heather, gorse, their cottage, the simple realities of their daily lives. Around her, the strange air billowed, ruffling her hair, at times chilling, at others warm. She had a sensation of moving, but in what direction she didn't know. She wasn't walking but seemed propelled by some kind of magnetic force. Upward, downward, left, right, straight on. Her disorientation became complete. All control had been taken from her. Palpable fear. She could taste it, touch it, hear it. Her mind filled with it. What if she could never escape its clutches? She didn't even know what to call it. Lady Mandolyne was a figment of Claire's imagination. Whatever had caused these illusions had used that as a conduit.

Something changed.

No billowing air, all sense of movement suspended.

Evelyn opened her eyes.

And screamed.

She was in a small house. No, the house wasn't small. *She* was. Cardboard figures, exquisitely painted, sat on cardboard gilt chairs. A cardboard woman played a cardboard piano. No one moved, but she heard the music. A Strauss waltz.

Evelyn raised her hand, and, as she did so, the whole scene came alive as if she had orchestrated it. The people were real. They were listening to the music. The woman's fingers flew across the piano, showing herself to be an accomplished player.

Evelyn looked down at herself and saw she was dressed as she had been when she went out for her walk with Claire. She was sitting on a chair, like the rest of the audience.

Claire! Where had she gone? Frantically, Evelyn looked around at the strangers, none of whom took any notice of the inappropriately dressed guest. The women's jewels glittered. The men's brilliantined hair gleamed in the light from the chandelier. Such a strange scene. So real and yet unreal.

So much like...The Garden of Bewitchment.

She daren't even think that. Maybe the people couldn't see her. Evelyn stood and pushed her chair back. She almost trod on one of the other guests. He showed no reaction, not even the briefest acknowledgment of her presence. She must be invisible to him. Across the room, tall windows gave a view out onto an immaculate garden, filled with a myriad of colors brighter than she could ever have imagined.

There was no point denying it further. This *was* the house and garden Claire had described from the toy. The one she had stumbled across the previous day. Now Claire had disappeared and Evelyn was in the house.

But why?

She left the room, crossed a wide hall and opened a wood-paneled door into a library. She gazed around the deserted room. In the fireplace, a fire burned brightly.

Evelyn made her way to a central table on which a few books were scattered. She picked one up and gasped at the title. *The Chronicles of Calladocia.* No authors were credited. She opened the leather-bound volume. The illustrations were exquisite. Someone had gone to a great deal of trouble. Neither she nor Claire was capable of such fine work.

Lady Mandolyne, resplendent in her flowing gown, gazing wistfully at the reader, yet with a madness in her eyes that surely Claire had been about to detail. Evelyn turned the page. Sir Dreyfus Monroe had been brought to life exactly as she had imagined him. Tall, strong and handsome in his uniform, but sad. This must be him after his return from battle when Lady Organdia had been unfaithful.

On the next page, the evil and sly Lord Estival Drew-Cunningfort leered at his new love. There was much work for Evelyn to do with this part of the story, but, as she turned page after page, she saw it all laid out before her. The *Chronicles* was written. She decided to keep the book. Whatever happened, at least she would have that.

She must find Claire. Was she somewhere in this house?

Evelyn left the library, still clutching the book. Back in the hall, a long, wide staircase would take her up to the bedrooms. Maybe Claire had secreted herself in one of them.

She ran up the stairs as fast as her long skirt would allow. At the top, landings stretched left and right. She took the one to the left and opened door after door. Each room was identical. Soft green curtains, Regency upholstery and furniture. Even the Indian rugs on the polished floors were the same. Back at the top of the stairs, she tried the doors on the right-hand landing. Here again, all were the same and all empty. All but one. In that room, an old lady lay in bed, her face a mass of wrinkles. Her eyes were closed, and she was... sleeping?

No rise and fall of the coverlet to indicate breathing. Evelyn tiptoed to her bedside. The woman's translucent skin held a bluish tinge. Dead.

The woman's eyes flashed open. Pupils like black slits set in red irises. A faint reptilian hiss emanated from the semi-corpse, and then she fell quiet again.

Evelyn quit the room, her heart pounding out of control. She caught a brief glimpse of a man in evening dress disappearing into another bedroom. Should she follow him? Maybe he could tell her how she came to be there. But what if he was like the old woman?

The brief glimpse she had gained of him disturbed her. He had reddish-brown hair and, seen in profile, his nose...so much like...

Branwell.

More stairs, which probably led up to servants' quarters. Evelyn must go up there.

Here all the rooms were plain, each one sparsely furnished with an iron bed, cheap wooden dresser, ewer and bowl for washing. Nothing to see here. Nothing to help to explain the mystery. Yet always the feeling someone was watching her. That someone or something close by could see her every move. Anticipate it even. Evelyn returned to the first floor.

Bypassing the man's bedroom, she went down to the hall. The music had stopped. She went back into the drawing room to find no one there. The chairs were arranged as they had been, and the lid on the piano now covered the keys. Outside, the sun was going down on a lovely day, the sky tinged with pink and orange.

Where had everyone gone?

Evelyn left the drawing room and returned once more to the hall. The front door was shut. She opened it and inhaled the sweet evening air, scented with honeysuckle. All around her, birds fluttered. A bright purple butterfly flew past her, and, in the distance, she heard the unmistakable sound of a woodpecker tapping away at a tree.

Evelyn left the house and entered the garden. The trees seemed to welcome her, their branches parting to let her through.

But that shouldn't happen.

An instant's panic. She spun around. The branches had closed behind her, blocking her view of the house. If she went any farther she would lose track of herself.

I must keep calm.

Swallowing hard, she started back in the direction she had come from. This time the branches didn't part. She had to struggle through them. Twigs tangled in her hair, and her hat caught on a particularly stubborn one. Her dress snagged and ripped. A branch sprang back, nearly knocking her over. She pushed harder and harder. Another branch scratched her cheek, and she felt a warm trickle down her face. Blood.

Still she pushed on until at last she caught a glimpse of the house. She pushed harder. A large butterfly alighted on her outstretched hand. It fluttered its wings once and then transformed. A hideous, grinning, black imp sat where it had been. Evelyn let out a cry, and it opened its mouth wider, revealing sharply pointed green teeth. It emitted a heinous laugh and took off, wings beating and buzzing like some monstrous fly.

One final shove, born of sheer desperation, and she made it through, clear of the wood and into the garden. Scratched, torn and bleeding, she staggered up to the entrance of the house but stopped before she opened the door. What would she do now? She had no plan, no apparent means of escape and no idea of Claire's whereabouts. She was about to reenter a house about which she knew nothing, except something felt badly wrong with it and its inhabitants. She looked back over the garden. Such tempting beauty. It looked so innocent and inviting. But what if she had plowed on through the trees as they clearly wanted her to? Where would she be right now? An image of the horrible grinning imp flashed through her brain. She shuddered. No, nothing was as it seemed in this place. At least in the house, she had something between her and whatever waited out here, ready to trap her.

But even in the house, everything felt wrong. Maybe that was the trap itself.

The sun had almost set, and, all around her, the shadows lengthened. *Shadows of evil.*

With a shudder, Evelyn opened the door and closed it behind her. In the distance, the tinkling of glasses and the sound of another Strauss waltz being exquisitely played on the piano. She forced herself to follow the sound. The drawing room door stood slightly ajar. She grasped the handle and tugged it. It opened smoothly.

The music stopped. The cardboard figures were each frozen in mid-action. Some seemed about to sip a glass of champagne. Others were laughing. Instead of sitting and listening politely to a piano recital as before, this had all the hallmarks of a party in full swing. Or it had been until she had opened that door and somehow ended it.

Should she enter? Could she? The floor looked like painted cardboard too. She put her toe on the edge. All sensation drained out of it, as if it too was taking on the texture of her surroundings. Numbness shot through her foot and up her leg. She pulled back, and feeling returned. Blood flowed through her veins once more. Now what could she do? She had come no nearer to finding Claire, and this strange world was no place for her.

A baleful howl shattered the silence. It came from beyond the garden. A wolf perhaps, or a large dog.

Heavy footfalls approached. Steady but thumping so hard they shook the house.

The voice, when it came, seemed to be in slow motion. Like a gramophone that needed winding up.

"Ev... Ev..."

So loud she thought her eardrums would explode at any moment. She clamped her hands to the sides of her head.

"Claire." It had to be her. For all it seemed distorted and out of time, she would know her sister's voice anywhere.

Evelyn screamed as a massive eye filled the window. Every detail magnified. The threadlike red veins. The enormous blue iris and black-as-night pupil. The long tendrils of lashes.

Claire's eye. But enhanced a hundredfold.

"Claire." Evelyn's voice could hardly reach her. It must sound like no more than a squeak.

A rush of wind threatened to topple the house. Evelyn staggered. Some of the cardboard figures fell on top of each other in an untidy heap.

The wind died down. Until Claire took her next breath.

The cardboard windows bowed. The whole flimsy wooden house shook. "Claire. Move away. *Please.*"

"Ev. I can see you there." The voice boomed out. Evelyn had to make her stop. At the same time she had to convince her sister to get her out of there. But carefully. Claire didn't know her own strength. One false move and Evelyn would be broken. Dead.

"Claire. Listen to me."

"I can't hear you."

"Don't speak. You're killing me!"

Her words must have reached Claire because her sister withdrew. Evelyn waited, anxious to know what she would do next. She didn't have to wait long.

With a loud, tearing sound, the roof of the house disappeared, along with the upper stories.

Two fingers, thick as massive tree trunks, probed the drawing room.

"I'm here." Evelyn waved from the hallway. The fingers moved closer until Evelyn was able to catch hold and clamber onto them. Her sister's skin felt warm, reassuring. The hairs Evelyn knew to be virtually invisible, when she was of normal size, appeared long, almost like fur.

Evelyn clung on as Claire stood and brought her fingers up to her face. Behind Claire a shape moved. Dark, indistinct and larger than she was. A giant among giants.

"Claire!"

Her warning came too late. A strong arm encircled Claire's waist and tossed her aside. Evelyn was thrown into the overgrown and all-consuming forest of trees. She hit her head and blacked out.

★   ★   ★

"You're mine, Claire. All mine. Don't ever forget it."

"Branwell..."

"Take my hand. We have work to do if Lady Mandolyne is to escape."

"Escape? Escape from where?"

"The creature. The Todeswurm."

"Todeswurm?"

"Death worm. She saw it in the mist. You remember. You and Evelyn argued over what she had seen. You and I worked it out. She had seen the Todeswurm. Now it is here, and we must rescue her."

"But, Ev—"

"She is sleeping. Unconscious. But she will be fine when she wakens."

"Something happened to her. She—"

"I know, Claire. I know. It too is the work of the Todeswurm, which is why we must find it. Kill it if necessary. Then all will be as it should be."

"I don't remember...Todeswurm. I don't remember writing any of that."

"Because you didn't. And neither did your sister. I wrote it. Perhaps now your sister will believe what you have told her all along. I am Branwell Brontë, and I am very much alive."

★   ★   ★

Evelyn's head swam as consciousness returned. She lay curled in a fetal position on damp grass – the only patch of grass in a sea of heather and gorse. She struggled to lean up on one elbow, squinting at the pale sun as it emerged from behind a dark cloud. She shivered. The dampness had penetrated through her clothes, chilling her to the bone, but she must get up. What had happened to her?

Memory swirled back. A strange house. Her sister tall as a giant. The man who had grabbed her. And he *was* a man. At least… But Evelyn could not remember any distinctive features. Just a shapeless form that had grabbed Claire and tossed her aside.

Everything seemed perfectly normal now. The peaceful, bleak moorland. The curlew crying to its young.

No sign of the house and garden or of the trees that seemed to have a will of their own. Could she have dreamed it? And where was Claire now? She prayed her sister had made it safely home, waiting for her, probably wondering what had happened to her.

Evelyn struggled to her feet. Her dress – stained with grass and mud. Her hair had come loose, and she had lost her hat.

She must get back home. As she set off, she prayed she wouldn't see any of the neighbors. How would the normally well turned out Miss Wainwright explain her current state of dishevelment?

She hurried as fast as her tired feet would allow, reaching the cottage in a few minutes. When Evelyn had shut the door firmly behind her, she breathed deeply.

She called out to her sister. No reply.

Evelyn tucked a lock of hair behind her ear and stopped. Something had tangled itself up there. She tugged at it, wincing as strands of hair came out at the roots. After a few more tugs, she examined her hand. Lying in her palm lay a small twig. Not heather or gorse. This was unmistakably pine. And there were no pine trees on the moor.

But there were in The Garden of Bewitchment.

She trudged up the stairs as a wave of exhaustion overtook her. In her room, Evelyn yawned and laid the twig on her dressing table.

She must have a bath. She felt so dirty and stale. Maybe relaxing in the soothing hot water would help restore her fevered brain to something like sanity.

She discarded her filthy clothes. Even her underwear hadn't escaped the grass stains. Her hair was tangled with more bits of twig and leaves, none of which belonged on the moor.

She heated large copper pans on the range and dragged the hip bath from the corner of the kitchen. Only at times such as these did Evelyn question her decision not to employ staff. Her mother would have had a fit if she had seen her daughter drawing her own bath.

Much later, refreshed and dressed in clean clothes, she sat in the drawing room, her long hair lying over her shoulders where she had draped a towel. She brushed it as it started to dry.

Still no sign of Claire. It would be teatime soon.

The sound of a key scraping in the lock made her jump. Her sister's face lost its worried expression almost the instant she saw Evelyn.

"Thank God you're all right," she said.

"I think so. But I'm so confused. What happened up on the moors?"

"You were in the house. The toy house. I took it apart, and something grabbed me from behind. Then Branwell came."

"What?"

"Branwell came. Ev, you have to believe me. Look, I'll show you."

Claire picked up the manuscript containing her part of *The Chronicles of Calladocia*.

"See? On this page. Branwell has written something, and he's drawn it too."

Evelyn said nothing. She remembered how she had grabbed the

completed *Chronicles* in the house. Where was it now? She must have dropped it when she was flung out of Claire's hand. Evelyn took the book from her sister and peered down at it.

The slithering creature oiled its way towards Lady Mandolyne, who could do nothing to escape. She took in the slimy body, scales overlapping and pulsing as it moved. The stench from its foulness made her retch. Any moment now and it would be upon her. It had left its cloak of mist and forbidding darkness, and, out in the open, it must feel its increasing strength. Strength given by Hell itself. Fearing no one, but feared by all who came into contact with it, the Todeswurm prepared to strike.

Lady Mandolyne prayed. But there was none there to save her. Soon it would be upon her and she would be no more.

The Todeswurm opened its hinge-less mouth wide. Wider, until she could only see a vast and bottomless chasm. Its foul breath choked her with its sulfurous odor.

Two final words issued from her frozen lips. "Forgive me."

And then all became darkness for Lady Mandolyne Montfera.

Evelyn pushed the book aside on the table.

"Well? Isn't it magnificent?"

"Who wrote that, Claire? It isn't your handwriting or mine."

"I told you, Branwell. He did it when we were out. It solves the problem perfectly, don't you think? And what an excellent creature the Todeswurm is. I had never heard of one before, had you?"

"That's probably because it doesn't exist. Claire, this can't be Branwell's writing. You and I both know it."

"No. You're wrong." Claire's eyes filled with tears. "How can I make you believe me? This is Branwell's writing."

"Then where is he? Why doesn't he show himself to me and explain himself? Because he can't, Claire. That's why."

"He can't come to you. You're right. But he can come to me, and he does. We belong together, Ev."

"Look, I don't understand what is happening to us any more than you do. Something happened up on those moors. That much we do know. And we seem to remember pretty much the same sequence of events, but Branwell can't be any part of this."

"There's no point in arguing with you when you are in this mood, Ev. I know that. Just as much as I know Branwell wrote that and he comes to me. He loves me. He told me so."

Evelyn shook her head, conscious of a nagging ache behind her eyes. Her vision swirled. "I'm getting a migraine. I shall have to lie down for a while. We'll discuss this later." Although, why bother? Claire would not be moved, and with everything else happening to them, was it really so impossible she could be right?

*   *   *

Evelyn tossed and turned, her head filled with hammering, nauseating throbbing. Wild thoughts clashed against each other. Matthew Dixon. Did he have some role in this? That box he had buried and then dug up. They still didn't know what it contained or whether they could trust the man. Lady Mandolyne, who had somehow become all too real, at least for an instant. And the terrible toy that had somehow transformed into reality. Evelyn had been in the house and the garden. Either she had been vastly reduced in size or her sister had been transformed into a giant.

Nothing made any kind of sense, and the more the thoughts whirled and clashed, the worse the pain became until she would have given anything to smash her head against the wall until it stopped.

The door opened softly. Claire appeared, carrying a cup of tea.

"I thought this might make you feel better, Ev."

"Thank you." Evelyn struggled to sit up, every motion kicking off renewed agony.

"I put plenty of sugar in. I know you say it helps sometimes."

Evelyn took the cup and saucer, noting how her hands trembled.

"Is there anything else I can get you?"

"No, thank you, Claire. This was very thoughtful of you."

Claire left her, shutting the door softly behind her.

Evelyn sipped her tea, feeling the hot liquid soothing her. When she had drained her cup, she lay back against the pillows and closed her eyes. Her troubled thoughts faded into the background until she fell asleep.

*   *   *

She awoke to darkness. The migraine had lifted, leaving the familiar feeling of physical tenderness behind. She heard voices and sat up, straining to listen.

Claire's room. Talking to herself again. The words were indistinct, but she recognized the timbre of her voice.

And another voice. The hairs on the back of her neck stood on end. Her breathing came fast and shallow. A man. Claire was talking to a man. There could be no mistake this time.

She must go and confront him. What was he doing in Claire's room in the middle of the night?

She made to push the sheet off her, but her head started to throb again. Too soon. She lay back, praying for the pain to subside.

Claire's laughter rang out. Evelyn heard the scrape of her door as it opened.

"Good evening, Evelyn."

The man's voice. Distinct. Directly in her ear.

Evelyn screamed, but Claire didn't come.

CHAPTER TEN

The morning was a uniform gray. A thick blanket of cloud hung low over the village, and Evelyn moved heavily in the humidity.

In contrast, Claire seemed alive with enthusiasm, humming a song Evelyn didn't recognize and busying herself dusting shelves.

"Good morning, Ev. Feeling better? Did you sleep well?"

"Not particularly. I had a nightmare."

"Oh?"

"Hardly surprising given the sort of day we had. Don't you feel as if you're losing touch with reality in some way? I know I do."

Claire lowered the ostrich feather duster. "I don't think I know what you mean, Ev. I mean, it all seems perfectly clear to me. The toy has come alive somehow and exists in some way we don't understand up there on the moor. But always in the same place, so all we have to do is avoid going there. Branwell is helping with *The Chronicles of Calladocia*, and it is all the better for his intervention. And, as for Matthew Dixon…he is a man with a lot to hide and we should keep out of his company. Branwell warned me about him, by the way."

Too tired to protest his existence anymore, especially after the previous night's bad dream, Evelyn settled for, "Oh, really, and when did he do that?"

"Last night. After you had gone to bed. He came to me."

"In your room?"

"Yes."

She had said it as if it was perfectly natural to have a ghost – a male one – visit her alone in her bedroom. "And what exactly did he say?"

"He told me Matthew Dixon had come here for a reason. Not to recuperate. There's nothing wrong with him. The stick is for show, to give him an alibi. He's here to separate us from our inheritance."

"Oh, rubbish, Claire. Granted I don't know what's in that box of his, but I'm going to find out. The man had an accident, and he is recovering. I think we're reading far too much into this, so I have determined I shall tell him I saw him burying the box and ask him straight out what was in it."

Claire's look of horror was instant. "You can't do that. You'll put us both in mortal danger."

"Oh, don't be so melodramatic. You sound like one of your penny dreadfuls again."

"I'm being serious. Branwell said Matthew has been hired by someone. He doesn't know all the details yet, but we must be careful and stay away from him. He said he came into your room to warn you, but all he managed to say was 'Good evening' and then you closed your mind. You mustn't be scared of him, Ev. He's our friend. He loves me, and he wants to help."

Evelyn stared at Claire. Memories of that voice so close to her ear. The voice she thought she must have dreamed...

"I need some air. I'm going out."

"But you haven't had any breakfast."

"I'm not hungry."

With Claire's warnings and protests still ringing in her ears, Evelyn tugged on her walking shoes, grabbed her hat and coat and left. Outside, the air hung still and heavy. She smelled the mist and tasted its earthy woodiness, tinged with decay. Straight off the moors. Even so, it felt better than the claustrophobic restriction of the cottage, where truth and fantasy were becoming hopelessly interlocked and impossible to separate.

She knocked on Matthew's door before she could talk herself out of it. He answered almost immediately, a look of genuine surprise on his face as he saw who his visitor was.

"Evelyn. Please come in."

She looked all around her, making sure neighbors weren't twitching their lace curtains.

"Thank you, Matthew. I'm so sorry to call unannounced, but something is troubling me and I had to ask you about it."

"Something's happened, hasn't it? I can tell by your face. You look so tired, Evelyn. Have you been sleeping?"

"Not too well."

Matthew closed the door and beckoned Evelyn into his front room.

"I'll make us some tea."

Evelyn nodded and sat on a comfortable easy chair, grateful for the cushions she sank into. Weariness almost overwhelmed her, and she felt her eyes grow heavy as Matthew reappeared, carrying a tray.

"I'm afraid the only biscuits I could find were Rich Tea. I hope they will be all right for you?"

"They will. Thank you, Matthew."

He handed her a strong cup of tea, which she relished. As she sipped the scalding liquid, she felt some strength returning. Matthew waited, watching her every move. She set the cup and saucer down on a small table.

"I have to ask you something, but first I must make a confession." It was now or never. She couldn't fathom his expression. Did he have any clue what she was going to say next?

"A few days ago, I saw you up on the moors, near the crags, burying a box. You didn't see me as I was sheltering from the rain and it was very misty." His expression didn't change. Not even a flicker.

"I remember the day."

She waited for more, but he said nothing. Evidently he had no intention of making this easy for her. "You are going to think me extremely impertinent, but I need to ask. So much has happened in the past few days. So much neither Claire nor I can explain. We think it may have something to do with the contents of that box. Would you be prepared to tell me what is in there?"

Matthew sat back and crossed his legs. He steepled his fingers in front of him and studied Evelyn.

"You're quite a dark horse, aren't you?" His voice wasn't unpleasant, and he certainly didn't have the attitude of someone who had been caught misbehaving.

"I'm not sure I know what you mean," Evelyn said.

"I wonder why you thought it necessary to conceal your presence from me. I thought we were friends."

"I... I didn't want to intrude. Really it was none of my business. It was only afterwards..."

"It's all right, Evelyn. All I can tell you is there is no need to worry about the box. It has nothing to do with you. Merely a keepsake for a friend. I made a promise, and I kept it. That's all."

He offered her the biscuits, but she declined. So that was it. He wasn't going to elaborate. Should she tell him Claire and she had been back and tried to dig it up only to find it had been taken?

Evelyn mulled it over as they sipped their tea in silence. She squirmed, feeling uncomfortable. Maybe he hadn't dug it up. Maybe he would be shocked to find it had been taken. But how would she explain their actions in the first place? These were not those of a friend. He would never forgive her.

She drained her cup. "I'm so sorry to have intruded in this way. It was unforgiveable of me." Perhaps her contriteness might encourage him to take her into his confidence.

"There is no apology necessary, I can assure you. Thank you for being so honest with me. Eventually." He smiled. "I'm sorry I cannot divulge the nature of the contents as I would breach the trust of my friend. I'm sure you understand."

"Yes, of course."

His words were said kindly, but she couldn't mistake the wedge she had driven between them by her actions. He didn't believe her excuse for not revealing herself to him that day, and she couldn't bring herself to tell him of the inexplicable experience she and Claire had shared up on the moors. Trust had been broken between them. It could not be undone.

As she left, Evelyn turned back, feeling suddenly more alone than she could ever remember. "Goodbye, Matthew."

He seemed shocked for an instant. Maybe her goodbye had sounded as final as she felt it would be.

"Goodbye, Evelyn."

The visit had been for nothing. She knew no more than before she had knocked on his door. Now, in addition, she had probably lost someone she had begun to think of as a friend, even with the doubts she still harbored about him.

★   ★   ★

Once home, she called out, "Claire?"

No reply. A small white envelope lay on the table, addressed to her, in Claire's distinctive writing.

I'm sorry, Ev, but I can't live this way any longer. I need to be with Branwell, and you will never accept him. Please don't try and find me. Simply know, wherever I am, I will be happy and Branwell will be with me. Goodbye, Claire.

The tears streamed down her cheeks as she crumpled the letter, holding it to her breast.

"You can't leave me, Claire. You can't. You were never meant to be alone and neither was I."

She sank down onto a chair and wept, for her sister, for herself and for an uncertain future alone.

Finally, the tears dried and Evelyn mopped her face. Her practical side took hold. She went upstairs and opened Claire's closets and drawers. Sure enough, her clothes were missing, as were her books. Evelyn sat down on her bed. Where would Claire go? Who would she go to?

She had money and access to more when she needed it. Perhaps she would put up at a hotel nearby for a few nights until she decided on her future. Evelyn thought hard. In her obsessed state of mind, she would go somewhere Branwell would be certain to find her. In her mind, at least. Any number of hostelries and ale houses would fit the bill, and a number of them offered accommodation. Indeed, Branwell had probably stayed in most of them, too inebriated to make his way home to the parsonage.

Haworth seemed likely. The Lamb perhaps, or the Crown and Anchor. In her delusional state it would be easy for Claire to imagine Branwell with her.

Without a moment's hesitation, Evelyn packed an overnight bag.

Within an hour she crossed the threshold of the Crown and Anchor, where the sound of laughter and men clanging pewter mugs of ale rang in her ears.

A few stared at her as she passed them. An unusual sight. A respectable woman, on her own, entering a hostelry in the afternoon.

The landlord looked at her askance. "Yes, miss?"

"Do you have any rooms for the night?"

"For yourself, is it, miss?"

"Just myself, yes. I wondered... Has another lady, who looks much like me, also been in here today?"

"Oh, no, miss. I am quite sure I would have remembered if she had."

One or two sniggers earned a sharp look from the publican.

Evelyn ignored them. "I understand there are a number of inns where she might stay in Haworth?"

The publican looked at her with a perplexed expression on her face. "Forgive me, miss, but wouldn't she be more likely to stay at the Temperance Hotel? I would have thought that a more appropriate lodging for a lady such as yourself."

Evelyn had indeed considered it but dismissed it out of hand. No way would Branwell ever cross the premises of such an establishment, even if he *had* been secretary of the local Temperance Society in his younger days. No, Claire, in her befuddled and besotted state, would stay somewhere her 'lover' would frequent, which meant somewhere where alcohol was readily available.

"Thank you," she said. "But it's inns I am interested in. I believe my sister may be staying in one of them in Haworth. There are a few, I understand?"

"Indeed there are, miss. Apart from here, there's The Lamb, the Black Lion, the Cross Keys. They're all within a few minutes' walk of here. Did you want to check them and see if your sister is staying at one of them?"

"I shall do so, but, in the meantime, if I could take one of your rooms for tonight, I would be most grateful."

"Well, Sam, there's an offer you don't get every day." The well-built man with the ruddy face and bulging belly – which had no doubt cost him more than a few pounds in beer over the years – made a lascivious gesture that was lost on Evelyn. It wasn't on the landlord.

"If you can't keep a civil tongue in your head in the presence of a lady, Thomas Wagstaff, I'll have you out of here. Now apologize."

"Sorry."

"Not to me, you great lummock. To the lady."

Evelyn gave him what she hoped was a cold stare. One she was famous for. Claire said it turned her blood to ice whenever her sister looked like that at her.

"I'm sorry, miss. I suppose the ale got to me."

Evelyn nodded her acceptance of his apology.

Sam glared at the man again, almost daring him to say one more word out of line.

"Now, miss, if you'll come with me. I'll get Mary to show you your room. I'm afraid I have to ask you for payment in advance. It's nothing personal, only we've had a few problems in the past."

"Not at all. Thank you," Evelyn said, ignoring the whoops and parodies behind her as she followed Sam.

The room was small, pleasantly furnished and, much to Evelyn's relief, spotlessly clean. Mary kept bobbing unnecessary curtsies, and Evelyn wished she wouldn't. Although her parents had always employed servants, none had been encouraged to bow and scrape before the Wainwrights. Mary's extreme deference sat uncomfortably with her, and Evelyn gave a small sigh of relief when the girl left, closing the door quietly behind her.

She sat down on the edge of the bed, unpinned her hat and laid it beside her. Why had she come here? No wonder the men had enjoyed themselves at her expense downstairs. It simply wasn't done for a woman in her position to enter a public house alone, and, as for taking a room... Why hadn't *she* checked in at the Temperance Hotel? Because, with everything that was happening to her, she might want a little nip of strong liquor herself. Besides, it was only one night. It would give her enough time to call at each of the hostelries in turn and enquire after Claire and give her sister a chance to show up, assuming she might have stopped off somewhere else first. Haworth was a small village. Pretty much everyone would know everyone else, and anything out of the ordinary, such as a new face, was bound to be noticed. No doubt her own presence would currently be in circulation, along with any number of theories as to her purpose in being here.

Evelyn unpacked her few belongings, re-pinned her hat and made her way downstairs. The men who had been there had left, presumably to return to their families for the evening. The bar was quiet, with just a couple of old men who eyed her disapprovingly. She ignored them and marched straight up to where Sam was polishing glasses.

"Can I get a meal here this evening, Sam?"

"Aye, you can. Martha is cooking up a nice mutton stew. Would that be to your liking?"

Not having eaten mutton stew in a considerable while, Evelyn couldn't remember whether it was to her liking or not, but she nodded and smiled. "Thank you. What time would be convenient?"

He looked at the clock. "Seven o'clock should do it. You'll have a couple of hours to wander round and see if you can trace your sister. If you find her, bring her back and she can join you for dinner. There'll be plenty. Martha always cooks for a battalion."

"That's very kind of you, Sam. Thank you. I will be sure to do that. If I find her."

Judging by Sam's expression, he would be the grateful one. It looked as if he already regretted his decision to allow an unescorted woman to stay the night. Maybe Martha, his wife, she assumed, had given him some harsh words on the subject. No, it would be far more respectable if Evelyn were to dine with a female companion.

Evelyn left the public house and stepped out into a gloomy and breezy late afternoon. Her first port of call was the Cross Keys. It too was virtually empty, and her enquiry brought no results. No one there had seen Claire. Then followed The Lamb, with the same result. Farther down the steep Main Street, the pleasantly cozy Black Lion boasted a hearty middle-aged woman behind the bar who looked as if she wanted to adopt Evelyn.

"I haven't seen her, dear, but are you sure she would want to stay here on her own?"

"The truth is, I don't know," Evelyn replied, deciding not to tell the woman where she intended to spend the night. "She didn't say where she was going and was probably a bit upset."

"Why would she come to Haworth? Do you have relatives here?"

"No. She is...well we both are...great Brontë lovers. We have read all their books so many times, and I know she is particularly fascinated by Branwell Brontë."

The woman smiled. "Branwell, eh? Yes, he was a rum one. I remember him. Only vaguely, of course; I was no more than a kid at the time. My father kept this place then. Many's the time he's asked him to leave. 'Don't you know who I am?' Branwell would ask. 'Don't you know who my father is?' 'Yes, Branwell. I know. I know,' my father would say, 'but you've had enough, and I'm not serving you any more tonight. Go home, lad. Go home.' Off he'd stagger, falling about all over the place. I used to watch him from my bedroom window and laugh. I was too young to understand then. Such a sad business, and his poor old father never got over it."

"I'm sure my sister would love to hear your memories of him," Evelyn said. "I think she has a fairly starry-eyed impression that doesn't match the facts as we know them."

"Yes, I can see how that would happen. He did have a charming manner when he was sober, and he was a great character. Such a sense of humor he had. He'd have the whole place in fits of laughter. They'd all buy him drinks. Worst thing they could have done, of course, but people think they're being friendly, don't they?"

"They do indeed. Thank you, Mrs....?"

"Lingard. Jessie Lingard." She stuck out her hand, and Evelyn shook it. The woman had a firm grip.

"Evelyn Wainwright. You have been most helpful."

"Oh, I doubt it. I've never seen your sister, and I'm so sorry I couldn't help. I will keep an eye open for her. Where can I get in contact with you if she comes in?"

Evelyn hesitated, but why lie? "I am staying at the Crown and Anchor tonight and intending to return to Thornton Wensley tomorrow. That's where we live."

Jessie's eyebrows were already raised. "You're staying at the Crown and Anchor? Sam Whitbread's place? On your own?"

"Yes."

Jessie leaned forward. "You do know the place is haunted, don't you?"

"No. I hadn't heard."

"Well, it is. There are plenty of folk who've upped and left in the middle of the night complaining of strange noises and seeing things that couldn't be there. I'll bet old Sam took your money as soon as you arrived, didn't he?"

"Yes."

"I'm not surprised. He's been caught out more than once. That wife of his, Martha, she gave him such a telling off I reckon his ears must have been ringing for days afterwards." She laughed a hearty roar. "Seriously, though, Evelyn. Be careful. A woman on her own...and there's more to that place than meets the eye. It was one of Branwell Brontë's old haunts, and some say it still is. Mind you, I suppose that applies to most of the drinking places in the West Riding." Jessie laughed again.

Evelyn wished she had asked to stay at the Black Lion. "I'll be careful, Jessie. If I decide to stay another night, would you be able to accommodate me here?"

Jessie patted her hand. "Of course, dear. Just let me know. We'd be happy to have you."

Evelyn smiled, nodded and left.

That was it. No more public houses. No one had seen Claire.

With nowhere left to try, she trudged back up to the Crown and Anchor and went straight up to her room.

★   ★   ★

Dinner was well cooked, hearty and full of flavor. Whatever else Martha was, she certainly had a way with food. 'A good plain cook', her mother would have called her.

After she had finished, Evelyn felt tiredness overwhelming her. It had been a difficult and disappointing day, leaving her bereft and confused. Where could Claire have gone to, if not here, in Haworth?

She retired early, grateful for the cool, soft pillow and clean, sweet-smelling sheets. She drifted off within minutes.

Her dreams were of moorland and swirling mists. She was searching for Claire, calling her name again and again. The curlew circled overhead, and she too seemed to echo Evelyn's cries as if she had joined the search.

Then she heard it, a faint answering cry, coming from far in the distance. Evelyn ran, skipping over rough grass and heather. The curlew continued to circle overhead, keeping pace with her. Claire's cries were nearer now. More desperate.

"I'm coming, Claire. Hold on, I'm coming."

And then she saw her. On the ground, her face dirty and blood-streaked, her ankle caught in a vicious-looking mantrap.

Evelyn knelt down beside her and took her in her arms. "How did this happen?"

"*He* did it to me. He isn't who he seems to be. Oh, Ev..." Her sobs tore at Evelyn's heart.

Claire shuddered and pulled herself away from her sister's grip. "He's back. He's come for me. He'll take you too. Oh..." She pointed ahead of her, her hand trembling, eyes wide and staring.

Evelyn turned. A man stood mere feet away, dressed from head to toe in black, his face indistinct...until he moved slightly.

"*Matthew?* But..." No, it wasn't him. It was...

The face seemed to drift out of focus. As if someone were manipulating a camera lens.

The features settled. Claire whispered. "Branwell. It's Branwell, Ev. Only it's not really him."

"I know it can't be."

The man's features softened again, became unfocused, then clear as again Matthew Dixon stood in front of them. He said nothing, but a smile twitched the corners of his mouth.

Evelyn stared incredulously. "How can this be?"

He reached into an inside pocket and pulled out a sharp-pointed stiletto. He raised his arm, and Evelyn knew it was meant for her. She screamed.

She sprang up in bed, sweating and breathing hard. A nightmare. But it had been so real. Too real. Every image, every second of it replayed in her mind, and her hands trembled as she clutched at the sheets.

The room was bathed in darkness, black as pitch. She reached for the candle, nearly knocking it over in her anxiety. After fumbling for the matches, she found the box and struck one. It burst into flame, and she lit the wick.

She picked up the candleholder and shone the meager light around the room. The flame threw up flickering shadows, and Evelyn wished she had an oil lamp to provide more illumination. The shadows only made her more scared. That dream had really unnerved her.

Then a sound. Someone was in here with her. She swore she could hear them breathing. Still clutching the candle in one hand, she edged herself higher in bed, drawing her knees up.

"Is there someone there?" Her voice trembled. She must control it. No reply.

She shone her candle around, slowly, dreading what it might reveal but forcing herself.

A wardrobe at the far side of the room seemed almost alive in the flicker of the candle. The chest of drawers next to it. Had it moved, ever so slightly? No, it had to be her imagination. Farther around the room, the small dressing table gave her a fright, until she realized the other flame and shadowy person she saw was merely a reflection of herself in the mirror.

She moved the candle still further, until she shone it next to her.

A sudden movement. A rush of air. A pair of bloodshot eyes staring into hers, right before the light snuffed out. Evelyn screamed and threw the useless candle to the floor. She stuck her head between her knees, clutching them tightly to her.

A hammering at her door. Evelyn was too scared to move or cry out again. Voices. Sam's and a woman's. Martha's. Someone threw the door open, and she dared to look up.

Martha rushed to her side, holding an oil lamp. "Miss Wainwright, whatever's the matter? What happened?"

Sam hovered by the door, also with an oil lamp in his hand. Evelyn was grateful for the light. It showed her the room was empty.

"You're shaking."

"I saw. I think I saw. Eyes. Staring at me. Mad..." She couldn't carry on.

Martha exchanged glances with her husband. "Maybe you had a bad dream. They can be very realistic."

"No. I *was* asleep, but I woke up. I heard someone in the room."

"Did you see anyone?" Martha asked.

"Only eyes. Terrible eyes." Evelyn shuddered.

Once again the look that passed between her and Sam was not lost on Evelyn. "What are you not telling me?"

Sam left and closed the door quietly behind him.

Martha sat on the edge of her bed. "You're not the first person to see him, and I dare say you won't be the last. Old Jeremy Ackroyd has haunted this place since the 1700s. He was the landlord here, but a fearsome man he was. Almost destroyed the business because people were too scared of him to come in. Then one day he disappeared. No one ever saw him again. Not alive anyhow."

"Do you think someone murdered him?"

"Who can say? If they did, no one ever found his body. Mind you, I don't think they looked too hard. When the place had been shut up for a week, folk assumed he had up and gone. New people came and ran the place, and all went quiet. Over time everyone pretty much forgot about Jeremy Ackroyd...until the hauntings started."

"Have you seen him?"

Martha shook her head. "No. And neither has Sam. It seems

he doesn't bother with whoever is running the place. He likes to frighten guests, and he does a pretty good job of it too." She sighed. "You should be all right now. He's had his fun for one night. Try and get some sleep. I'll leave you the lamp."

"Thank you." The thought of being plunged into total darkness had not been one Evelyn relished. Now at least she would have a little light to comfort her.

Martha closed the door softly behind her.

Evelyn slept only fitfully, waking at every slight noise. At dawn, the sound of birds chirruping brought her comfort. She had made it through the night here. Despite Jeremy Ackroyd's best efforts.

Now remained the issue of whether to stay another night in Haworth. If she did, Evelyn was certain she wouldn't remain here.

By breakfast time she had decided. She picked up her packed overnight bag and made her way downstairs where the welcoming smell of frying bacon greeted her. Martha smiled as she passed her coming out of the kitchen. "It's all ready for you. I'm so sorry you had such a fright in the night. Did you manage to sleep at all?"

"A little. Thank you for the lamp. It helped."

"You'll be leaving us today, then?" Martha indicated the bag.

"Yes." It wasn't a complete lie.

"Such a shame you didn't find your sister. I do hope she turns up soon."

"So do I. Thank you, Martha."

★   ★   ★

After breakfast, Evelyn made her way down Main Street and knocked on the door of the Black Lion. Jessie's beaming smile made her feel truly welcome.

The landlady seemed riveted by Evelyn's story of the ghost in the night. "I had heard he was up to his old tricks again. Pretty fearsome sight by all accounts."

"He was. It's so strange. Until recently I've been quite skeptical about that sort of thing, but so much has happened lately..." She paused, realizing she had been about to tell Jessie everything. The woman's easy, almost maternal, manner made her a natural person to confide in. But a story as fantastic as Evelyn's? She didn't know her nearly well enough. "I mean this Jeremy Ackroyd business. I know what I saw."

"Oh, it would have been him, right enough. Fortunately we don't have anything like that here. All our ghosts are harmless ones." She smiled at Evelyn. "You'll sleep soundly in your bed tonight, I can assure you."

Evelyn took in the neat room, pretty with floral curtains and bedspread. A small dressing table, single wardrobe and chair completed the simple but perfectly adequate furnishings.

She set down her bag and sat on the edge of the bed. The day stretched before her, and, having exhausted all the places Claire could have stayed, she had few options and no clue as to where her sister might be. Maybe if she walked around the village... Evelyn remembered Claire's secretive solo trips she never spoke about. What if she had come here? What if Claire knew someone here and would come to meet them? Or maybe one of the shopkeepers would remember her. Of course her trips could as easily have taken her sister to Halifax, Leeds or Bradford. Keighley even. But a nagging feeling wouldn't leave her. Haworth, with all its connections to Branwell, would be the one place Claire would choose to escape to.

Evelyn left her room, went downstairs, out onto the street and nearly barreled into Matthew.

He caught her. "Evelyn, what a pleasant surprise. What brings you to Haworth?"

Surprise? It certainly didn't look like it. If Evelyn hadn't known better, she would have sworn Matthew knew exactly where he would find her.

"I'm looking for Claire. She's missing."

"Missing?"

He still didn't appear as shocked as he made out.

"She left me a note saying she was going and I wasn't to look for her. Naturally I had to try and find her. I don't think she's well."

"And you thought you'd try here."

"She's obsessed with Branwell Brontë. It seemed the obvious place. Why are *you* in Haworth?"

He avoided her eyes. "A short break. I thought I would try the moors here for a change."

A lie. But for what reason? "They're pretty much the same as in Thornton Wensley," she said.

"Ah, but on *these* moors Emily Brontë was inspired to write *Wuthering Heights*."

Suddenly Evelyn didn't want to stay in his company. She didn't want to hear him lie to her anymore. After their last parting – when she had assumed their brief friendship had been irrevocably tarnished – she had tried to put him out of her mind, and now, for some unknown reason, he had followed her here. No question about it. Should she challenge him?

"Matthew, I'm sorry, but I need to get along now. Have a pleasant stay." It was easier this way. She hurried off up the street, hoping he didn't follow her. At the top of the hill, breathless, she turned back to look down. No sign of him.

She called in at a few shops, but no one had seen Claire.

Evelyn mounted the steps to the church and opened the door. Inside, peace and tranquility reigned, giving her a chance to decide on her next course of action.

Why had Matthew followed her? By the time she left the church half an hour later, she had decided there was only one way to find out. She gritted her teeth.

He wasn't hard to find. Sitting in a café, drinking a cup of hot chocolate, right by the window where he could watch all the comings and goings on bustling Main Street. He smiled at her and beckoned her to come in and join him. She did so.

She sat opposite him, and a smartly dressed waitress appeared. "I'll have hot chocolate too, please," Evelyn said.

The waitress nodded and left.

"Any joy yet?" Matthew asked.

"None, I'm afraid."

Her cup of hot chocolate arrived, and Evelyn sipped the sweet, warming beverage. Matthew watched her every move. Evelyn set her cup down in its saucer.

"I need to ask you," she said. "Why are you really here?"

"I told you. The moors—"

"No, Matthew. I'm sorry, but I don't believe you."

"Then what do you believe?"

"That you knew I was here. You knew Claire was missing, and you came after me."

"Not strictly true," he said, steepling his fingers. "I knew Claire was missing, and I guessed you would come here looking for her."

"But how did you know she had gone?"

"Because she told me."

"She *told* you? When?"

"She pushed a note through my door." He fumbled in an inside jacket pocket and pulled out a crumpled piece of paper. He handed it to Evelyn, who immediately unfolded it.

Dear Matthew. I am finding it impossible to stay here in Thornton Wensley. Life with my sister is stifling me, and I need to break away. Please be a good friend to her. She needs one. Kind regards, Claire Wainwright.

Evelyn folded the paper and handed it back to Matthew, who pocketed it. Her feelings fought with each other. Sadness, worry, and above all a sense of incomprehension. What had gone so terribly wrong with their relationship that made Claire feel stifled? And why hadn't she spoken of it to her?

"Why would she deliver such a note to you? She barely knows you."

"Maybe that's the reason. She knows you and I are friendly and I would be unlikely to try to prevent her from taking such a drastic course of action simply because I wouldn't feel comfortable interfering in the life of a virtual stranger."

"Why didn't you tell me this earlier? All that nonsense about trying a change of scenery."

"You took me by surprise. I was about to enter the Black Lion to see if Jessie had seen you."

"You know the landlady, then?"

"Slightly. I have enjoyed the occasional beer in there on my infrequent trips to Haworth. You are staying there, I gather?"

"She told you that?"

"No, you did, when you came out of there at ten o'clock this morning."

Evelyn nodded. "I have decided to go back to Thornton Wensley tomorrow. It doesn't look as if my visit here is going to bring me any closer to knowing where Claire has gone. I can only hope she comes to her senses and returns home."

"You could report her as missing. I could accompany you to the police station."

"I doubt the police would be interested. She is a grown woman and has gone of her own accord. If she had been kidnapped or simply disappeared without a word, I wouldn't hesitate."

"Then I think you are probably right to return. In all probability she will come back when it suits her."

"I hope so, Matthew. I really do."

"Join me for dinner this evening? I have also taken a room at the Black Lion for the night, and it's a miserable business eating alone."

Evelyn hesitated, then smiled. He had a point. She had felt quite uncomfortable eating her solitary dinner yesterday, even if the food had been delicious.

"Very well, Matthew. Thank you. I would be happy to."

"And as for now, let's go and enjoy these wuthering moors."

Evelyn smiled. If only she knew she could trust him, but something still niggled at her and wouldn't stop.

They trekked up past the church and onto the moors, clambering over uneven ground. Matthew took her hand a few times to steady her over the more treacherous parts, until they came within sight of a lonely building standing next to a tall tree. The wind whistled around them as Evelyn took in the weathered gritstone house. Sturdily built, its color varying from sandy to gray to almost black, it showed every sign of having been added to over many years as the needs of its inhabitants changed. An L-shaped building had probably stabled a horse or two. Outbuildings in various stages of disrepair could have served a variety of purposes, and, some distance away, a small outhouse stood apart. The privy, no doubt.

The house stood entirely alone, an anomaly in a bleak landscape where little would grow. A few sheep grazed but nothing to indicate how anyone living there could earn enough to keep them.

"It's a fearfully isolated place," Evelyn said.

"That, my dear Miss Wainwright, is Top Withins. Inspiration for the Earnshaw family home in *Wuthering Heights*."

Evelyn studied it. Top Withins – built from the very stone of the Pennines themselves – asserted its right to be there. Solid, braced for all weathers and for everything the harsh elements could throw at it. Small wonder it served as inspiration for the fertile imagination of the parson's daughter from Haworth.

She cast her mind back to her well-worn copy of Emily Brontë's masterpiece. "She changed it a lot. From here it doesn't remotely resemble the house she described. But the landscape does. It's so bleak and empty. Almost devoid of life."

"Some might even call it desolate. Only fit for sheep. There's no arable farming around here. The soil is too acidic."

The wind whistled around them, fluttering Evelyn's skirt. The isolation of the place must make it hard to live in. Yet smoke curled up from the chimney. Someone was at home.

Evelyn fought an urge to proceed up to the front door and knock. Maybe Claire had been there. But she dismissed the thought. Whatever frame of mind her sister was in, she would be unlikely to make the walk to Top Withins all by herself. Reluctantly she tore herself away.

"I think we should start back now, Matthew."

"Yes, you're right."

They walked mainly in silence. Evelyn's feet ached. She hadn't walked this far in a long time. She welcomed the prospect of soaking in a nice hot tub and concentrated on the pleasant image to try to take her mind off her pain.

Matthew was a little ahead of her when he stopped dead and bent down. "How extraordinary," he said. "Have a look at this. Did you ever see anything like it?"

Evelyn caught up with him and bent down to peer at the large rock. She stared and didn't believe what she was seeing.

"Do you know what that is?" Matthew asked.

Evelyn took in the carved scaly serpent, its body coiled and its hinge-less mouth open, ready to strike.

"Todeswurm," she said.

CHAPTER ELEVEN

"Todeswurm?" Matthew asked. "What's that?"

"A death worm. I don't know much about it, but it's odd to see it up here. Maybe that's where he got the idea from."

"Who?"

"Branwell." Evelyn stopped, realizing what she had said. "No. I mean Claire. Claire wrote about it."

Matthew peered closer. "Looks a nasty piece of work."

"Yes."

If he wanted to know more, she wasn't about to tell him. As for the carving, hundreds of carved rocks existed all over the country and usually many hundreds of years old. That this one happened to closely resemble the drawing Claire had insisted was Branwell's had to be pure coincidence. Nothing else.

The long trudge back to Haworth did little to calm Evelyn's fractured nerves. They were within sight of the village when Matthew broke the less than comfortable silence between them.

"I hope you realize I'm your friend, Evelyn. If there is something I can help you with, I'll be happy to."

"Thank you, Matthew."

"When we return to Thornton Wensley, I will need to dispose of that toy. The Garden of Bewitchment. It's still up in the cave."

"With all the worry about Claire, I had put it out of my mind. But it can't be destroyed, can it? We've tried twice to burn it and failed."

"Then we'll have to try another method. Pack it in a lead-lined box and bury it, perhaps."

Evelyn bit her tongue. She longed to mention the other box,

the one Matthew was so secretive about, but he said he had made a promise to a friend. He wouldn't reveal its contents.

★   ★   ★

Dinner consisted of a steak and ale casserole with fluffy mashed potatoes and carrots. Evelyn found an appetite she thought she had lost.

"Going on long walks over the moors always makes me hungry," Matthew said as he helped himself to more potatoes.

"Your leg seems much better now. I notice you no longer carry the stick."

"It is indeed. I'm a bit tired today, though. Perhaps I did overdo it a little. Still a good night's rest and I shall be fighting fit again."

Jessie Lingard came in. "I see you made short work of that." She indicated the empty dishes.

"Delicious, Jessie," Evelyn said. "Thank you."

"I'm glad you enjoyed it. There's jam roly-poly and custard."

"Perfect," Matthew said as he took his last mouthful.

Jessie collected the plates and left them, and returned soon afterward with bowls of delicious dessert.

Evelyn tasted the jam-filled suet pudding, which instantly transported her back to her youth. Meals with Nanny. Cook used to make all the traditional children's desserts, and, of all of them, jam roly-poly, with homemade raspberry conserve, was her favorite. She couldn't remember how many years had elapsed since she had last tasted it.

"You can't beat a good suet pudding, can you?" Matthew said. "And Jessie makes the best."

"It's probably a good idea to go back tomorrow. I should be the size of a house if I stayed here much longer."

Matthew looked at her thoughtfully for a second. "You know, Evelyn, things will settle down. I'm sure of it."

"I wish I could be so certain. If only I knew where Claire was and why the strange things that have happened have occurred. I mean, the ransacking of Claire's room. The awful toy, which just happened to be the same as the one you experienced as a child. And there's more."

Matthew set down his spoon.

Evelyn took a deep breath. She would tell him. "The toy came to life. I was in it. In the house. And there was something evil in the woods and the garden. Claire rescued me."

Matthew looked at her as if she had suddenly grown an extra pair of arms. "The Garden of Bewitchment? Where did it come to life?"

"It seemed to start with a man I saw when I was having a sleepless night. He was standing on the path up on the ridge outside the back of our house. I saw him again the next day and he looked so familiar. Then Claire told me she had been through a frightening experience up on the moors. She told me something had attacked her, knocking her unconscious, but her memories of the event were so incredible, she doubted herself. Perhaps the injury to her head had resulted in some strange imaginings. We decided to return there and that's when everything became so strange. Nothing was right. We had somehow wandered into The Garden of Bewitchment and it had become real. That's when I lost Claire. Then, suddenly, somehow I was in the house, but I had been reduced to the size of one of those figures you could see through the windows. I seemed to become like one of them for a moment or two, as if I too were made of cardboard...or at least my foot was when I touched it to the floor of the drawing room. I was terrified. Not only because of what I had become or where I was... There was something outside, you see. Something that threatened me. I could feel it. Then Claire appeared at the window, only she was normal size, like a giant to me. She rescued me. Oh, you must think I am completely mad. Only an insane person could possibly believe what I am telling you."

"I can assure you I am far from insane," Matthew said. "Remember I have had my own experiences with that devilish toy. I believe everything you have told me. Was this before or after we took that thing up to the crags?"

"After."

"And have you seen the man again?"

Evelyn shook her head. "At least, I don't think so."

"Can you describe his features at all?"

"Not really. Except…"

"Yes?"

"This too will make no sense, but to me he resembled the picture Claire has of Branwell Brontë."

"Did he have a slightly hooked nose?"

"Yes. I would say so. In fact that was the only feature of his that didn't quite match Claire's print. Branwell, I believe, had a somewhat longer nose. Why did you ask?"

"Because my uncle had a hooked nose, and for some time now I have wondered if he had something to do with The Garden of Bewitchment."

"What makes you think he might?"

"Because just before I escaped from the attic, I'm sure I saw him."

"In the attic?"

"Yes, but more especially in the garden itself. Your experience of finding yourself in it means you will understand probably better than I do. I caught a glimpse. Only a fleeting one, but enough to be as sure as I can my uncle was standing behind a tree, peering round it and watching my distress with a smile on his face. I dismissed it for years, but since everything has started happening with your experiences, I am more convinced than ever. What I saw truly was him."

"It was in his attic, after all. Someone must have put it there."

"Quite possibly, but you also know that thing is capable of manifesting itself at will."

They sat in silence, each absorbed in their own thoughts. Evelyn yawned. "I'm sorry, but I will have to get to bed."

Matthew stood, and Evelyn left the table. "Good night, Matthew."

"Good night, Evelyn. I'll see you at breakfast."

★   ★   ★

In her room, Evelyn undressed and climbed into bed. Sleep came quickly, and by morning she felt refreshed and ready to face the challenges of whatever lay ahead.

Matthew did not look as if the same could be said for him. Dark circles had appeared under his eyes, and he looked drawn.

"Did you get any sleep at all?" Evelyn asked. "You look exhausted."

"Barely an hour. Someone kept banging on my door, but when I got up to answer it, there was no one there."

Jessie came in, bearing a rack full of hot, golden toast.

"Jessie, are there any other guests staying here?" Matthew asked.

"No. Why?"

"So there is just you and your husband?"

"Yes. Mr. Dixon, you don't look very well, are you all right?"

"As right as any man can be who has had virtually no sleep. Someone – or something – kept banging on my door, right through the night."

"I can assure you it wasn't either of us." Jessie looked at Evelyn.

"Nor me," Evelyn said.

"Come to think of it," Jessie said, "I did hear something. About one o'clock, it was. I put it down to the wind. Of course our room is on the other side of the inn to the guest rooms."

"Maybe you're right. Maybe it *was* the wind." Matthew sat down wearily. When Jessie had gone, he leaned forward. "That was no wind. In fact I can tell you there was no wind at all last night. It was perfectly still. Did you hear anything?"

"Not a thing. I slept soundly all night."

"Your room was at the opposite end of the corridor to mine, wasn't it? With these thick doors you probably wouldn't have heard much even if you were awake. Some of the bangs were really loud, though. Another unexplained occurrence to add to the collection."

"It's fast growing into a catalog." Evelyn picked up a slice of golden toast. "I want to make a final check of all the hostelries in the village before we leave. Just in case Claire has turned up."

"I wouldn't hold out too much hope."

"No, I shan't. Just clutching at a very tenuous straw."

Outside, the weather had turned misty and heavy with impending rain. The tour of the inns produced nothing, as did a check on the final few shops, so Evelyn and Matthew returned to the Black Lion to collect their luggage and pay their bills.

Jessie greeted them with her usual cheerful smile. "I think I have solved the mystery of the door that kept you awake last night, Mr. Dixon."

"Oh yes?"

"My husband reminded me. It's so long since he has been heard I had almost forgotten about him. You see, we all have our resident ghosts around here, and the Black Lion Boy is ours. He's a mischievous little imp that one. About every ten years or so he puts in an appearance. He'll bang doors, switch boots around that our guests leave outside their doors for polishing. He spills flour all over the kitchen. Nothing malicious, just naughty. My husband has given him a sound talking to, so hopefully he'll be on his way again."

Evelyn and Matthew exchanged bemused glances. Would that the spirits they were dealing with were so benign.

Having bid Jessie goodbye, Matthew carried their luggage down the hill to the station.

★   ★   ★

Back in Thornton Wensley, Evelyn opened her front door. "Claire?"

Silence. Only the ticking of the clock. She would need to wind it today.

In the kitchen, she set about lighting the range. A cup of tea would go down well.

Having encouraged the little flame to burst into life, Evelyn divested herself of her coat, hat and shoes and went upstairs. She paused outside Claire's room and gave a light knock. No response. She opened the door and gasped at the sight.

The room resembled the drawing room in the house of The

Garden of Bewitchment. Everything in its usual place. Piano, chairs – but no people – fireplace and mantelshelf. All full size. And all wrong. These items weren't real. As in her own experience, they were cardboard but lifelike and able to support themselves. She went over to the piano and touched the keys. A light tinkling sound, but the keys did not depress. The piano itself swayed as if it might fall over at any moment.

The chairs too were self-supporting, but Evelyn had no intention of testing them out by sitting on one of them. She knew it would give way and send her crashing to the floor.

She went over to the window, which was resplendent in long velvet-looking drapes. These turned out to be paper. They made a crinkling noise when she touched them.

The view looked all wrong too. Instead of the backyard, steps and moorland, the exquisite garden stretched out before her, surrounded by trees. Those same trees that had tried to trap her. Evelyn backed away. She must get out of this room.

She bolted for the door, dragged it open and shut it tightly behind her. Her own room was mercifully normal, but she couldn't help wondering if Claire's disappearance and the transformation of her room were inextricably linked, and, if so, didn't that mean Claire was trapped in that evil garden?

Eventually Evelyn came out of her room, stopped and looked at Claire's door. She needed help, and the only person who wouldn't think she had lost her reason was Matthew. She would have to swallow her doubts about him and enlist his aid.

Her fingers trembled so much she could barely button up her boots. She winced as she snagged a nail, the sharp stab of pain adding to her discomfort.

A sudden scuffling sound from upstairs stopped her in her tracks. It had come from Claire's room. Evelyn swallowed hard and grabbed the stair rail. Taking care not to make a sound, she hitched up her skirt and slowly mounted the staircase.

More scuffling. What if that…thing…the Todeswurm was in there?

Evelyn reached the top of the staircase and listened.

More scuffles, footsteps. Coming closer. Evelyn watched in horror as the door handle turned. The door opened.

"*Claire!*"

"Hello, Ev."

After all she had put her through. *'Hello, Ev!'*

"Where have you been? Why did you go off like that? How did you...? Your room!" Evelyn pushed her sister aside and peered in. But all seemed as normal. No sign of the evil garden. Only Claire's furniture exactly where it should be. Evelyn stood back, words momentarily failing her.

Claire seemed in a placatory mood. "I'm sorry I worried you. I felt stifled. I needed to get away, but I'm feeling much better now. I fancy a glass of milk. How about you?" Without waiting for an answer, she started down the stairs with Evelyn close behind her.

"Claire, you're behaving as if nothing happened. You've been away for days. I came looking for you in Haworth."

"Oh, you wouldn't have found me there."

"So I discovered. I thought you might go there for Branwell."

"Oh, no. He came with me."

"So where did you go?"

They were in the kitchen now. Claire filled the kettle and placed it on the hob. She seemed to take an age, and Evelyn's impatience grew until she wanted to both hug and shake her sister.

Claire looked at her steadily. "Do you know? I really can't remember."

"You can't remember? Have you been ill? Lost your memory?"

"I don't think so." Claire considered this for a moment, her face a mask of concentration. "No, I'm pretty sure I remember everything. I just can't place where I was."

"But Branwell was with you?"

"Part of the time. Yes. I remember a beautiful garden... Oh don't look so horrified, Ev. I was perfectly safe."

"Your room. Earlier, I opened your door and the entire room

had transformed into the house in The Garden of Bewitchment. Don't tell me you were in there somehow. Like I was when you rescued me?"

"Was I? Yes, I think maybe you're right. But I wasn't in any danger. Branwell protected me until it came time for me to return."

Evelyn sat down heavily and accepted the glass of milk Claire poured out for her. "How did you get into that place anyway? The Garden of Bewitchment wasn't in your room when I went to Haworth."

"I'm not exactly sure. I remember writing a note to you, oh, and one to Matthew, and then the drawing room went dark. Shadows appeared everywhere, as if night had fallen quicker than it should. Then Branwell came to me. He took my hand and told me not to be afraid. The shadows were our friends. They would protect us."

"Protect you from what?"

Claire shrugged and frowned. "It all made perfect sense then. Not so much now, though."

"So you went with Branwell into the shadows?"

"Yes. The room. It sort of…changed somehow. Instead of walls, it opened up, and soon we were in the garden and I saw the house. I heard music playing."

"And did you meet anyone else there?"

Claire thought for a moment. "No. Not really. I mean there were other people there, but they didn't speak to me. I don't think they could see me."

The same experience Evelyn had met with.

"Oh, there was something else, though. Something in the garden with me, but Branwell told me I mustn't fear it. It wouldn't harm me as long as I did what he told me to do."

"And what was that?"

"Oh, nothing really. Branwell gave me a knife."

Evelyn stared in horror at her sister. "A *knife*? Whatever did you need a knife for?"

"In case anything got through. Anything that shouldn't. But

Branwell said it was most unlikely. He simply wanted me to be prepared for every eventuality."

"Didn't this frighten you?"

"A little. At first. But Branwell reassured me."

"And how did he do that?"

"He kissed me. He told me he would always watch over me, even if I couldn't see him. Then he told me he had to go away for a while but he would return."

"And did he?"

"I don't know. I stayed in the house for a bit and lost track of time, I think. Then a little while ago, I decided to go for a walk, came outside and found myself back here in my room."

Evelyn tried to absorb it all. Here was her sister telling her the most incredible story in such a way as she might be describing a walk to the shops. True or not, she had little doubt her sister believed every word of her fantastic tale.

★   ★   ★

Matthew exhaled loudly. "Some story, Evelyn." He stood and looked out of the window of her cottage. Claire had taken herself upstairs for a lie down when he knocked at the door.

"I know," Evelyn said. "I wouldn't believe it if I hadn't had strange experiences with that garden myself, but I don't understand why this is happening or how to make it stop."

"She is utterly convinced she sees Branwell, isn't she?"

"He is as real to her as we are. At first I thought it was a mere fantasy taken too far. Now I don't know what to believe."

"You've heard of possession, I expect. Where a person's body is taken over by a spirit, usually a malevolent one."

A memory clicked into place in Evelyn's mind. "I read in the newspapers about a woman from Falkirk called Ellen McNulty – a perfectly normal housewife and mother who suddenly turned into a violent and bloody murderer. It was said her body had been possessed by an evil spirit."

"Yes, I remember the story. It didn't end well. They convicted and hanged her, I believe?"

Evelyn nodded.

"Claire's situation is nothing like as dire, but if we are to believe there is true evil in this world, and I do, then it is highly likely such evil can infect the minds and bodies of the innocent and the vulnerable."

"And you think this is what has happened to Claire?"

"I don't know. I merely offer it as a possible explanation."

"In Ellen McNulty's case, they brought in a Roman Catholic priest who performed an exorcism. Do I need to do the same?"

"I truly don't know, Evelyn, but it may be worth considering, at least."

Evelyn sighed. "I never would have thought I would ever be having such a conversation about my own sister."

"In a village like this, who would? And yet..." He shivered and moved away from the window. "There *is* something about this cottage that disturbs me every time I enter it. I can't explain anything, but there is a feeling of darkness. With your permission, Evelyn, I would like to write to my cousin and ask him if he knows of any stories connected to this house that might give us a clue as to what is going on here."

"I should be most grateful if you would. Maybe we can find out a way to stop it and rid ourselves of that evil toy for good."

"It hasn't turned up again?"

"Not since Claire returned."

"That at least is something. I should tell you I went up to the crags and, as we might have expected, the toy wasn't there."

"Unless someone removed it."

"Too much coincidence. No, it somehow managed to relocate itself back here. It has a link to this place."

"Your uncle? Was he your cousin Gerald's father?"

"Yes. Why do you ask?"

"Did he ever live in your cousin's cottage?"

"Not that I'm aware of. He may have stayed there from time to time."

"Would you ask your cousin if he did and, if so, did he bring anything with him he may have left behind either in your cottage or mine?"

Matthew blinked a couple of times. "Why didn't I think of that? I will certainly ask him."

"Meanwhile, I have to try to restore Claire to some kind of normality."

"Are you sure I can't help? Maybe if I talk to her."

"Would you? I would be so grateful."

"Tomorrow perhaps? I don't want to disturb her now."

"I am quite sure tomorrow will be perfect. Around three o'clock?"

Matthew left shortly after, and Evelyn picked up her book. At least they were doing something. She prayed Matthew's cousin would have some answers.

★   ★   ★

Claire answered Matthew's knock in seconds. She stepped aside to let him in.

"Evelyn had to go out. She sent her apologies. She won't be able to see you this afternoon. Something came up. I don't know what. She didn't tell me."

"Nice to see you again, Claire," Matthew removed his hat, "It's actually you I came to see."

"She told me you wanted to talk to me. Cup of tea?"

"Yes, please."

"I made it ready for you. Please sit down."

Claire poured cups of tea and handed one to Matthew. Whatever Ev thought she might achieve by this meeting, she couldn't imagine. Still, her sister had been behaving strangely, as if she had some great secret she wasn't prepared to share. It didn't matter. Ev could keep her secrets. After all, Claire had her own.

"Evelyn tells me you have been seeing quite a lot of Branwell Brontë?"

Claire tucked a stray strand of hair behind her ear. "Yes. And please don't tell me it's impossible. I know he's dead. But he isn't dead in the way we know it. He lives on."

"In the afterlife?"

"Not really."

"I'm sorry. I don't follow you."

"If you don't believe, then I can't make you."

"Is he here now?"

"Can you *see* him?"

"No."

"Then, clearly, he is not." Tiresome man. Claire didn't trust him. She didn't care whether he knew it or not.

"Claire. I sense hostility from you. Please understand, I am only trying to help. Your sister has been so worried about you, and you have both been through a traumatic series of incidents."

"I don't feel traumatized in the least."

"Perhaps you should."

"Why would you say that?"

"Don't you feel it is a little unusual, shall we say, to talk matter-of-factly about having a relationship with a ghost?"

"Branwell isn't a ghost."

"Isn't he? Then what is he?"

"He's not a ghost." She wasn't about to tell Matthew something she had promised Branwell to keep between them.

"Claire, either he is alive or he is dead. He can't be somewhere in between. You know that, don't you?"

"Matthew, please don't patronize me. I don't appreciate it."

"I assure you I am not patronizing you. I'm merely trying to understand your version of what has happened to you. You disappeared for a few days and apparently spent the time in The Garden of Bewitchment. Is that right?"

"Yes."

"It's a toy."

"But you know, as does my sister, it is much more than that. Much more." Careful. She mustn't say too much. She must remember her promise to Branwell.

"I do know it possesses some remarkable powers and it seems to be exerting quite a hold on you, apparently with Branwell's assistance."

"And mine. I want it too." Now she really mustn't go any further. Already his expression had changed. He seemed to sense he was getting somewhere. She had let her guard down. Instantly, she shut up.

"Claire, please tell me what you know."

"There is nothing to tell. You know everything there is to know." Why couldn't he leave her alone? Couldn't he tell this was hard enough for her? The constant clamor of voices in her head. Ev eyeing her so suspiciously all the time, and now Matthew. What was he even doing here?

Claire stood. "I should like you to go now, please."

Matthew stood. "I wish you would trust me, Claire. Evelyn does."

"Does she? I very much doubt it. She can't decide whether you are friend or foe, but *I* know."

"What do you know?"

Ah, now he looked apprehensive. Well, so he should. "I know you are not what you claim to be. There is nothing wrong with your leg. Never has been. As for any accident that damaged your spine… No, it didn't happen either, did it, Matthew? If indeed Matthew is your real name."

His face had turned angry now. "I don't know where you got your so-called information, but you are wrong, Claire. So wrong. I assume Branwell has a hand in this?"

"At least you acknowledge his existence, which is more than my sister does."

"Oh, he exists, all right, more's the pity. He exists but not as you would have him."

"I don't know what you're talking about." He mustn't turn things around on her like this. "You are merely using him to deflect from your own duplicity. Now, please leave." Claire opened the door and motioned him to exit.

He gave her the briefest of nods and strode out. Rain began to fall as she closed the door on him.

A handclap started up behind her. "Well done, Claire. I am proud of you. You stood up to him perfectly. His sort only know how to bully and attack, but you wouldn't be cowed."

"Never, Branwell. Not while you are at my side anyway."

"Never it is then. For I shall always be at your side."

Claire smiled and moved closer toward him. He put out his hand to her, and she took it.

"Come, my dear, Lady Mandolyne awaits us by the lake."

"She is really there?"

"Of course. You wanted her to be there, don't you remember?"

"Yes, but I never thought it was possible."

"But you saw her that other time. And so did Evelyn."

"I thought I did. Oh, Branwell, sometimes I'm not sure what is real and what is fantasy."

"All you need to know is, this is real. You are with me, and we are going to see Lady Mandolyne. Everything is going to be perfect."

"Yes, Branwell. Everything is going to be perfect."

The walls seemed to melt away until they were no longer in the cottage. Trees surrounded them, their branches gently swaying in the light breeze.

Claire walked beside Branwell. He tucked her hand into the crook of his elbow and patted it. Soon the trees parted, birds sang and butterflies fluttered. The heady perfume of a thousand roses filled her nose and made her head swim. She had never felt so blissful.

The crystal waters of the lake gleamed before them, and, at the water's edge, Lady Mandolyne waited for them.

"See, my lady? I have brought Claire to see you. You will have much to talk about, I am sure." Branwell gently disentangled Claire's arm from his and stepped aside.

Lady Mandolyne extended a long white arm with tapering fingers toward Claire, who took a step closer. The woman's eyes sparkled like sapphires. Her head tilted at a slight angle as she studied Claire and beckoned her to move closer.

As she did so, the woman's eyes became brighter still, glittering and hard. She opened her mouth as if to speak, but no words were formed. Only in Claire's mind.

I have waited for you. Now you are here, we can begin. But no one is to know of this. On pain of death.

This couldn't be right. Lady Mandolyne should not be threatening her, and how could anyone threaten in such a soft voice?

"My lady, I—"

Lady Mandolyne put up her hand to stop her from saying more. She nodded toward Branwell, who put his arm around Claire.

"Come with us, Claire," he said. "We have something to show you."

His eyes looked warm and sincere, but, for the first time, Claire felt unsure in Branwell's presence. He seemed to sense her resistance and tightened his grip on her shoulders.

"You have nothing to fear, Claire. I am with you. I will always be with you."

And for the first time, Claire felt his words not as a promise.

But as a threat.

CHAPTER TWELVE

Later that week, Matthew motioned for Evelyn to sit in a chair by the fire in his cottage. Urgent business had taken him to Leeds for a few days and, as Claire had refused to discuss her meeting with him, Evelyn was anxious to hear what had transpired between them. Matthew's expression did little to raise her hopes.

"I am so sorry," he said. "I did my best, but she wouldn't open up to me. She won't hear a word against Branwell and won't admit there is anything wrong."

"I suppose we do have to acknowledge there is an entity, or call it what you will, that goes by the name of Branwell Brontë?"

"Yes, Evelyn. I'm afraid we do. I think we also have to acknowledge he is, in some way, linked to the toy, and I do have other news."

"From your cousin?" Evelyn took a deep breath, preparing herself for whatever might come.

"Gerald said Uncle Mortimer became quite eccentric in his later years. He spent a great deal of time in the attic, and my aunt became most concerned about his mental state. He would come down from there, tangled in weeds, twigs, and muttering vile oaths against someone or something he called Dakraska. When my aunt questioned him about it, he would fly into a rage so severe she actually feared for her life. A few minutes later he would be his old, quiet self again. She said it was as if he had been possessed by this Dakraska."

"And it only happened when he had spent time in the attic?"

"Yes. My aunt tried padlocking the door so he couldn't get in. She even threw away the key. He promptly went out and took an ax from the garden shed and proceeded to hack the door down. And then things turned much worse."

"What happened?"

"That thing...Dakraska...came after her. She woke up one night to find herself staring into the vilest yellow eyes she had ever seen. The creature resembled a serpent or worm."

It had to be. "The Todeswurm?"

"From what my cousin wrote, I think so. It reared up and opened its disgusting mouth. My aunt said it was like looking into a vast chasm, dark, stinking and foul. She screamed, and my uncle raced in from his room, brandishing a poker. He hit it, and it lashed out at him. Then it vanished, as if it had never been there. My uncle died the next day – officially from a heart attack – but my aunt swore to her dying day that the thing had scared him so much he died of fright."

"How terrible. And you knew nothing of this?"

Matthew shook his head. "There's one more thing. My uncle *did* stay with Gerald at the cottage. My cousin said he brought a toy with him, but the rest of the family weren't in the mood for playthings. While he was staying here, though, he became friendly with one of the locals. Gerald can't remember his name, but he does remember his father going out one rainy day with the intention of visiting his new friend, who was the tenant of your cottage. And he had The Garden of Bewitchment with him. But he brought the toy back home with him. He didn't leave it at the cottage. We know that. Gerald can't remember ever seeing it again. Then we only have my aunt's recollections of the terrible effect it had on him at the end of his life."

"But given it was only here such a short time, how can it manifest itself here again and again? Unless it infests wherever it has been and leaves something behind. Like a footprint. Only, in this case, it's a creature. A Dakraska, or Todeswurm. Where does the name Dakraska come from anyway?"

Matthew shook his head. "I don't know. I have heard of ancient legends of death worms, and people have described them in minute detail. We could try the library and see if they have any reference material on the subject."

"I'll do that," Evelyn said. "I suppose we have to say we have made progress today, but every move forward seems to present new problems. There is still the strange man I saw."

"I have no answers. Apart from the possible facial similarity to my uncle, and, indeed Branwell Brontë."

*   *   *

Dusk had descended by the time Evelyn made her way back down the lane to her cottage. Inside, Claire hadn't yet lit the lamps, and the gloom-filled room lay shrouded in shadows.

Evelyn set about lighting the wicks. As she did so, a warm glow began to lighten the darkness. The corners remained in shadow. Growing darker by the second.

"Claire?" she called, her anxiety level rising.

"I'm in my room, Ev. I'll be down in a minute."

Relief wiped away the fear. When would she ever be able to return home without worrying whether her sister would still be there?

The night felt chillier than it had been even a few moments earlier, too cold to remove her coat and hat yet. It grew colder still as her breath misted in front of her.

A lamp flickered, sputtered and went out. Then another, plunging the room into darkness.

"Claire? I need you now. Please come down, with your lamp."

Evelyn tried to relight the lamps, but the matches sparked, and then extinguished as if someone had blown on them.

Claire didn't reply, but Evelyn heard footsteps on the stairs.

"Claire, thank goodness, I don't know what—"

The man approached her, and, as he did so, she saw he wasn't as tall as he seemed on those stairs.

Her heart hammering, Evelyn tried to keep her voice steady. "Who are you?"

The man smiled and came yet a step closer. It was still too dark to make out his features. He didn't speak but held up his hand. Invisible hands pinioned her in a grip cold as ice and impossible to break. No matter how she struggled, they stayed firm and unyielding.

"Get them off me," Evelyn yelled, more angry than scared. How *dare* anyone lay their hands on her? "I don't care who or what you are. Release me. Now."

"Oh dear, Miss Wainwright," the man said. "I couldn't possibly do that now, could I?"

"Why not?"

"Because I have to take you somewhere."

"And if I don't want to go?"

"Not your decision."

Propelled forward, she either had to put one foot in front of the other or risk stumbling. Blackness consumed everything ahead. Aware of no doors opening, or even of the ground beneath her feet changing, she smelled fresh air and knew they were outside. Still the unnatural blackness persisted as she was pressed onward by something she could not see.

She lost track of how long they had been walking. Her arms ached from the tight grip her captors maintained. She couldn't turn her head, had no idea if she was being held prisoner by humans, animals or machines, only that they would not release or slacken their hold, and trying to break free only resulted in more discomfort.

Still they moved on. Branches brushed her hair. In the distance, the sound of water. A waterfall perhaps. The scent of jasmine and honeysuckle floated toward her as the night became warmer. The garden. They had taken her back there, wherever it was now. She prayed as hard as she could that they weren't taking her to the Todeswurm.

Sudden, bright light stung her eyes. The darkness evaporated in less than a second and so did the vise-like grip around her and the man who led her here. Her wrists burned. Bruises where she had been gripped began to bloom. All around her, the beautiful garden blossomed in such tranquility. Such deadliness. Mere yards from the house and with nowhere else to go, she made her way toward it.

The front door stood open, inviting her to enter. Inside, the magnificent hall was silent and empty. No music came from the drawing room. She opened the door and found the room deserted. The furniture looked real, and when she ran her hand across the piano, the wood felt solid under her fingertips.

A shuffling noise. She turned.

Creeping along the floor, a hideous wormlike creature gained ground upon her. She put her hand over her mouth to stifle the scream that so wanted to escape, and she backed up against the wall. Still the creature advanced. Its eyes open and focused on her. Its mouth gaped, an all-consuming blackness, drawing her ever closer to its hideous depths. She sensed intelligence in its gaze, but only of the most evil kind. It had meaning and purpose. It knew what it was doing. And it wanted to kill her.

Cornered, desperate, Evelyn beat on the walls. The slithering worm stopped. It reared up cobra-like, hissing and spitting at its prey. Evelyn caught sight of a small handle on the wall a few inches away from her. She grabbed it, and, in one twist of her hand, a door opened. In a second, she was through, slamming the door behind her, and grabbed a heavy box covered in cobwebs. She pushed hard, its weight resisting every shove, until she had wedged it behind the door. She leaned against the box, panting.

The creature had no fingers, so with any luck it couldn't open doors. God alone knew how great its strength was, but it had powerful muscles.

Her breathing eased, and Evelyn listened for any sound from the other side of the wall. Silence. Maybe it had given up, unless... Perhaps it was waiting for her. Lulling her into a false sense of security. She wouldn't fall for that one.

Evelyn took in her surroundings – a long, narrow room. Dim light squeezed through a small window at one side, sufficient to illuminate a mahogany desk. Evelyn made her way over to it. Old, yellowing papers littered the floor. She ignored them for now, intent on discovering what the many drawers contained. She opened them one after the other. All contained yellow parchment or other high-quality paper. All pristine. She opened more drawers in front of her. These held pens of varying types, including expensive-looking fountain pens and quills.

She came to the final drawer, to the right of her. Inside lay a manuscript. She had seen it before. The one she had found in this house but not this room. This time, it had a new cover, with *The Chronicles of Calladocia* picked out in gold lettering on green board covers. Although not properly bound, it gave every impression someone had taken a great deal of care over it. She turned to the first page. As before, authorship wasn't credited. Also as before, the stories went far beyond what she and Claire had written. The pictures too were of high quality and in exquisite detail. Each one reflected the characters she knew so well. Lady Mandolyne once again appeared identical to the ethereal creature she had encountered.

Evelyn lost track of time. Here, at least she was safe, or so it seemed. For now anyway. She turned her attention to the papers strewn all over the floor. She picked them up one by one. Most held little of any interest. They appeared to be early, discarded drafts of the parts of the story neither she nor, to the best of her knowledge, Claire had written. There were heavy crossings out, as if the author had become frustrated at his or her inability to tell the tale.

Evelyn laid them neatly on top of each other on the desk. Soon, she had amassed a pile as big as the finished work itself.

By now the light had begun to fade. Evening must be drawing in. She needed to find an escape from the Todeswurm. Picking up the book, she made her way past the desk, along the narrow room, grateful for the occasional window, however small, so she could see where she was going. Shadows lengthened all around her, and she had the impression of moving in an anticlockwise direction. This space must extend all around the house. There didn't seem to be any doors to the outside world, and, so far, she hadn't found another internal one such as the one she had entered by.

She had to escape soon or risk spending the night here. Although, at least that would be preferable to encountering the beast again.

She reached a dead end. It appeared the only way in and out of this place was through the door leading to the drawing room. Did the Todeswurm know that? Maybe it was waiting for her there right now, knowing she would have to come out sooner or later.

Evelyn swung around and made for the nearest small window, high up on the wall. She couldn't reach it without standing on something, and, apart from the box she had used to wedge against the door, and the desk, which might not take her weight, there was nothing.

Panic welled up inside her, and she swallowed hard. She mustn't pick now, of all times, to give in to useless fear. She must be practical.

It became ever more difficult to see. The shadows darkened by the second.

And then she heard it.

Scuffling.

Pray God the thing hadn't made it in here with her.

Evelyn shrank against the wall, holding her breath. The scuffling came nearer. Not the slithering she had heard in the drawing room. This sounded more human.

"Ev?"

Never had she been gladder to hear her sister's voice. "Claire. Thank God. How did you get here? How did you find me?"

"I...don't know. I..." Claire's face appeared before her. For a second she seemed devoid of a body, as if *only* her face could manifest itself. In an instant the moment had passed and her sister stood opposite.

"I was suddenly here, and I knew I had to find you. I knew where you were, although I haven't the faintest idea how."

"Are you...alone?"

"I think so. I'm not sure. It's all a bit confusing. I was with

Branwell. We were by the lake. Lady Mandolyne was there, as real as you and I. But there was something wrong, Ev. She didn't seem… right somehow."

"We wrote her as having gone insane, don't you remember?"

"Yes, well, that would fit. And there was something not right about Branwell either."

"In what way?"

"Oh, Ev, I've always felt so safe with him. But he was different this time. As if I was with another man entirely. One who had taken over Branwell's body." Claire caught sight of the book, tucked under Evelyn's arm.

"What's that?"

Evelyn held it out to her. "The completed *Chronicles of Calladocia*. Only we didn't complete them. Someone else did."

"Let me see." Claire opened the book and flipped over the pages. "This is his handwriting. Branwell's. These are his drawings too. I recognize the style. They're like the ones I showed you, and you wouldn't believe me when I said I hadn't written that scene or drawn the pictures."

"Well, I believe you now. Or, at least, I believe you didn't write them, but, if your suspicions about Branwell are correct, it could be neither did he. Someone else is possessing him."

"*Possessing* him? How? Why?"

"To get at us for some reason, I presume, although I have no idea why. Matthew seemed to think possession was a likely answer, and I think he's right."

"Is he here? Matthew?"

Evelyn shook her head. "Did you come in through the little door in the drawing room?"

Claire nodded. "I don't know why. I felt drawn to it somehow. I didn't even know it was there."

"The same thing happened to me. The Todeswurm threatened me, and I found it."

"Lucky."

"Yes." A bit too lucky perhaps. It certainly seemed to have given up all too quickly. "Did you see any sign of the worm or anyone else?"

"No. The place was empty. Branwell and Lady Mandolyne disappeared somewhere."

"Then we must try and get away."

"Unless we can reach a window, open it and squeeze through, we'll have to go back the way we came. Through the drawing room." Claire looked up at the nearest window. "There is no catch. No way of opening it without smashing it, which would give the worm another means of getting in. We might need this place as sanctuary in the future."

"You're right. The drawing room it is, then."

Evelyn led the way back down to where the desk stood, the neat pile of papers still there. "Could you carry those?' Evelyn asked. "There may be something in them I've missed. I only had a quick look. Besides, last time I tried to take this book back, I failed."

Claire helped Evelyn heave the box aside and then picked up the sheaf.

"What's in this box?" she asked.

"I have no idea. I don't even know if I can open it." Evelyn felt around. Nothing. "Right, let's not waste any more time. The light's almost gone."

Reluctantly, Claire joined her at the door, and Evelyn turned the handle, taking care to make as little noise as possible.

She peered around into the drawing room, and a pair of familiar eyes made her jump.

"Matthew!"

"Hello, Evelyn. I've come to get you out of here."

Evelyn pushed the door wide and stepped out into the room. "I'm so relieved to see you. Come on, Claire. Matthew's going to get us out of here."

Confusion covered Matthew's face. "Who are you talking to?"

"My sister. Claire. You remember."

"Evelyn. There's no one there."

CHAPTER THIRTEEN

"I don't understand." Evelyn peered back into the room. "She was right behind me."

"No, Evelyn. You were on your own. There was no one with you." He pointed to the book. "What's that?"

"Something Claire and I have been working on that seems to have been completed by someone else. Matthew, I don't understand where she's gone. She was there. She came for me."

"This place. It plays havoc with your mind. I don't know how I got here, but I do know how to get us out. We must hurry."

"But what about Claire? I can't just leave her here. The Todeswurm is about."

"Trust me, she's not here. If she ever was."

Evelyn followed Matthew reluctantly. But she had to acknowledge what he said was right. This place could destroy anyone's sanity. She must trust Matthew, at least for now. He was all she had to get her out of here.

The garden gave way to trees, and, as before, Evelyn felt them closing in on her, their branches tugging at her clothes, pulling her hair, scratching her face. Matthew strode on ahead, and Evelyn had trouble keeping up. She clung fiercely to the book and concentrated on not tripping on the uneven ground, where roots lay waiting for an unwary footstep.

The sun had gone down, and a half-moon cast inadequate light, which struggled to make it to ground level.

Then they were through the trees, back onto moorland.

Evelyn was alone. No sign of Matthew, the garden, the house. Only the bleak moorland stretched before her.

Gray clouds rolled in; the wind picked up and nearly blew her off her feet. Still she stood there, her mind reeling. Could she trust herself anymore? Had she been in that garden? That house? No sign of any of it now. Could she believe anything she thought she saw anymore?

Buffeted by the sudden gale, the onslaught of rain brought her to her senses. She couldn't stay out in this weather. She must get back. At least the crags looked familiar.

She picked up her skirts and remembered. The book. Had she dropped it? She searched all around but could not see it anywhere. If it had ever existed, it had once again disappeared.

Evelyn hurried as best she could, by now soaked to the bone. Her hair escaped its clips, tears mingling with the rain and half blinding her.

Finally she made it to the path, which fast became a quagmire.

The path gave way to the lane, and Evelyn dashed along to her cottage. With trembling fingers she unlocked the door. Once inside, she stripped off her sodden coat and hat, shivering uncontrollably.

"Claire," she called half-heartedly. She wouldn't be there. Claire was lost.

"Ev?"

Her sister bounded down the stairs and took Evelyn in her arms. "Where have you been? I've been so worried about you."

"But you were with me. In that house. Then Matthew came and…" Evelyn read the confusion on Claire's face. "It doesn't matter. I'm home now. You're home. Everything's going to be all right."

"I have to show you something," Claire said. "But you must get out of those wet clothes or you'll catch your death. What were you thinking of, going up on the moors in this weather?"

"How did you know I was on the moors?"

Claire pointed at Evelyn's feet. She looked down and saw the mud plastered all over her boots.

"It wasn't raining when I went up there."

"You've been gone so long I've been really worried."

Evelyn said nothing. She followed Claire up the stairs.

★   ★   ★

The next morning, following a night when sleep had been hard to come by, Evelyn wandered into Claire's room. Her sister looked up from where she had been staring, apparently at the floor.

"Notice anything?" she said.

Evelyn gazed around the room. "Apart from being much tidier than usual, no. What's changed?"

"Firstly, I didn't tidy it, and secondly, look at this."

Claire went over to the corner of the room and picked something up. She brought it back to show Evelyn. A tiny wormlike creature wriggled in Claire's hand.

Evelyn recoiled. "For heaven's sake, Claire. What is it? Some kind of maggot? Get rid of it. I don't even think you should be touching it."

"Oh, I'll get rid of it, but watch what happens when I do." Claire opened her window and flung the tiny creature out. She shut the window tightly. "Now go over to that corner and look carefully."

Evelyn did as she was bid. At first nothing happened. Simply an ordinary skirting board and the edge of the rug. Then, slowly, a bubble appeared in the paintwork. It squirmed for a moment and then popped open. Another of the tiny worms fell onto the floor. Evelyn backed away. "Oh my Lord. How is this happening? Where are they coming from?"

"I have no idea. But it's been going on for a couple of hours now. When I dispose of one, another appears."

"No. No. It's not natural. We must go to the apothecary and get some poison. Arsenic or strychnine."

"I suppose we can try, but I'm sure they would simply keep coming back. I don't know what they are or why they come, but I don't believe they're natural, and it looks like we're stuck with them. For now, at least."

"I'm not living with maggots or worms or whatever they are. And you can't sleep in the same room as them."

"Oh, but I can. Look." Claire picked up a tumbler and placed it over the squirming creature. It wriggled around, trying to locate a way out. Finding none, it seemed to give up and lie still.

"Is it dead? Asleep?"

"Definitely not dead. When I take the glass off, it starts wriggling again. But at least this way I only have to contend with one. As long as you don't get rid of them, and I assume that also means killing them, they leave you alone."

"This is all connected to that infernal toy. Matthew's uncle brought it to this cottage. He made a friend here, and the two of them used to play with it. Goodness knows what they discovered. When we moved in, our presence somehow activated something, and that's why it appeared. Everything we have experienced since then is linked to the disgusting thing. Including your new friend." Evelyn pointed to the glass where the creature lay quiet.

A wave of extreme tiredness swept over Evelyn and she stifled a yawn behind her hand. "I'm going to have to lie down again for a little. I feel as if I haven't slept in a week."

"Don't worry, Ev. I'll look after everything here. I'll make us a salad at teatime. That way you can eat whenever you're ready."

A knock sounded at the front door.

"I'll get it," Claire said. "You rest. You look worn out."

Gratitude overwhelmed Evelyn, and she could have kissed her. She wandered into her room, and Claire made her way downstairs.

★   ★   ★

"Matthew," Claire said.

"Evelyn?" He looked uncertain.

"No. Claire. Goodness, I would have thought you could have told us apart by now. I'm the messy one. You would never catch Ev with her hair like this." Claire indicated the untidy ponytail lying half over her shoulder and half down her back.

"Is Evelyn in?"

"She's having a lie down. She had a traumatic time yesterday by all accounts. But then you were with her, weren't you? In The Garden of Bewitchment? "

"Me? No. I don't know anything about that."

"Oh, really? That's not what she said."

"I can assure you it's true. I didn't come to argue with you, Claire. I have some information for Evelyn. Can you ask her to contact me when she is rested?"

"Or you could tell me. Don't you trust me to relay your messages to her?"

Matthew hesitated. Claire knew exactly what that meant.

"Very well," he said at last. "If you will let me in, I will do my best to explain."

Claire stepped aside. Matthew seemed to have aged in the past few days. She would have sworn he hadn't had any gray in his hair, but now little flecks of it had begun to appear at his temples. It suited him in that irritating way men had of being able to look distinguished as they aged, whereas most women merely looked older.

He sat down. Given the easy way in which he moved, his leg must be feeling much better. But then, he had invented the so-called accident, hasn't he? Remembering this sent little shock waves of anger flowing through her veins.

She sat opposite him. "So what is it you want my sister to know?"

"I told her about The Garden of Bewitchment and how my uncle used to play it with someone at this cottage. My cousin told me."

"Yes, I'm aware of that."

"I have received another letter from my cousin this morning, apologizing for getting some of his information wrong. Uncle

Mortimer didn't befriend the *tenant* of this cottage; he befriended the *owner*. Squire Aloysius Monkton. They used to meet here, as the squire had taken to staying down here. He preferred it in the winter months to the draughty manor house."

"I can see why he would. I'll see Ev gets the message." Claire stood.

"Oh, no, that isn't all. There's much more. I'll read it to you." Matthew retrieved a letter from his inside jacket pocket. "He says, 'Your recent communication set me thinking about things I'd never given a passing thought to for years. I went through some of my mother's old diaries and found the entries where she talks of my father's friendship with the squire. Aloysius Monkton died a few years later, and he is the same one who is said to haunt the village to this day. He was, by all accounts, an eccentric old cove, mostly preferring the company of his dogs to his fellow humans. My mother remarks on this. For some reason, he and Father hit it off. When Father brought that toy we spoke of – The Garden of Bewitchment – the squire was fascinated. He said he had owned one himself when much younger but hadn't seen it for years. He said it held a special fascination for him because it had been based on his home and garden. His own father had commissioned it as a special birthday present but had died before he was able to give it to his only son. The squire expressed his amazement that Father had one, as he had been sure only one had ever been made. Father got the impression he would very much like to have it, having lost his own, but the old man was reluctant, eventually refusing altogether. My mother writes it caused a big argument between the two men, with the squire accusing Father of having stolen the toy from him. All very childish and petulant. Later that year, she notes the squire never returned to the manor house – Monkton Hall. He took ill and died.'" Matthew folded the letter and returned it to his pocket. "So, you see, Claire. This puts a very different complexion on things. I have asked my neighbor Mr. Skelton, and he informs me Monkton Hall is a mere two miles away, practically derelict as it hasn't been lived in since old Monkton died. There were no children to inherit, so it just lies there. Mr. Skelton has promised to escort me there tomorrow, and I wondered if Evelyn would like to come along. It's not a difficult ride apparently, and Mr. Skelton has two horses he can lend us."

"So I'm not to be included in this invitation?"

"Only because there wouldn't be a horse for you to ride. Although it's not difficult terrain for a horse, it would be hard to get a carriage up there."

Inwardly, Claire seethed. How presumptuous of the man. She broke the awkward silence. "I will relay the information to her, and if she is well enough, I am sure she will want to accompany you. If she is not, then I shall take her place. Agreed?"

"Agreed." Even though he didn't look as if he meant it.

★　★　★

"At last. Maybe we're getting somewhere," Evelyn said. She felt rested after her long sleep and ready for the delicious pork pie and salad her sister had prepared. "If this toy was based on a real house, we can at least have an opportunity to explore it and maybe we will find some answers."

"Hurrah for Matthew's cousin." Sarcasm dripped off Claire's words like treacle.

"Oh, don't be like that. I'm sorry there aren't enough horses for you to come along too. We did discuss bringing ours when we left Sugden Heath, but we agreed they would have so little to do. Living so close to the railway station, we simply have no need of them, and it's not fair to the horses to have them live a boring existence stuck in a field all day, every day."

"It's all right, Ev. I understand."

If only she sounded as if she meant it. "I'll be able to tell you all about it when I return. If it looks as if we need to go back again, then we'll hire some horses and you can come too. Agreed?"

Claire nodded and helped herself to some fruit cake.

★　　★　　★

The air smelled fresh and damp, and an aroma of moist earth permeated the air as Matthew, Mr. Skelton and Evelyn set off, this time away from the moors to the other end of the lane and onto the narrow road.

Mr. Skelton turned out to be in his element as a tour guide. "We travel along here for about a mile, and then we turn off down a lane. You'd miss it if you didn't know it was there. Of course, in the old squire's day it would have been well tended."

Riding sidesaddle on a placid bay horse, Evelyn took in the scenery. Trees lined the route, and the air filled with the sound of birdsong. How could anything be wrong on such a perfect day? The heavy morning dew was drying in the warm sunshine, and the smell of grass and wildflowers pervaded the atmosphere.

"Here it is." Mr. Skelton encouraged his horse to turn off the road. Matthew and Evelyn followed close behind. The first thing that struck her was the silence. "Where have the birds gone?" she asked Matthew, who was slightly ahead of her.

He turned back. "I've been wondering the same thing."

"Anything wrong?" Mr. Skelton called out from the front.

"It's much quieter down here," Matthew said. "No birdsong."

"By Jove, I believe you're right," Mr. Skelton replied. "How strange."

They trotted on for a few yards. The trees grew denser with each hoofbeat. The silence grew heavier. As if waiting for something.

Matthew turned back to Evelyn. "Are you all right back there?"

She nodded, but she felt anything but all right. She wanted to turn and gallop away as fast as her mare would allow, but she had to keep going.

Finally the dense cover gave way to a partial clearing, hopelessly overgrown but still possible to make out some features of what once must have been an exquisite garden.

"Goodness," Mr. Skelton said. "It never occurred to me how many years must have gone by since I was last here."

"When was this, Mr. Skelton?" Evelyn asked as they dismounted from their horses. Matthew assisted her. Each of them took the reins of their horse and walked them on.

"Let me see now. The old squire had just died. Gracious. It must be twenty-five years or maybe more. There had been rumors, you see, and I was intrigued."

"What sort of rumors?" Matthew asked.

"Oh, the usual whenever someone slightly…shall we say, unusual, is involved."

"You mean the hauntings?" Evelyn asked. "The squire is supposed to haunt the village with his dogs?"

"That's the one. And the other stuff, of course."

"Other stuff?"

"Pure nonsense. This house and the garden were reputed to be haunted by a separate ghost. Well, sort of a ghost, more of a fantastic creature actually."

"My cousin didn't tell me about that," Matthew said, exchanging glances with Evelyn. "What was it all about?"

"Some sort of snake, I believe, massive and not of any known species, which supposedly appeared when a group of young people trespassed on the property. I suppose much as we are doing. Not that there is anybody around to see us off these days. I don't even know who it belongs to now. Squire Monkton had no family. Not a one."

"And has anyone reported seeing anything like this recently?" Matthew asked.

"Not to my knowledge. Not for many a year. The last sighting I heard of was probably over fifteen years ago. No one comes here anymore, you see. No reason to."

Evelyn looked around at the wilderness. "I think we should go on. Try and find the house if we can get there."

"Good idea," Matthew said. "Are you happy to proceed, Mr. Skelton?"

"Oh, dear me, yes, indeed. This takes me back years, even if it is difficult to distinguish anything. Oh, look, there's the old fountain."

Evelyn touched Matthew's arm, and he looked at her. "It's the same one. I recognize the gargoyles and that pineapple carving around the top. I've seen it before and it's the same as Claire described as being in the toy."

"What was that?" Mr. Skelton asked. "I'm sorry. I'm a bit deaf these days."

"Evelyn said she has seen the pineapple and the gargoyles before. On the fountain. And they're the same as in the toy Garden of Bewitchment."

"Oh, yes," said Mr. Skelton. "Yes, I see. Well, that really proves it then, doesn't it? The toy was made for the squire and is unique to this house. You must have the same one."

"It looks likely, but let's press on. I want to see the house."

Tree roots had spread across once-manicured paths, making walking hazardous. The grass of the lawns had grown and stood six inches high. Roses and hibiscus mingled with sunflowers, hollyhocks, delphiniums and dahlias in a wild profusion of color and natural abandon. Laburnum and lilac trees spread their branches as an arbor. Evelyn bent down so as to avoid their scratching, almost inquiring, twigs. Memories of her encounters with the trees in The Garden of Bewitchment flooded back. But this was real life and late spring. Hibiscus should barely be in leaf yet – if at all – let alone flowering, and it wasn't the only anomaly. So many of these plants needed a gentler climate. They didn't belong together on a West Riding moor, however well cultivated it might have been once.

"There it is!" Mr. Skelton sounded like a young boy making an important discovery. "The house. It's still standing."

Evelyn and Matthew pushed aside fronds of wisteria. Even with the decay – broken windows, a front door hanging off its hinges and ivy, which had taken over the walls – Evelyn recognized the elegant mansion.

"It's real," she breathed.

"Let's see what it can tell us."

Now they were there, Evelyn's old fears resurfaced. What were they going to face inside?

Matthew sensed her hesitation. "You're all right, Evelyn. We are all here. This isn't fantasy. This is real."

Evelyn nodded, took a deep breath and followed them. They tied their horses up to the veranda, then had to clamber over fallen timbers and years of autumn leaves covering the once-magnificent hall in a blanket of decay. Mr. Skelton stood, a slight smile of recognition on his face.

"Do you remember it when it was at its grandest?" Evelyn asked him.

"I have some memories, yes. The family threw a ball for the Coronation in 1838. I was only eighteen then. Such a grand affair, I can tell you." He seemed to slip into his memories for a moment. "Yes, indeed. A happy day. I met my dear wife then, you know. We were married the following year, much to my father's disapproval. He thought we should wait until I had established myself as a doctor. But, young love." He sighed. "We've been married for fifty-four years now, and we are just as happy as the day we first started courting."

"That's a wonderful achievement, Mr. Skelton," Evelyn said.

"I'm surprised you've never married, Miss Wainwright. Such a handsome woman as you. Oh, pardon me if I presumed..."

"Not at all. The situation hasn't presented itself, that's all."

Matthew had wandered off into the drawing room. The sound of running footsteps and he appeared at the doorway. "I think you should see this, Evelyn."

Evelyn and Mr. Skelton followed him into the drawing room. Like the hall, the room had been wrecked or fallen into decay. Broken chairs were scattered all around, a piano covered in cobwebs, the wood dull and lifeless. But one thing stood out from the debris. A table Evelyn didn't remember from her encounters with the toy. It stood in the center of the room, and on it stood a dolls' house.

"Come and look at this, Evelyn," Matthew said, pointing at the dolls' house.

"It's this house," she said. "Just as in the toy."

"Except this one is much bigger and the figures aren't made of cardboard. Have a look inside."

Evelyn moved cautiously nearer to the table. Matthew beckoned her, and she approached more closely. She took in the detail. Exactly the same as The Garden of Bewitchment and as this house must have looked in its heyday. Even down to the color of the paintwork.

Matthew opened the right-hand door to reveal the three floors of the house on that side. The drawing room was laid out with the piano, female pianist, and chairs – each one occupied by a doll, all apparently listening in rapt attention to their entertainer.

"Now look more closely at the dolls," Matthew said.

Mr. Skelton approached and looked over Matthew's shoulder. He gave a sudden sharp intake of breath.

"I don't believe what I'm seeing." He reached forward and picked a male doll off one of the chairs. He examined it closely. A young man, dressed smartly in evening dress of the early Victorian style.

"Someone you recognize, Mr. Skelton?" Matthew asked.

"But don't you see?" He held it up to his face.

Evelyn took in the high cheekbones, the light brown hair parted at the side.

"Oh my heavens," she exclaimed.

"What is it?" Matthew asked.

"It's me," Mr. Skelton said. "The doll is me as I looked many years ago. But how is it possible?"

Evelyn felt her face blanching. "You've never seen this dolls' house before? Or any of these figures?"

Mr. Skelton shook his head, replacing the doll back on its chair with trembling fingers. He wiped his hands on his trousers as if trying to rub off any contamination. "Never."

"That's not all," Matthew said, picking up two more dolls. He handed them to Evelyn.

Evelyn took one look and thrust them back at him. She backed away. "Oh, no. No. This can't be."

Mr. Skelton took her arm as she swayed a little off-balance. "Whatever's the matter, Miss Wainwright?"

Evelyn pointed at the dolls, which Matthew was now replacing on their respective chairs. "It's Matthew, and the other one is the image of me."

Mr. Skelton released her arm. "Whatever is going on here? Where did these things come from?"

Matthew brushed his hands. "I have no idea. But it all seems linked to a series of unbelievable events that have been occurring here since Miss Wainwright, her sister and I all came to this village."

Mr. Skelton looked at Evelyn in a way that made her feel uncomfortable, although, for the life of her, she couldn't understand why.

"I don't think I have had the pleasure of meeting your sister, Miss Wainwright."

"Oh, but you helped her. On the moor when she collapsed."

Mr. Skelton looked confused. "But I thought that was you, Miss Wainwright. Goodness me, how alike you two young ladies are."

An innocent enough remark. After all, people were always getting the two of them confused. Even Mama and Father had made the odd mistake. So why did Evelyn feel there had been more to her neighbor's words than appeared on the surface? *It's because of everything that has been happening. I'll be jumping at my own shadow next.*

Even still, Evelyn chose not to remind him of the brief encounter he had with her and Claire when he was returning from the public house that day. No doubt, at his advanced age and with a number of whiskies under his belt, Mr. Skelton could be forgiven for the odd memory lapse.

The old man continued. "But these events, as you call them, they are all linked to this house?"

"Yes," Matthew replied. "And to that infernal toy, The Garden of Bewitchment. I didn't tell you I also played with it when I was a child. Only once, though. Things...happened. I never wanted to see it again, but it turned up here, at Miss Wainwright's cottage, which is where the squire was staying, I understand, at the end of his life."

"Oh, yes, indeed. He grew to hate this house. He never told me why, but with advancing years he became ever more eccentric. I suppose it comes to us all one day." He smiled wryly.

"And now this." Evelyn indicated the dolls' house. "I have the impression something is playing with us. A sort of game of cat and mouse."

"I think," Mr. Skelton said, "if you don't mind, I would like to get off home now."

"But there is so much to find out," Evelyn said. "Please stay a little longer."

"No. I'm sorry." The old man was shaking, trembling from head to foot.

Evelyn's heart went out to him. "Then we mustn't detain you. I'm sure Matthew and I can find our own way home now you've got us here. We'll bring back the horses as soon as we return."

"Before dusk. I really wouldn't stay out here after then. It's so dark. And lonely."

The man seemed suddenly terrified. Matthew saw it too. She could tell by his concerned expression and by the gentle way he spoke.

"Of course. I can assure you I have no intention of remaining here after dark."

"Very well then. I will take my leave of you. Please be careful. Something doesn't feel at all right here." With one final, disturbed glance at the dolls' house, Mr. Skelton turned and sped out of the house.

Presently, they heard his horse whinny, followed by the clip-clop of hooves as their neighbor walked him the first few yards away from the house. By the sound of it, Mr. Skelton had broken into a run, unexpected in a man of his age.

Evelyn found herself riveted to the dolls' house. "What now?" she asked.

"I don't know," Matthew replied. "But I think we should look around the house and see if we can find anything to give us a clue as to what has been happening. What other rooms did you go in when you were in the miniature house?"

"I went all over the house, but most of the rooms were empty. Judging by the state of the staircase, I think we should rule out the upper floors. It doesn't look too safe up there to me."

"Agreed. Let's try the room on the opposite side of the hall."

He led the way across the hall and through another broken door. Bookshelves lined the walls just as Evelyn remembered, only instead of row upon row of neatly stacked volumes, the books were scattered everywhere, as if someone had ripped them out in a fit of uncontrolled rage.

Evelyn bent down and picked one up. *Gulliver's Travels*. But why would anyone rip the pages out like this? She showed Matthew the torn and shredded book.

"They're all like it. Someone, or something, has gone wild in this room," Matthew said.

"The Todeswurm?"

"Maybe. I suppose." He didn't sound convinced.

Certainly the creature didn't seem to have the wherewithal to physically rip books apart. It could have used its mouth, with its sharp fangs, but this looked like the work of someone with hands and fingers or, at the very least, claws.

A sudden noise from outside gave them both a start.

"That sounded like…" Evelyn began.

"Wolves. At least two of them, maybe more."

"But there aren't any wolves around here."

"Not alive anyway. Remember the legend of Squire Monkton and his dogs."

Evelyn shuddered. "But surely they are heard around the village. Not here."

"Just because there's usually no one to hear them here doesn't mean they don't come."

"We'd better get out of here."

Matthew hesitated, then nodded. "Let's go."

They raced out of the house and stopped on the doorstep.

"Where are the horses?" Evelyn cried.

They were nowhere to be seen.

"Mr. Skelton must have taken them when he left."

"But I only heard the sound of one horse, not three."

"So did I."

"Then who—"

The sound of howling cut her off.

"They're getting closer," Matthew said. "Back to the house."

Back in the drawing room, Evelyn's heart raced. "Now what do we do? This house hardly provides any protection. The door's wide open, and we have no way of barricading ourselves in."

"We need to search for a room with an intact door."

"No, wait. I've just remembered," Evelyn said. She made for the far wall and started feeling along the paneling. "In the miniature house, I found an entrance. A doorway leading to a room, well, more of a wide corridor actually. It ran all around the house and came to a dead end, but at least it kept the Todeswurm at bay."

"I'll help you." He joined her. "What are we looking for?"

"Found it." She turned the little handle. "It's so small and well camouflaged you could easily miss it." She opened the panel. "Come on."

The howling sounded much closer now.

"They're practically at the door," Matthew said and joined her, closing the door firmly behind him.

"We'll push this box up against it. That should keep us safe."

They did so.

"What's in the box?" Matthew asked. "It's heavy enough."

"I never discovered. Claire and I needed to get out."

"So will we at some stage. We can't stay holed up here forever."

"Listen." Evelyn pushed her ear close to the wall and put her finger to her lips. Outside she heard sounds of heavy paws scuffling in the detritus. Two, maybe three animals sniffing, searching. "They're here," she mouthed.

Minutes ticked by. Evelyn hardly dared breathe, and her lungs ached for want of a good deep breath.

One of the beasts sniffed at the wall, the sound so close. Could it smell them, or at least sense their presence? More snuffling noises. The sounds of a tongue licking lips. Panting. Evelyn closed her eyes and prayed.

At last, the noises moved away, grew fainter. Evelyn's knees ached from crouching in an awkward position, but the risk of making a noise and attracting attention if she shifted herself was too great.

Matthew flinched. His leg must be troubling him.

How much longer?

Evelyn could hear nothing from the room. Then they both heard a long, baleful baying, clearly some distance from the house.

Evelyn breathed and relaxed her aching limbs. Matthew did the same.

"Now let's discover the secrets of this box," he said.

Evelyn felt all around the lid. "I can't find a way to open it."

"Let's see if sheer brute force will work." Matthew tugged at the lid. It didn't budge. "I need a crowbar or some such tool."

"I don't remember seeing one." Evelyn looked around, noting the desk and the papers strewn across the floor as they had been when she had entered the other house. Without looking at them, she knew what they were, and this time she would hang on to them and find the bound manuscript.

"This will do." Matthew brandished a claw hammer.

"Where did you find that?"

"Down here, amongst all this junk." Matthew indicated a dark corner Evelyn couldn't remember searching. He proceeded to claw at the box, and the wood splintered. He pulled nails out, and finally the lid flew off. Matthew threw the hammer down. Evelyn moved closer to see what was inside.

"Oh, Squire Monkton, whatever were you up to?" Evelyn muttered.

Matthew took out a long, black velvet cloak with a wide hood, followed by a heavy gold chalice studded with precious jewels. Thirteen brass candlesticks followed and then a massive black leather-bound book.

"It must be hundreds of years old," he said, turning the pages. "It's in Latin, and mine's rusty, but from what I can gather, it contains spells and incantations. The etchings are exquisite. If bizarre."

"Let me see." Evelyn tried to lift the book, but its weight took her by surprise. "No wonder that box was heavy."

"Look at this." Matthew indicated a full-page drawing. Evelyn leaned over his shoulder. The etching depicted a room, not unlike the drawing room of this house. It showed the piano, chairs, table and the miniature replica of the house.

"It's uncanny. So much like…" Evelyn clapped her hand over her mouth. "Oh, look, Matthew." She pointed to a section of the wall in the picture. A small door stood open, and two faces peered out.

"It's us," Matthew said.

"But how?"

Matthew hurriedly turned some more pages. Evelyn gasped at the next drawing.

There, clearly depicted, were the two of them standing exactly where they were now, peering down at the book and at the picture of themselves.

Matthew's eyes met Evelyn's. "I don't know how this can happen," he said, "but this book has to hold the key to everything going on here."

"But can you read it? I never studied Latin, so I am no help at all."

"Let's get it over to the desk. There's a candle there. The light is fading too fast over here."

Matthew heaved the book onto the desk and reached in his waistcoat pocket for matches. The glow from the candle lit up the copperplate writing. He studied the words in front of him. "It's so long since I studied it, and I'm not sure I can make sense of it. This section doesn't appear to be a spell. *"Qui antea vixerunt expectant quos hodie vivunt."* Those…those who live – no – those who have lived before…await…those who live today. *Qui vitam in proxima saecula cupiunt eum adsectuentur qui antea est et sempiternam regnat.*" He paused, struggling with the text. "I think it's, those who want…desire maybe…life in the next world…shall follow the one who is before… or perhaps it's the one who went before. *Domini nunc sempiternamque totam fidem promittent.* The master…they shall…swear – no – *promise* allegiance…their full allegiance…to the master now and for all time. Does that make any sense?"

"Indeed it does. I think it explains quite a lot as well. It would appear the squire had become a devil worshipper, if I'm not mistaken. He was conjuring up the devil for his own ends. Again, if I'm not mistaken, he got rather more than he bargained for. Don't you see? He played with fire and got more than his fingers burned."

"You think something came through?"

"Something he could neither control nor get rid of. It would explain why he left this house for good, wouldn't it? He thought he could leave the evil behind here."

"But instead, it latched on to that toy."

"If I'm right, the reason all these things are happening to the three of us is because the one thing we all have in common is our contact with The Garden of Bewitchment. And we can add a fourth – poor Mr. Skelton, because he brought us here."

"And this book is the key." Matthew closed it. "We have to get it out of here and take it to someone who can interpret it for us."

Evelyn looked up at the window. "We certainly can't leave now. It's dark."

"At least the wolves have stopped howling."

"I still wouldn't risk it. I know Claire will be worried, but she would worry even more if she thought we were trying to get through those woods in the dark."

Matthew opened the book again. Evelyn watched as he turned the heavy pages. "They're parchment, I suppose," she said.

"I hope so."

"What do you mean?"

Matthew fingered the page he was on. "They could be vellum, which would be fine, but I can't help wondering…"

"Wondering what?"

"Some of the pages are different. Darker. Like this one, see?" He indicated a light tan page. Evelyn touched it and recoiled. It had a vaguely rubbery consistency.

"What is it?"

Matthew shook his head. "I've heard of books being bound in it but not pages made from it. I must be wrong."

"Tell me what you think it is."

"Human skin. But I must be wrong."

"I pray God you are." But inside her, Evelyn doubted it. "What sort of a monster was he? This squire?"

She couldn't look at the book anymore. Instead, she busied herself collecting up the sheets of paper, which lay exactly as they were in the miniature house. When she had finished, Matthew was still poring over the volume. He moved slightly to allow her to open the desk drawers. She found *The Chronicles of Calladocia* and, flicking through the pages, saw they were identical to the ones she had seen in that other house.

Matthew stirred. "Have a look at this." He pointed to another illustration.

On the facing page, Evelyn made out the word 'Calladocia'. The picture showed Lady Mandolyne gazing out into the mist. Some distance away, a tall, dark man, too shadowy to make out his features, stood with two women. One was clearly Evelyn and the other, less distinct, Claire.

"This book shouldn't exist," Evelyn said. "It can't exist. It goes against all the laws of nature."

"Only the ones we know about, and clearly it does exist. We are both looking at it, and this is the real Squire Monkton's house."

"And we're trapped here."

"Only until dawn. At first light we can get away from here. What's that?" He indicated the bound manuscript and the loose pages.

"Something that really shouldn't exist. At least not like this. Something my sister and I were working on but which seems to have been…taken over…by someone else. Someone she believes to be Branwell Brontë, but, as far as I am concerned, the writer's identity remains a mystery."

"But your sister truly believes it to be Branwell Brontë."

"Yes. But what connection could he possibly have with that book and this house?"

Matthew shook his head. "I have no idea. Unless the spirit of Branwell is being conjured by Squire Monkton's mischief and used as some sort of hold on Claire. She is infatuated with him, isn't she?"

"Yes. I suppose that makes sense. In as much as anything else does here."

"She is depicted as almost ghostly here."

Evelyn looked again at where Matthew was pointing. "Do you suppose that has any significance?"

"I don't know."

But the look on his face said more. Right now, Evelyn didn't dare ask. She looked down at the figures assembled, as if in conversation, and the picture of Claire seemed to fade with every second. Evelyn turned away. Invisible bonds clenched her throat and constricted her muscles – her feeling of loss almost too much to bear. Yet for the life of her she didn't know why. She would give anything to bury her head in her hands and weep.

A hand on her arm brought her back to reality.

"Evelyn, what's the matter? I mean, apart from the obvious."

His concern brought tears to her eyes. She blinked them back. "I can't explain it. I had this overwhelming feeling something was happening to Claire. I don't have any idea what."

Matthew's eyes strayed back to the book. "You had better see this," he said.

Evelyn looked down at where he was pointing. She saw herself, the tall man and…

"She's gone. Claire's not in the picture anymore. Oh, Matthew, what does it mean?"

"I don't know. I wish I had an answer, but I don't."

Evelyn continued to stare at the page, willing the image of Claire to return, but it didn't.... Everything remained the same. Lady Mandolyne continued to gaze out over the lake. The tall man appeared to be deep in conversation with Evelyn. Only the three of them were there. As if Claire had never existed.

"I can't help feeling... No, I mustn't say it."

"Say what, Evelyn?"

"I feel as if I am never going to see her again."

Matthew put his arm around her, and it felt the most natural thing in the world. For a moment.

"What was that?" Evelyn pulled away. She and Matthew listened.

"Did you hear it?" she whispered.

"A cough?" Matthew whispered back. "Yes, I heard it. A man's cough."

A deep voice rang out, echoing through the wall.

Evelyn gave Matthew a questioning look. She couldn't understand a word.

"Latin," he whispered. "He's summoning something. I can't make it out."

A creak.

Evelyn pointed to the door. The handle turned. She held her breath. The door opened a fraction and then hit the box. Not as heavy now that the book had been removed. It shifted slightly.

In a flash, Matthew heaved the massive volume off the desk and, trying not to make a sound, lowered it back into its resting place. Someone continued to push at the door, but now they hit the heavy obstacle of the box.

The pushing and shoving stopped. Matthew and Evelyn stayed silent, straining to hear the slightest sound from behind the wall. Nothing.

More minutes ticked by. Evelyn had lost all track of time. She longed for sunrise. Somehow things didn't seem as frightening in the light. Somewhere in the distance the wolves howled again. The moon cast a beam of silvery light through the window. Matthew's face appeared ghostly. Ethereal.

He edged his way closer to her. His whispers were so quiet she could barely make out his words.

"I think we have been paid a visit by Squire Monkton," Matthew said.

"I feared as much. What can he possibly want with us?"

"We have something he doesn't have and presumably his infernal master wants."

"What's that?"

"Our life force. It would make sense of what I read in the book. 'Those who have lived before await those who live today.' Why would they await them? To take their spirits."

"We have to get out of here, and we need that book, but at the moment it's the only thing keeping him out of here."

"Then we'll have to lift the desk and haul it over there to take the place of the box."

"But that still leaves us trapped here."

"We need to find a way of getting past the squire. I believe all the answers lie in the book, and it is doing no good at all acting as a doorstop."

It made perfect sense, although Evelyn had no idea how they were going to manage to carry it out of here and evade the squire, not to mention the Todeswurm or Dakraska, or whatever it was properly called. But they could not afford to be overly cautious. They needed the information in that book. "All right," she said. "I'll help you."

No sound came from the drawing room. "Maybe he's gone?" Evelyn asked.

"Perhaps. We must be as quiet as possible."

Evelyn nodded. She removed the manuscript and loose pages from the desk and stood at one side of it. Matthew took the opposite side, and together they lifted it closer to the door. It should hold him off for a bit, or at least warn them of his presence. They then shoved the box out of the way and replaced it with the desk – Evelyn, for one, relieved to rid herself of its weight. It was far more solid than it looked. She flexed her aching arms.

They listened. Still no sound.

"I think he must have gone," Matthew said. "Even though we were being as quiet as possible, we still made a noise he could have heard if he was still there."

"How would we know, though? It's not as if he has a body. Surely he can materialize whenever and wherever he chooses."

"I'm not certain that's true. He may have boundaries. He may be doing someone else's bidding. The book would certainly indicate that."

"If only we knew more about it."

"Let's get it out and have another look. The candle's burning a little low. We mustn't waste it."

The moonlight had disappeared, and the flickering glow of the candle was the only light they had. Evelyn stood aside while Matthew laid the book down. He opened the heavy cover, and the pages rippled. Evelyn remembered a childhood visit to the zoo. She had been horrified and fascinated by the reptiles. The snakes slithered around, their forked tongues flicking in and out of their mouths, their skin…*rippling*…as they moved. *Just like these pages.* She and Matthew watched in horrified fascination as they settled.

Another picture. This time of Evelyn's cottage. There she stood in the corner of Claire's bedroom, looking down at The Garden of Bewitchment laid out on the floor. No sign of Claire.

"I look so sad," Evelyn said. "I think I may be crying." As before, the feeling of abject loss filled her, and tears pricked her eyes.

Matthew peered closely at the toy. "Claire's there," he said, pointing at a small figure standing by the fountain. "You can just see her. She's smiling."

"You're right. She looks happy." Evelyn stood back. "That doesn't make sense either. Why would I be so unhappy when she is clearly perfectly fine?"

"Because you can see what she can't," Matthew said. "Look."

In the woods, the Todeswurm waited.

Evelyn blinked, and each time she did so, she could have sworn the creature inched closer toward Claire.

"We have to get her out of there. What if this means she is actually outside?"

"I don't think so," Matthew said. "If she was outside, the real house…this one, it would be overgrown, but this garden is pristine."

"So she's in the toy."

"Or it's playing with us. I don't know."

"The book opened at that page. It wanted us to see that image."

"It could be trickery. It probably *is* trickery."

"I can't take the risk. I have to go to her." Evelyn started toward the door and grabbed hold of the desk.

"Stop. What are you doing? It's still pitch dark out there. You'll never find your way to the fountain, and even if you did, what are you going to do? Take on the Todeswurm single-handed?"

She had hoped Matthew would come with her, but it seemed he wasn't prepared to. A sudden wave of anger swept through her. But he was right. In the dark, they could do nothing. The Todeswurm had the element of surprise. Even assuming Claire was there in the first place. And then there were the wolves…and Squire Monkton. "Oh, this is impossible." She forgot any need to keep quiet and slammed her fist down on the desk.

Matthew caught her hand before she brought it down again. "That won't do any good, Evelyn. We must be calm and rational. Only then will we have any chance of helping Claire, who may not need our help anyway. She's probably home and in bed right now."

"I wish I could believe that."

"Look again at the picture."

Evelyn swiped her eyes with her hand. She didn't want Matthew to see the tears threatening to spill over onto her cheeks.

Evelyn looked. "I can't see her anywhere."

"It's all right. Don't panic, Evelyn. There she is."

On the edge of the picture, outside the woods, Claire, clearly in the process of walking home, safely out of the garden.

"Where's the Todeswurm?"

Matthew pointed. The vicious-looking creature. Exactly where it had been. "See? Claire's safe from it."

"As far as we know."

"Agreed."

★　　★　　★

Time moved slowly until, at last, a finger of dim light shone through the window.

"Dawn. Thank goodness," Matthew said. "We'll wait a few minutes until the sun comes up properly and then make a move."

"Yes," Evelyn said, gathering up the manuscript. Matthew closed the book. "This is going to be quite a weight without the horses," he said.

A few minutes later, the sun had gained strength and they caught a glimpse of pale blue sky through the small window.

"Time to leave," Matthew said.

Together they shifted the desk aside, and Matthew tentatively opened the door. He peered out. "All clear, as far as I can tell," he said, heaving up the book. "Let's go."

Clutching the bound manuscript and the sheaf of loose pages, Evelyn followed him out into the drawing room, swiftly across the floor, into the hall and outside, where they were greeted with brilliant sunshine.

From close by, they heard a whinnying.

"The horses!" Evelyn took off at a run. Oblivious to the trailing branches and with Matthew close behind, she sped off down the garden, past the fountain. The two horses stood side by side, grazing on the long grass.

They slowed down and approached the animals gently so as not to spook them. "If only you two could tell us what happened to you yesterday." Evelyn stroked the bay's mane. The horse blinked gentle brown eyes.

"I'll help you up," Matthew said.

Once mounted, Evelyn took the reins. Matthew stuffed the manuscript and pages into saddlebags and shoved the book as best he could into a saddlebag on his chestnut gelding, and within a couple of minutes they were trotting back toward the main road. They were in the depths of the wood when Matthew's horse suddenly shied and reared up.

"Whoa, boy. Easy." He fought to bring the frightened horse under control.

Evelyn's horse skittered and bucked. She flew through the air and landed inches from a fallen tree. Her horse bolted through the undergrowth.

"The manuscript!" Evelyn yelled, trying to sit up, while the world spun around her, faster and faster.

Matthew clung on, but his horse was having none of it. He kicked and bucked, and Matthew slipped off. He lunged for the book and almost lost it, grabbing it at the last minute as the horse took off at a gallop.

Evelyn let the tears flow. Tears of anger and frustration.

Matthew stared around. "I can't even see what spooked them."

"Can't you? I can." Evelyn pointed a shaking finger. A few yards away, a tall man watched them. His features shadowy as always.

"I saw him in the book."

"And I have seen him before. Matthew, are there any photographs of Squire Monkton?"

"I expect so, why?"

"If I'm not mistaken, I think that may be him."

Evelyn stared at the man, who slowly turned and walked back toward the house. Soon, he had disappeared from sight.

CHAPTER FOURTEEN

Evelyn came down the stairs of the cottage to where Matthew waited. "Just as you said. She's tucked up in bed." She looked at the clock. "Gracious. Eleven o'clock. She's having a long lie in."

"As a concerned sister, she probably waited up for you half the night and only went to bed when she couldn't keep her eyes open any longer."

"Or she found herself in The Garden of Bewitchment, exactly as we saw her in the book."

"Either way, she can surely be forgiven for sleeping late today."

"She's certainly dead to the world." Evelyn flinched at her misjudged choice of words. "She didn't even stir when I went in. Usually Claire is such a light sleeper."

Matthew seemed locked on to her eyes. Evelyn felt a twitch of discomfort. "Is there something wrong?"

"No. No. Not at all."

"Which means there is. Will you tell me?"

"Not yet. I think I'm being foolish, and I need to be sure first. I think I should leave you now." He stood and immediately made for the door.

Before she could find out what troubled him, he had left. As she watched him hurry down the lane, Evelyn's consternation grew. Matthew Dixon kept too many secrets, and she couldn't help feeling this was another one of them.

★   ★   ★

Her sleep that night consisted of a series of unsettling catnaps. Each time, she awoke with a gasp, aware of some nightmare that escaped her grasp the moment she regained consciousness. She had the impression the tall man had something to do with it, but nothing tangible remained.

Finally at dawn she gave up the effort and went downstairs. In the kitchen she busied herself with boiling the kettle for a cup of tea. As she stood in front of the kitchen window, tea caddy in her hand, she caught a movement up on the track above the cottage.

The man had come back.

Heedless of being clothed only in her nightdress and dressing gown, she wrenched open the back door and raced out into the yard. The man was walking away from her in the direction of the crags.

"Excuse me, sir," she called.

He stopped. Turned. His face indistinct. Even allowing for the distance between them, she should have been able to make out more detail in his features, but they seemed sheathed in some sort of mist.

He started to move toward her. Slowly. Taking his time, like a cat stalking its prey.

Her natural instinct of self-preservation kicked in. She should get back inside and lock the door. Barricade it even. But Evelyn stood firm, drawing her robe tighter around her. She would not show fear to this man, whoever he might be.

He was mere yards above and beyond her when he stopped. He seemed to study her for a moment, then reached into his ankle-length coat.

"Squire Monkton?" Evelyn asked.

The figure did not answer. He stood, statue-like, his hand inside his coat, searching for something from an inside breast pocket.

He withdrew his hand and extended it to her. His arm seemed to lengthen, or maybe he moved closer toward her, although she didn't see him move his legs.

His hand had been curled in a fist, which he now opened, revealing something that glittered in the early-morning sun. He started down the steps. Evelyn wanted to back away, but she wouldn't let herself. She would stand her ground.

His face came into view, and she could see his yellowed eyes. The man looked sick. Ill enough to die. If he wasn't already dead. His skin was pockmarked and speckled with tiny lesions oozing pus and blood. Evelyn had to work hard not to recoil from the stench of putrefaction emanating from him. He opened his mouth to reveal a few remaining teeth, all of which were brown and broken.

He offered the glittering jewel to Evelyn. She shook her head. "It isn't mine to take. But please tell me why your Garden of Bewitchment has entered our lives."

He considered her question for a moment. "Lives? One life. Only one life."

"I don't understand."

"You will. Take it." He pushed the jewel at her.

"No. It isn't mine, and I don't know what you want of me."

He closed the palm of his hand with a snap of dry skin and bone.

"Then be damned," he said and was gone. Vanished, as if he had never been there.

Evelyn stood, staring at the space where he had been moments earlier. The chill morning air penetrated her body until she had to give in and go inside. Claire was pouring a cup of tea for herself.

"What were you doing out there, Evelyn?"

Evelyn told her.

"It must have been the squire. From your description, it most certainly wasn't Branwell."

"Branwell," Evelyn said. "The last time you saw him you were a little afraid of him, weren't you?"

"I thought so, but the more I went through it in my mind, the more I am sure it wasn't him. I think it was Squire Monkton up to his little tricks again. I think he is behind all the strange things that have been happening."

"So you finally acknowledge it. Branwell is dead and buried?"

"Oh, no, the real Branwell is as alive as you and I, but I believe

Squire Monkton somehow transformed himself into someone who looked like Branwell to trick me."

It made a strange kind of sense, but Evelyn kept coming up with the same, unanswered question time and again.

Why?

★   ★   ★

Evelyn didn't see Matthew for two days, and when he arrived on her doorstep, he was full of apologies. "I took the book to Leeds to see an eminent academic at the university. Professor Lawrence Mapplethorpe is a classical scholar, and he is fascinated by it. He wants to meet you because he believes he has quite a lot to tell us about The Garden of Bewitchment and everything else that has been happening. He also knows a lot about ancient myths and legends. When I mentioned the Todeswurm and Dakraska, he knew what I was referring to. Apparently they are, as we suspected, one and the same. Dangerous entities, with a long pedigree. Can you pack a bag now and be ready to leave within the hour?"

"But what about Claire? She's as much involved as we are."

"Professor Mapplethorpe only wants to meet *you*."

"But—"

"We don't have time for an argument, Evelyn. Please do as I say. I am convinced the professor has the key to solving our dilemma."

Evelyn paused. How would she explain this to Claire? One look at Matthew's face told her she would have to find a way somehow. He was deadly serious, and, after all, if this professor knew about the book, it would be to all their advantages.

"Very well. I will be ready in an hour."

Matthew seemed relieved. Almost too relieved.

After he had gone, Evelyn called Claire from the kitchen.

"But why am I not to be included?"

"I wouldn't think any more about it, Claire. Besides, you know you are not overly keen on mixing with strangers."

"And you know I am getting better. I go out and about on my own here. You don't know where I go."

"No. That's what worries me. When you do go out on your own, you seem to be a magnet for trouble. You've never properly told me where you went when you disappeared."

"I told you I couldn't remember. I still can't. Anyway, I wouldn't be on my own. You and Matthew would be there. Not to mention this Professor Mapplethorpe."

"I'm sorry, Claire. It wasn't my decision, but I do have to abide by it if we are ever going to find any peace."

"Oh, very well, go and see your precious professor. You probably only want to be alone with Matthew anyhow."

"Don't be childish. It's not true and you know it. Matthew and I are friends, and that's all."

"You didn't trust him not so long ago. Remember you still don't know what he keeps in that box of his."

"I'm continuing to reserve judgment. Now, please. Let's drop this. I need to pack or I'll be late."

"You're impossible." Claire hitched up her skirts and stamped up to her room. She slammed the door so hard the building shook.

Maybe this was why the invitation hadn't been extended to her. Matthew had been on the receiving end of Claire in a mood, and whatever they would discover in Leeds would require cool heads.

*   *   *

"Can we at least say goodbye and kiss like sisters instead of parting as enemies?" Evelyn said.

Claire's lips were in the annoying pout that infuriated Evelyn so much. Really, there were times when she could have believed her sister was much younger than her.

Evelyn leaned forward and gave her sister a light peck on her cheek. It wasn't reciprocated. "Goodbye, Claire. Please try to stay out of trouble and get rid of this ridiculous mood you're in. When

I get back I hope to have some positive news for a change, and it would be nice if you could greet my return with a smile."

Claire blinked at her. Her stubbornness refused to let her go.

With a resigned sigh, Evelyn left her and joined Matthew, who was waiting in a hired carriage.

"How were things with Claire?" he asked.

"She wasn't happy at not being included. As you can see, she didn't even bother to see us off."

"I expect she'll get over it."

"With any luck."

"I thought we could take rooms at the Metropole Hotel. It's stylish and comfortable. Modern too."

"When are we due to meet the professor?"

"Tomorrow morning at eleven. He is studying the book now. He's really very excited about it."

Evelyn managed a wry smile. "He doesn't have to live with the consequences."

*   *   *

The following morning, a cab took them to the university. Crowds of male students milled around, talking, laughing. Matthew and Evelyn alighted from the cab, and Matthew led Evelyn away from the main building to an elegant Georgian townhouse on the university grounds, where he introduced Evelyn to a short, dapper man with a shock of white hair and thick glasses. He wore tweeds and continually puffed at a small meerschaum pipe. The aroma of rich tobacco scented the room. Floor-to-ceiling bookcases, groaning under the weight of hundreds of leather-bound volumes, lined his cozy study. A fire blazed brightly in the hearth, which Evelyn welcomed, since the day felt more like autumn than late spring. A chill, gray mist had dampened everything it touched, and she wished she had remembered to pack a warmer coat.

"My dear Miss Wainwright, do come and warm yourself. I shall ring for tea. Or would you prefer hot chocolate?"

"Hot chocolate will be perfect, thank you." Evelyn sat down in a comfortable leather armchair and felt the warmth returning to her chilled feet.

Their drinks arrived, brought in by a man wearing a servant's uniform and a surly expression. He set down the tray and left.

"Jacobs," the professor said. "He's in a bad mood. I think his football team lost at the weekend."

Evelyn liked the professor. His manner indicated a much younger man than his appearance portrayed, and a sense of humor had created the many wrinkles around his eyes. There was something timeless about him and his manservant. As if they belonged to an earlier part of the old queen's reign. No doubt, the academic environment they were in accounted for that. They were, after all, cushioned away from the ever-changing outside world.

Matthew sat opposite Evelyn, and the professor came to sit between them on a chair that, judging by its battered state, was clearly his favorite. He leaned forward, tapped his pipe in an ashtray and took a tobacco pouch out of his pocket. He proceeded to fill his pipe, talking all the while.

"Now this most interesting volume Matthew has brought for me to look at is highly intriguing. I studied demonology in my youth, and, as a result, I was aware such works existed, but never, until a couple of days ago, did I ever imagine I would be able to hold one of my own, and it's heavy, isn't it? By the heavens. Quite a weight. Of course the leather binding conceals a layer of lead, which doesn't help matters. You didn't know that?"

Matthew and Evelyn shook their heads.

"Oh, yes, indeed. Lead. Also copper, silver, tin and gold mixed in with it. All highly significant. In ancient hooniyan tradition, these metals were frequently made into nails to be driven into a wax image of a person destined to be harmed in some way."

"Hooniyan?" Evelyn asked. "I've never heard of it."

"Not surprising really. Hooniyan tradition hails from Ceylon. Of course, this book isn't from there. Oh, no. Although it is certainly well traveled. In addition to the Latin text, it seems to have Sumerian, Egyptian, Hindu and Jewish roots, and those are only the origins and influences I have encountered thus far. I still have much to read and discover. I do hope you will allow me to keep the book while I do so."

"Of course, Professor. We are anxious to know what has been causing the phenomena I outlined to you on my previous visit. It's most important to us, and to Miss Wainwright's sister."

The professor looked at Evelyn curiously. "Ah, yes, your sister. Miss Claire Wainwright, I believe?"

"Yes," said Evelyn, "she has also been affected by this book and the toy."

"The Garden of Bewitchment," the professor said. "Which is also laid out in this book. At least, the instructions on how to create it are given."

"Really?" Evelyn exclaimed.

"Most assuredly. Everything anyone could want to know about creating their own devil's garden is in here." He reached behind him and tapped the book, which lay on an untidy desk, in a space he had created between unruly piles of papers. "In fact this entire book is centered on that very phenomenon. Essentially this is a handbook into the process of summoning demons and creating your own version of the anti–Garden of Eden. Or, shall we say, the Garden of Eden after the serpent had persuaded Eve to entice Adam into eating the apple."

Evelyn exhaled. "We believe he had some strange ideas and was a practitioner of the occult, but how would Squire Monkton acquire such a book?"

"Ah, now there's the interesting thing. The book chooses who it possesses."

"Who *it* possesses?" Matthew's words echoed Evelyn's thoughts.

"Indeed," the professor said, lighting his pipe. He puffed for a moment or two. "You see, this book relies on people for its survival. You could say it feeds off them. Don't ask me how it works, who wrote it or what its origins are. I couldn't possibly hazard a guess. Nor could I tell you if human hands created it, although I suspect not. In order for this book to survive, it must be in the possession of someone vulnerable. Someone who possibly has something to hide or has a secret in their past they would rather remain buried. Possibly even someone with a mental condition of some kind."

"Do we know if Squire Monkton fell into any of those categories, Matthew?" Evelyn asked.

"I wouldn't know. My cousin might, I suppose, but he didn't mention anything, apart from an increasing tendency towards eccentricity. I could ask him, but I rather think our own experiences outweigh Gerald's knowledge of him by now."

The professor laid his pipe in the ashtray next to him. "It is of little importance to us anyway. Whatever the squire may have been or may not have been, the fact is the book found him and, in coming into his possession, proceeded to possess him."

"Which could well explain his foray into the dark arts," Matthew said. "But the Garden also belonged to my uncle. He certainly became difficult, even violent, towards the end of his life and obsessed with it, but I never heard anything about this book, and my cousin never mentioned it, so I suppose it unlikely to have featured in my aunt's diaries. As we know, he has been through them recently."

"Oh, your uncle certainly would have had it," the professor said. "He couldn't have built the Garden without it."

"I managed to build it without," Matthew said.

"As you told me when we first met, but I can assure you the book was there, in the same room as you when you did it. You felt its power. It even trapped you until you escaped from it. Its hold wasn't strong enough over you then."

"But what about my sister's experiences?" Evelyn asked. "We never saw the book in her room when the Garden appeared."

"Simply because you didn't see it means nothing, Miss Wainwright. It can manifest itself at will – or hide in plain sight."

"And then the strange man I saw—"

"The one with the hooked nose? Matthew told me about your strange encounter. Apparently this character fills two – even three – descriptions, at least partially. Matthew's Uncle Mortimer, Squire Monkton and, quite probably, the late Branwell Brontë. None of whom were related and, in life at least, did not resemble each other sufficiently to be mistaken for one another. Your sister is, I believe, quite besotted with the late Mr. Brontë."

Evelyn glanced at Matthew, feeling momentarily that he had betrayed her confidence, but then reminded herself there was little point in hiding anything from the one person who might actually be able to help them. "What can we do?" she asked. "With every passing day, we seem to be drawn deeper into a mire."

"I understand your fears, Miss Wainwright, and I wish I could answer all your questions here and now, but I need a little more time to complete my studies."

"We should destroy the book," Matthew said.

"On no account must you do anything of the sort." The force of the professor's words startled Evelyn. Until that moment he had been calm, collected, talking about this evil manifestation as if discussing the price of a loaf of bread. But now... His face had turned quite red.

"If you were to do that, you can be sure the book would release all its evil out into the world. Scatter it like leaves. Who knows what would happen then. At least this way it is contained and limited only to those people currently in possession of – and possessed by – it."

"How should we protect ourselves?" Evelyn asked. "As yet neither of us is possessed by the book—"

"Now you are wrong there, dear lady. One of you most certainly is, and the others are caught up by association."

Evelyn became aware of Matthew staring at her. His gaze felt like hot needles pricking her skin. "But which one of us is it?" she said.

"I'm not sure. All I can say for certain is one of you is not who they appear to be."

Evelyn knew it wasn't her, so it had to be Matthew. All the evidence pointed to it, but she still had to ask. "Are you including Claire, my sister, in your list of suspects?"

The professor looked at her seriously. His gaze made her feel uncomfortable. "Possibly. There is something…" He shook his head. "No, that couldn't be possible."

Evelyn wanted to shake him. "What couldn't be possible?"

"A thought came to me, but it is too ridiculous to utter out loud. Forgive me. The ramblings of an old man." He smiled.

"So where do we go from here, Professor?" Matthew asked.

Was he a little too keen to change the subject? Evelyn's thoughts drifted back to the small box he had buried and then dug up. A promise to a friend kept him from revealing its contents. Now she was as sure as she could be. He had been lying.

The professor relit his pipe. Evelyn waited. "My advice to you is to keep away from the house and garden belonging to the late squire. Nothing good will come of you visiting there, and, indeed, you will be putting your lives in danger. Miss Wainwright, I suggest you and your sister stay close to your cottage except where dire necessity forces you to make an excursion. Then, do not go far. When I have made my final conclusions, I will contact you, Matthew. If I may, I believe it would be best if I came to Thornton Wensley. Do you have a spare room I could avail myself of?"

"Of course, Professor. It would be an honor."

"But what of The Garden of Bewitchment?" Evelyn asked. "The miniature one? What if it should appear again?"

The professor tapped his teeth with his pipe stem. "That is something for which I have no answer but is precisely why I urge you and your sister to stay close to home."

His words chilled her blood. Staying close to home might appear to be a good idea, but the Garden had materialized in the cottage in the past, so there was no reason to suppose it couldn't do so again in the future. They would simply have to be more vigilant. Somehow.

"The man I saw...the one Matthew told you about. You said it could be one of three people, but who do *you* believe it was?"

"Quite probably any one of them. In fact, there are entities that can take on any number of forms, depending on who they are appearing to at the time."

"But why did he appear in the yard behind the cottage?"

"You invited him there, didn't you, Miss Wainwright?"

"No, I didn't, I—"

"You called out to him. You might as well have issued an invitation and, if I may say so, did a most foolish thing. Once he has set foot on your premises, he will come again."

"Then Claire and I must leave the cottage."

"And go where, Miss Wainwright? He will only follow you. No, you have to stay where you are, and when he returns, you must tell him, in no uncertain terms, he is not welcome and must remove himself."

"And what of the jewel he showed me?"

"That too is mentioned in the book. It is part of the ritual outlined there. You were wise not to accept it, for then you would surely have been its next victim. I believe your squire is looking to pass his possession on – if he hasn't already done so. He will use any means to rid himself of any lingering effects. He wants to be at peace, but to do so he must meet the book's demands."

Matthew shifted in his seat. Evelyn continued. "This raises another question for me. Is my sister's obsession with Branwell Brontë putting her at risk of serious harm?"

The professor paused before replying. "Almost certainly. She would do well to reject him as you must reject your ghost. Matthew told me she disappeared and has only a partial recollection of where she went? Such a practice is outlined in the book. Her ghost took her away. He showed her who was in charge. I am oversimplifying a little here, and bear in mind I haven't finished my study of the book yet, but that is my current belief, although I am aware something doesn't quite add up. It's nothing I can discuss yet until I have all the facts."

"And when will that be?" Matthew asked.

"Why, when I have finished translating the book. As you know, it is a thick volume." As before, his tap on the book's cover produced a hollow sound.

"Thank you, Professor," Evelyn said. "This has been most... enlightening."

"Not at all, my dear. I trust in a few days I will have got to the bottom of the mysteries of this amazing work of literature."

Matthew shook his hand. "Knowing what you do of its power, are you not even the slightest bit concerned for your own safety? After what you have told us today, I know I wouldn't want that thing under the same roof as me."

"Oh, but you see, I *am* safe."

Something about his tone made Evelyn's skin prickle. "How can you be so sure?" she asked.

"I know it doesn't want me. It could never want me."

"But how do you know?"

"Trust me, my dear. I know this seems strange to you, but it will all make sense in time."

"Believe me, Professor, this is no stranger than anything else that has been happening," Evelyn said.

★   ★   ★

Back home, the wind howled all through the night, rattling the windows, keeping Evelyn awake. She looked out of her bedroom window in the early hours to see leaves swirling in the gale. Throwing a warm shawl over her shoulders, she drew it tightly around her. Up on the track no one stirred. Evelyn was about to withdraw and go back to bed when something caught her eye.

Down in the yard. Something moved.

She hurried down the stairs and into the kitchen. She peered through the window.

Nothing. Blackness. Still the wind howled.

She leaped back. A hand, its fingers splayed, pressed against the window. The nails long and ragged. A man's hand. Bluish gray.

Evelyn cowered at the back of the kitchen.

Thumping. On the back door. The hand had gone. Whoever owned it was banging. Determined to get in.

Claire appeared in the doorway. "What is it, Ev? Who's out there?"

Evelyn clung to her sister. "I don't know, but I have a horrible feeling it's Squire Monkton." More banging. The wind howled stronger, and somewhere dogs were baying. Dogs? Or wolves?

It was *her* fault. She had called out to him. The professor said so. Now she must tell him to go. "Stay there, Claire."

Evelyn swallowed her fear and advanced toward the door.

Her tongue felt thick and dry as she tried in vain to moisten her lips.

"Go!" she cried. "You're not welcome here. *Go!*"

The banging ceased. An earsplitting roar rattled the glassware on the shelves.

"Go, I tell you! Leave this place and do not return."

The roars grew louder still until Evelyn's ears rang and her head ached.

Then... Silence.

The sisters waited, not daring to move or speak as the wind died down to a gusty whistle. Sleep was out of the question. They drank tea until a pinkish-gray dawn broke and they finally felt calm enough to go to bed.

★   ★   ★

Evelyn came downstairs a little after one. Hunger had invaded her dreams and robbed her of any chance of falling back to sleep. She found Claire in the kitchen, sitting at the table, a worried expression on her face. "What's the matter?"

Claire shook her head. She put her hands to her face, and tears dripped through her fingers. "I'm so scared, Ev. I don't know what to do."

Evelyn sat down and took one of her hands in hers. "We're in this together, Claire. However frightening it all seems, you're not alone. I'm scared too."

"But you don't have this, do you?" Claire's fingers trembled as she unbuttoned the sleeve of her blouse. She turned her arm over and showed it to Evelyn.

"My God. What *is* that?" Evelyn stared in horror at the crisscrossing network of thin red veins running up and down her sister's arm, each one pulsing as if with life waiting to be born.

"I don't know. I woke up with it a couple of hours ago." Claire's terrified face demanded a response, but, for the life of her, Evelyn didn't have one.

"Hospital," she said at last. "We must get you to hospital."

Claire shook her head vigorously, buttoning up her sleeve again and wincing. "No, I won't go to hospital. I'll never come out alive."

"Oh, nonsense. This isn't the Dark Ages. Hospitals are places where people go to recover."

"No."

"But this isn't natural, Claire."

"Don't you think I don't know that? I won't go to hospital. This isn't natural any more than The Garden of Bewitchment. Don't you see? This is supernatural too. It's all linked to that damned toy."

"I don't doubt it, but it's a physical manifestation and the doctors might be able to treat it."

"And they probably won't. You don't know what I'm feeling inside."

"Tell me."

"It's as if a thousand voices are all speaking at once. I can't make anything out. But they are all trying to possess me at the same time. Make me do things they want to do."

"What sort of things?"

With no warning, Claire flew at her sister, snarling, biting, scratching. Evelyn shielded her face with her hands and did her best to fight her off. She fell, and the two of them rolled around the floor.

Claire's hair wound itself around Evelyn's throat, choking her. She coughed, tugging at the thick mane, which grew ever tighter. Slivers of light danced in front of her eyes. She was slipping away, even as she clawed the air, desperate to fend off the screaming creature her sister had become.

A sharp knock at the front door.

It seemed to startle Claire back to reality. Her horrified face blanched as she realized what she had done. Then her eyes darkened and the beast returned within her. She dragged her hair off Evelyn's throat, gave her sister one last vicious punch in her stomach, jumped off her with the agility of a cat, raced up the stairs and slammed her door.

Another knock rattled the door. Evelyn struggled up, her throat burning. She staggered to the door.

Matthew took one look at her and caught her as she fell, dizziness overwhelming her.

"Whatever's happened?"

"Claire… She tried…to kill me."

Matthew half carried her inside and laid her on the settee. "Is she up there?" He pointed to the stairs.

"Yes."

He charged up the stairs. Evelyn heard him calling Claire's name. Presently he was back down. "She's not there."

Evelyn tried to sit up, but another wave of dizziness stopped her. She struggled to speak. "Not possible. She went up there when you knocked at the door. She can't have got out."

"I'm sorry, Evelyn, but I've looked everywhere – under the beds, in wardrobes… She isn't there."

Evelyn sank into the cushions, her head throbbing.

"I'll get you some water and some aspirin."

Another knock at the door. Matthew answered it.

"Mr. Skelton. Hello. Please come in."

He did so. "I'm sorry to intrude, but it was merely to tell you… Oh, my dear Miss Wainwright, whatever is the matter?"

"She's had a bit of an accident," Matthew said quickly.

"I hope it's nothing too serious. You look very pale. I only came round to tell you the horses came back by themselves yesterday. I don't know where they had been for the past five days, but they were perfectly safe and sound, and I also wanted to apologize for leaving you. Most cowardly of me."

"Don't mention it, Mr. Skelton," Matthew said. "To put it mildly, we've all had quite an unnerving experience all round. And one I don't think any of us want to repeat in a hurry."

"Very wise, if I may say so. You know, old Mrs. Sutcliffe at the bakery said she heard the wolves again. She always likes to be the first with any new gossip."

"We heard them too," Evelyn said before she could stop herself. "Not long after you left us."

The neighbor looked inquiringly at Matthew. He nodded.

"Goodness me," Mr. Skelton said.

"Did you happen to find anything in the saddlebags?" Evelyn asked. "A manuscript?"

Mr. Skelton looked at her curiously. "No, nothing of that sort. Did you lose it?"

"No matter." Evelyn waved her hand dismissively.

Matthew brought her the water and laudanum. She accepted them gratefully.

Matthew straightened his waistcoat. "I sincerely hope I never hear those beasts again."

"Oh, Mrs. Sutcliffe had more to tell. Apparently she reckons she saw the ghost of the old squire in your yard, Miss Wainwright."

"When?" Evelyn croaked.

"Last night. The weather kept her awake, and she was making herself some hot milk when she chanced to look out of her kitchen window. She saw him in the lamplight from your window. Clear as I am standing here. She had seen an old photograph of him, so she knew who she was looking at, and it wasn't the first time she had seen him either. She saw him in your yard a few days earlier, on the same day I took you to Monkton Hall. Once again, it was nighttime."

"He certainly had a busy time," Evelyn said.

"Indeed. He wasn't alone either."

"Who was he with?" Matthew asked.

"Now here's the strangest part. Mrs. Sutcliffe said he had a ghostly-looking girl with him. Wraithlike and almost transparent, but she looked so much like you, Miss Wainwright. In fact, Mrs. Sutcliffe was convinced it *was* you until she realized she could see right through her."

"Claire," Evelyn said.

"But your sister isn't a wraith, is she?" Mr. Skelton asked.

Evelyn thought back to the vicious animal Claire had become when she attacked her. No, her sister was no wraith. She felt the scratches on her neck and face. Tender, raw, stinging. And then there was Claire's skin... Whatever had caused that? Could it be consuming her body?

"I daresay we shall know more in time," Mr. Skelton said. "I had better take my leave of you now. I do hope you will soon be quite recovered, Miss Wainwright."

"Thank you," Evelyn said, wondering yet again why her neighbor's words seemed sorely at odds with the tone in which he uttered them.

Matthew saw him out.

"You realize this will be all over the village?" he said with a smile as he returned to her side.

Evelyn gave him a questioning look.

"Two single people of the opposite sex alone in a cottage together. The old ladies will be clacking their knitting needles."

"Claire," Evelyn said, pointing upstairs.

"True. They don't know she isn't up there. Come to that, I'll go and search for her now. Are you all right if I leave you alone?"

Evelyn nodded and smiled. She was glad he had offered to look for Claire. Despite what had happened between them, she was still her sister and in danger.

Matthew left, and Evelyn closed her eyes, exhausted.

"You didn't think I'd let him find me, did you?"

Evelyn's eyes snapped open.

Claire stood in front of her, a look of hatred on her face.

Evelyn tried to stand, but her body – still too weak after the battering it had received – wouldn't support her. She sank down again.

Claire sneered at her. "How does it feel, dear sister? To know you are the weak one and I am the stronger of us now?"

"Why are you doing this? What has happened to you?"

"Found your voice again, I see. Even if it is a pitiful squeak. I am doing it because I can. Because he whom I serve has given me the power. Branwell showed me the way. He shared the truth with me."

"What truth?"

Claire stared upward as if in prayer. "*Qui vitam in proxima saecula cupiunt eum adsectuentur qui antea est et sempiternam regnat.* Do you know what that means, sister?"

Evelyn had heard it before. It was in the book, and Matthew had translated it. "I know enough to recognize you are in league with the Devil."

Claire laughed. An unpleasant and raucous sound. "The Devil? How little you know, *dear* sister. But you will soon enough. For now, you are coming with me."

CHAPTER FIFTEEN

Evelyn was immediately struck by the coziness of the room, even if too many knickknacks led to an impression of being a trifle overcrowded. The mantelpiece virtually groaned under the weight of silver ornaments, an ornate clock with a glass dome and photographs of people Evelyn didn't recognize. Nor did she recognize the room – or remember how she had arrived here. She had been lying on her settee, her throat burning, and the woman who looked like her sister had threatened her. Then, without warning, she was here. Claire stood a few feet away, watching her every reaction. Evelyn touched her throat and felt the tender bruising.

"Where is this place?" she asked.

"Branwell's room. See?" Claire pointed at a wall covered with sketches, some only half-finished. "This is his work. He has such talent."

Evelyn nodded. They looked like the scribbles of a drunkard, in sharp contrast to a portrait hanging on the wall. An elderly man with white hair sat in profile, his long, elegant fingers curled around a prayer book or maybe a small Bible.

"Reverend Patrick Brontë, Branwell's father. An excellent likeness, don't you think?"

"I wouldn't know. I never met the gentleman and neither did you."

Claire laughed. An unpleasant, grating sound that set Evelyn's teeth on edge.

"What's happened to you, Claire?"

"To me? Nothing. To you? Everything."

Evelyn couldn't begin to understand what she meant. She only knew the woman standing in front of her was a stranger.

The door opened, and a man of medium stature, reddish-brown hair and a certain swagger entered.

"Ah, Branwell," Claire said, going to him and taking his hand. "You haven't been properly introduced to my sister, have you? This is Evelyn. Evelyn, meet Branwell Brontë. My husband."

"Your...husband?"

Branwell smiled, and his face transformed. His eyes narrowed until they were no more than slits. His nose peeled back, disappearing into his face, leaving only two small holes. He reached out his hand, and Evelyn recoiled from the sight of peeling skin, reptilian-like claws and scales and the overwhelming stench of sulfur.

All the while, Claire laughed. Louder and louder. "You may as well give in, sister. He has you. The master has you."

★　　★　　★

"Evelyn. Evelyn. Wake up."

Matthew's voice, a hand on her shoulder, shaking her. Evelyn opened her eyes to the familiar surroundings of her cottage drawing room. She put her hand to her head. "I had the nightmare to end all nightmares."

"You sounded like it. I came back, and you were thrashing around on the sofa."

Evelyn tried to clear the fog in her head. "Any sign of Claire?"

"No one has seen her. I'll check upstairs again in case she came back."

He left her and returned moments later. "Nothing. It's as if she simply vanished."

"Not for the first time."

"No." Matthew eyed her curiously. "How long has she had this fixation with Branwell Brontë?"

"Ever since we were children. We read prodigiously, and any books by the Brontës were always our favorites. Then we started to learn about them as people and Claire decided Branwell had become her favorite, even though he didn't write any books. Well, not as an adult anyway."

"There is a theory he wrote *Wuthering Heights*."

"We heard that too, but we dismissed it."

"Why? It sounds perfectly plausible to me."

"Have you ever read *Wuthering Heights*, Matthew?"

"Yes. Most of it anyway. I did grow a little tired of Cathy's selfish ways."

"Do you honestly believe a man could have captured that quite as effectively as the author of that book?"

"I can see we are going to have to agree to differ, because I detected a distinctly masculine tone in the story. I find it hard to believe a parson's daughter who had never been much further than her own front door could have written something quite so racy."

"But Emily Brontë ventured much further. She lived in Brussels with her sister Charlotte for a time."

"At school."

"True, but it expanded her mind. They were a highly intelligent family. Precociously intelligent, in fact. They wrote tiny books as children and invented their own worlds."

"Northangerland and Glass Town."

"That's right."

"Rather like your Calladocia."

Evelyn's breath caught in her throat. He knew about Calladocia? But if that were the case, was he...? "How did you know about that?"

Matthew smiled. "I know a little more than you think, Evelyn."

His tone unnerved her, and her skin prickled. "How do you know about Calladocia?"

"When we were in the house. The manuscript you picked up, the one you said you and your sister were working on. All those loose sheets. I saw what was written on them. Some of it anyway."

Evelyn sighed, relieved to hear a simple explanation for a change. "I see. Yes, you're right. Claire and I created Calladocia when we were children, and, rather like the Brontës, we continue to add little adventures from time to time."

"Involving Lady Mandolyne, I presume?"

"Sometimes. Yes. She is mainly Claire's character. I have my own." She remembered the completed manuscript. "Perhaps I should say I *had* my own. There seems little point in continuing with it now."

"Have you ever thought of writing something on your own?"

"No, I haven't." Strange, but until he suggested it, she had never considered writing without Claire.

"It would be the natural progression, though, wouldn't it? I mean, if you're following in the footsteps of the Brontës."

"But we're not. Not consciously."

"Aren't you? It seems to me to be exactly what you are doing."

Evelyn didn't like the way the conversation was heading. "Can we concentrate on Claire, please? My sister is missing again."

"Are you quite sure?"

"What do you mean 'am I sure'?" Evelyn felt her anger rising. What was this? An interrogation? "Of course she's missing. She isn't here, and I don't know where she's gone."

"That seems to happen all too frequently, don't you think?"

"I don't know what you mean."

Matthew inhaled deeply. "All right, Evelyn. I apologize. You're correct, of course. We must set about finding your sister."

"I'm worried she's been dragged back into that awful house."

"Surely she wouldn't be stupid enough to go out there by herself?"

"She might not have had any choice. Something is parading itself as Branwell Brontë and sucking her into its world. I'm convinced of it, and it's dragging us in with it."

"Interesting you should say that, because the professor has a similar theory." Matthew removed an envelope from his inside pocket and opened it. "This letter arrived earlier. He must have worked on the book during the night and written his response first thing this morning. He says, 'I have found a most curious section, which appears to relate to Miss Wainwright and her sister. Like you, I am experiencing changes within the book itself. It is as if it is a living thing. Roughly translated, it says the spirit of one shall enter the body of another. The two shall become one, as once they were. The one who shall remain will follow the master. It is written and cannot be undone. Though she may fight, she cannot prevail. The one who is inside her will push her onwards. It is written and it shall be.' He goes on to say, 'That section has appeared in the book since the last time I looked at it. Another illustration has appeared too. I think you should see it. Please be advised I shall arrive in Thornton Wensley tomorrow afternoon. I shall make my own way to your cottage and would be grateful if Miss Evelyn Wainwright also attends.'"

"Again he doesn't include Claire."

Matthew hesitated. He seemed to be about to say something else but settled for, "No, he doesn't. But as we don't know where she is at this moment, then that is probably no bad thing. Maybe the illustration will help us."

"The book is evil, Matthew. How can it possibly help us?"

"By making us aware of what is going on. You heard what the professor said and what we also know to be true. The book is sentient. It is able to adapt to changing situations."

"I still say it's like a cat playing with a mouse. It dangles a tantalizing amount of information before us and then snaps shut."

"Let's see what the professor has to show us. In the meantime, try not to worry too much about Claire. She'll turn up. Right now she's probably somewhere perfectly safe."

"I hope you're right, Matthew, but I can't help worrying. You didn't see her as I did the last time. I am convinced she is possessed. Whatever attacked me...whatever was in the same room as me, it wasn't my sister, and I want her back."

★   ★   ★

Professor Mapplethorpe rocked a little on his small feet. His pipe lay in his top pocket, and the book lay open on Matthew's dining table.

"This is the illustration I was referring to. No sign of it when I first looked at that section, but now, here it is."

Evelyn and Matthew looked down at the figures, clearly depicted in a Victorian room. Evelyn gasped and jumped back.

Matthew caught her arm. "Whatever's the matter, Evelyn?"

"I've seen that room. In a nightmare I had. I was there."

Matthew and the professor looked more closely at the picture.

Matthew straightened. "You're not in the picture now."

"No, but look. It's Claire, and she's wearing a wedding ring. The other character is Branwell Brontë." Evelyn stepped back. The sight before her revolted her.

"That creature is hardly a man," the professor said. "He doesn't have hands; he has claws, and the eyes are those of a reptile."

"And that's what he became in my nightmare. One minute Claire introduced him as her husband, and the next he transformed into…" She pointed at the engraving.

"She has a curious quality about her," the professor said. "Look, Matthew."

He bent lower. "Yes, I see it now."

"What?" Evelyn asked.

Matthew took a few steps sideways. "Come and see for yourself."

Evelyn took the few steps to the table and looked down. There Claire stood, smiling broadly, gazing proudly at the monster she called her husband. But, worse still, Evelyn could see the design on the wallpaper behind her. "I can see straight through her. She has no substance."

The professor took his pipe out of his pocket and began to fill it with tobacco. "And did she appear like that in your dream?"

"No. At least, I don't think so."

The professor nodded.

"What does it mean?" Matthew asked.

"I think Evelyn knows."

"I haven't the faintest idea."

"Oh, I agree you don't realize you know, but you do. It will come to you in time. I am confident of that."

"But what about Claire? Is she in danger? Where is she?"

The professor lit his pipe. He took so long over it Evelyn's fingers itched with the desire to wrench it out of his hand and throw it on the floor. Finally he spoke.

"I don't think you need to worry over your sister, Miss Wainwright. I am perfectly sure she is out of harm's way."

"But she's with that...that...thing." Evelyn stabbed her finger on the figure and winced at the shock hitting her with the force of a thunderbolt.

"Yes, it's probably wise not to do that," Professor Mapplethorpe said. "Remember, this book isn't like any other. It senses. It feels and responds. As for the creature with your sister, it won't harm her."

"How can you be so sure?"

"Because it's not her it wants."

"Who then?"

"Why, you, of course, Miss Wainwright. It's always been you."

Evelyn swallowed. "Why would you say that, Professor? How can you possibly know?"

The professor tapped the book with his pipe stem. "It's all in here. Down to the last detail."

"You're not suggesting the book mentions me by name?"

"Oh, no. Not at all. But the description is obvious. The plan was laid a long time ago. Many years before you came here. Before the two of you met. Finding The Garden of Bewitchment in your uncle's attic, Matthew, was no coincidence. You were meant to find it there."

"Really?" Matthew sounded as shocked as Evelyn felt.

"Most assuredly."

"But how did my uncle come to have it in the first place?"

"That is one question for which I have no answer. I have theories but no definite conclusion."

"And what would your theories be?" Matthew asked.

"Someone gave it to him. Someone connected to the book. From then on a chain of events was set in motion."

"But how do we break this chain?" Evelyn asked.

The professor sighed. "I'm afraid I don't have the answer to that either. As far as I can tell it will be difficult if not impossible to do so."

Evelyn clasped her hands tightly. "Then there is no hope, is there?"

"There is always hope, my dear," the professor said. "You've seen how the book changes to reflect the current state of affairs. It reacts as circumstances alter. Maybe that is how we can eliminate you from the danger it poses."

"My sister—"

The professor leaned over to Evelyn. "You mustn't worry about your sister. She is in no danger." He glanced over at Matthew, who had a bemused look on his face. The professor nodded once. "I must ask you, Miss Wainwright, have you ever been treated by a psychiatrist?"

"A psychiatrist? Never. What would I need a psychiatrist for?"

"Don't get upset, Evelyn," Matthew said, "The professor is only trying to help."

"But I don't understand. What in the world would I be doing seeing a psychiatrist?"

"Because you are not well, my dear," the professor said gently, straightening up.

"Not well? I am perfectly well apart from all this worry over Claire and everything that has been happening. And don't try to tell me I made it all up, because Matthew has been through a number of these experiences with me."

"I don't deny that," Professor Mapplethorpe said. "They certainly happened. The Garden of Bewitchment exists, and Squire Monkton is inextricably bound up with it. I am talking about something else entirely."

"Such as?" Evelyn knew she sounded defensive, but he had taken her completely by surprise. Mental illness? No, she was of sound mind and body. No question of that.

Matthew was watching her closely. Too closely for Evelyn's liking. Not for the first time, his expression was impossible to read, and when he spoke, his words did nothing to reassure her.

"It couldn't do any harm, Evelyn, could it?"

Before she could respond, the professor spoke. "I think that's enough for today. You are tired, and the stress is almost overwhelming. Now is not the time to pursue this further."

"You can't leave it like this. I need to know why you think I need a psychiatrist."

"Simply because you are not well. Miss Wainwright, I don't believe you have been well for some considerable time. Many years, in fact. You are aware Matthew here possesses a small box, the contents of which I understand you are most anxious to be made aware."

"You know about the box?"

"Of course."

Evelyn looked from one to the other. Matthew avoided her eyes. "What is going on here? I seem to be the only one who hasn't got a clue."

"Miss Wainwright, I told you earlier. All the events, your meeting with Matthew, the discovery of The Garden of Bewitchment, the world you created in your stories, Squire Monkton, Matthew's Uncle Mortimer, Branwell Brontë – all are linked together, and all are contained within the book."

"Yes, I understand that now."

"I am aware of the contents of the small box because it's mine."

"Yours?" Evelyn and Matthew exclaimed together.

"But how?" Matthew asked. "A friend gave it to me."

"The same friend who pointed you in my direction. Nicholas Lancaster."

"Yes, but—"

"I gave it to Nicholas when he was an undergraduate, with

instructions for him to give it to you for safekeeping. The box must never be opened, and you were not to know what was in it. Nicholas told you wherever you went you were to bury it in ground off your property. The box is made of gold, silver, copper and lead."

"Just like the book's cover," Evelyn said.

"Precisely."

"I know it's heavy for its size," Matthew said.

"You buried it as Nicholas directed?"

"Wherever I have gone, it has accompanied me. He was so adamant I must follow his instructions to the letter, and I owed him a big favor."

The professor puffed on his pipe. "And why did you owe him such a favor?"

"He saved my life. I was about nineteen at the time, and we were messing about on the river when I slipped and fell in. My foot twisted in some weeds, and the harder I pulled, the more they dragged me down. He dived in and saved me. The current was so strong he was nearly swept away more than once, but he dived underwater and released my foot."

"A strange accident as I believe you are normally a strong swimmer?" The professor puffed at his pipe.

"Yes, it was rather odd. As I say, I was dragged down, further and further as if the weeds were actually pulling me."

"Which indeed they were. Not long afterwards, he asked you to look after the box, didn't he?"

"A few weeks later. He said he needed to give it to someone he could trust never to let him down."

"Admirable qualities in a friend. Did he explain why it had to be buried in ground off your property?"

"Not really. He asked me to trust him. I thought it an unusual stipulation, but I went along with it. After all, it was no trouble for me."

"Where is the box now?"

"I originally buried it up near some crags on the moor, but I recognized that peat bog is unstable. I could have lost the box there, so I dug it up and buried it in the churchyard, too close to an existing gravestone to be disturbed when a new grave was dug."

"And you have never opened the box?"

"How could I? I don't have a key."

The professor reached into his top pocket and produced a small silver key on a chain. "Fortunately I do. Tomorrow morning I should like you to dig it up and bring it here. I believe Miss Wainwright will be most interested in what is inside it as it concerns her directly."

"Me? But how?"

"All in good time. Now have a good rest this evening, my dear. Tomorrow will be a busy day but, with any luck, a fruitful one."

Evelyn was not reassured by the serene smile on the professor's face, nor his words. "And what about Claire?"

"There is nothing for you to worry about. She is perfectly safe."

He kept repeating that reassurance, but how could he possibly know?

Evelyn left and wandered home.

Alone in her cottage, she sat, deep in thought while the shadows lengthened and night fell.

Eventually she stirred herself and lit the oil lamps before drawing the curtains.

Unprepared for the face that stared in at her, she screamed and jumped back. In a flash it vanished, leaving her trembling and shaking. But for one second, she had recognized that face. It hadn't morphed or been cloaked in shadow. It hadn't taken on a reptilian hue.

But it *had* been the image of Branwell Brontë.

CHAPTER SIXTEEN

With shaking hands, she poured herself a small brandy, downed it in one and poured another.

He had looked exactly like the man in her nightmare before he had transformed into the reptilian creature. The same as had appeared in the book before it too had taken on the features of the Todeswurm. But in the illustration, Claire had appeared transparent. Did Evelyn really need a psychiatrist? The professor seemed to think so, and Matthew appeared all too ready to go along with his suggestion. Evelyn shivered when she remembered newspaper reports she had read of the tortures these doctors put their hapless sufferers through. She had heard some even bored holes in their patients' heads to let out whatever demons lurked inside. Evelyn poured herself another drink.

She wasn't used to drinking brandy, and it made her head swirl. She must lie down. Try to get some sleep. Maybe when she knew what the box contained, things would start to make sense.

She swayed a little as she made her way up the stairs, clinging on to the bannister for dear life.

Once in her bedroom, she undressed, leaving her clothes in an untidy heap on the floor. Most uncharacteristic of her. She was normally so fastidious, a stickler for putting things back where they belonged as soon as they were done with. Claire was the untidy one. Claire...

Evelyn slipped on her nightdress and pulled back the covers. She climbed wearily into bed and fell asleep almost before her head hit the pillow.

★   ★   ★

She didn't know what woke her. In the pitch dark, she reached for the candle at her bedside. She struck a match, the dim glow barely penetrating the shadows. Surely they were darker, even denser tonight?

"Good evening, Evelyn."

Evelyn caught her breath.

He stood at the foot of her bed. Branwell.

"Don't be alarmed," he said. "I want to show you something."

The room shimmered. Evelyn rubbed her eyes with her free hand. She must still be asleep and dreaming. But she knew she wasn't. A faint headache served as a reminder of the brandy she had drunk. And Branwell Brontë was standing at the foot of her bed.

But then, in the next moment, she had been transported to the moor. In her nightclothes. The wind whistled past her cheeks, but she felt no cold. Branwell stood beside her.

"Take my hand," he said, offering his.

Evelyn shied away. "No. You're not real. None of this is real."

"It's as real as you are. As real as your sister is. My wife."

"That's not true. It can't be true. You're dead, and my sister—"

"Your sister. I shall take you to her."

The moor faded, and they were in the garden of Squire Monkton's house. The tangled weeds, overgrown trees, exactly as she remembered them. Fear churned in her gut.

"No. I won't go back in there."

"As if you had a choice. Of course you will. You want to see your sister, don't you?"

"Of course I want to see her, but not here. She mustn't be here either. It's too dangerous. Who are you, and what do you want with us?"

"You know who I am. I'm Branwell. Your brother-in-law, it would appear." He laughed.

"Take me back."

"Not until you have seen your sister. She has asked for you, and I must keep my wife happy."

"This is all wrong. Lies. Lies." Evelyn put her head in her hands, willing the scene to go away. Willing herself back in her bedroom. Safe.

Branwell took her arm and frog-marched her in through the ruined door and into the library. A woman stood, reading a book, her back toward Evelyn.

"See, Claire. I have brought your sister to see you. Just as you asked."

The woman turned. Evelyn screamed.

Claire's blackened face looked as if she had been severely burned. Her dress was filthy, covered in soot, but even more shocking, her eyes burned red, and, as Evelyn watched, she became less solid, less three-dimensional, and the shelves of books became visible behind her. Evelyn could see straight *through* her sister.

"No, no, no. This can't be happening!"

Branwell took his place next to Claire, raised her scorched, translucent hand to his lips and, without a word, lifted her in his arms as if she was weightless.

Under Evelyn's horrified, tearful gaze, she began to crumple like burned paper. Her body crackled and disintegrated in Branwell's arms, became ash and floated to the floor like gray snow.

"Claire!" Evelyn screamed, rushing toward her, heedless of Branwell, who laughed uproariously as he brushed flakes of ash off his jacket.

"What have you done?" Evelyn demanded, shaking him by the collar.

Branwell stopped laughing. A terrible transformation started with his eyes. The reptilian stare returned, and his claws dug into Evelyn's shoulders.

"It will be as if she never existed," he said and flung Evelyn across the room. She fell to the floor, hitting her head. Blackness descended.

*　　*　　*

"Evelyn...Evelyn."

Matthew's voice drifted toward her through a fog. Evelyn opened her eyes. She was back in her cottage, slumped on the floor of her hall. The front door stood wide open, and Matthew and the professor were bending over her.

"She's had a shock," the professor said. "Get her some hot, sweet tea. Plenty of sugar, Matthew, if you please, but first, let's get her onto the settee."

As the bright morning light streamed through the windows, Evelyn felt as if her limbs had become boneless and incapable of holding her up. Matthew and Professor Mapplethorpe eased her down onto the sofa, and she leaned back against the cushions. Matthew went off to make tea.

"Oh, Professor. It was awful. Awful. I don't know what to make of it."

"Tell me exactly what happened."

"It must have been a dream, I suppose, but it felt so real. All of it has seemed so real."

"That's because it was, my dear. Now, begin at the beginning."

Evelyn told her tale, haltingly. As she explained about Branwell she thought how preposterous it must sound to anyone who had not experienced what she had, but the professor sat through it all, occasionally tapping his teeth with the stem of his pipe, but otherwise silent.

"Then I heard Matthew's voice," she concluded.

Matthew returned with the tea, the cup gently steaming with the fragrant Ceylon blend. Evelyn accepted it gratefully.

"I heard most of that from the kitchen," Matthew said, sitting down. "You must have been terrified."

"It's what happened to Claire. I mean, I know it can't have happened, but to watch your sister..." She could not continue.

Matthew touched her hand. "It's all right, Evelyn."

The professor frowned and Evelyn shivered. "You don't agree with Matthew, Professor? You think something has happened to my sister?"

"Oh, no, not at all. Certainly not in the way you mean. Miss Wainwright, once again, I urge you to see a psychiatrist."

"Oh, no, not that again."

"Matthew, can you persuade her? It is most important."

"But why?" Evelyn asked. "Why is it important?"

"Because," the professor said, "with the right treatment, you would see things differently, and that is critical for you."

"You clearly suspect something, but you won't tell me what. Without an explanation I refuse to consult any medical practitioner and certainly not one who will try to get inside my head. Possibly even literally."

The professor shook his head, sighed and turned to Matthew. "I'm afraid there is only one course of action open to me. Please go and retrieve the box and bring it to me now. Let's not waste any more time."

Matthew nodded and left them.

"Miss Wainwright, I had hoped you would agree to seek medical help before I revealed the contents of the box, but, as it is, you leave me with no choice."

"I don't understand how you can possess any information on me. We had never met until a couple of days ago."

"But, as I told you, that is irrelevant. As I have told you before, all that has happened was laid down many years ago. Some of it even before any of us was born. Fate has dealt you a curious hand, a dangerous hand, even. How you play it will be critical."

"It's not as if I am anyone of importance. I am Evelyn Wainwright, spinster, living in a small village in the West Riding of Yorkshire with my sister. Why should that make me the center of so much intrigue?"

"Don't dismiss yourself so easily, Miss Wainwright."

★   ★   ★

Twenty minutes later, the door opened.

The professor stirred. "Ah. Matthew. Do you have it?"

Matthew handed over a small box, smeared with damp earth. "I'm sorry I haven't had time to clean it off."

"It is of no consequence." The professor produced the key and inserted it into the lock. It turned easily, and the box sprang open.

Inside lay some folded sheets of paper. The professor selected one and unfolded it. "I want you to listen without interruption, Miss Wainwright. Every word of this applies to you."

He began to read. "'The subject is a Miss Evelyn Wainwright, a fourteen-year-old girl from Sugden Heath in the West Riding of Yorkshire. She has been referred to me for consultation following a number of years when she has been suffering from delusions. Her parents reported these first started when she was approximately four years old and insisted she had a twin sister called Claire, even though Evelyn is – and always has been – an only child.'"

"But—"

"Miss Wainwright, please."

Evelyn closed her mouth. What was this drivel? Only child? Chicanery. It had to be.

Matthew cleared his throat. "Professor, I don't understand. I can vouch for Claire's existence. I have met her, spoken to her. I—"

The professor raised his hand. "Matthew, I urge you to let me finish reading out this letter."

Matthew nodded quickly, but he looked far from comfortable.

The professor continued: "'At first her parents considered her fantasy to be that of a child with an imaginary friend, common enough and something she would naturally grow out of in a year or two. This did not happen. So strong was Evelyn's belief in her imaginary twin sister, she was even heard having conversations with her, in two different voices. The personality of the other "sister" was distinctly different to that of Evelyn. Where the real girl tidied her room and took a great pride in her appearance, it would appear Claire was untidy, constantly leaving her clothes and toys lying around and proving something of a burden to Evelyn. Now, with her child at the age of puberty, her mother in particular is noticing differences in the relationship between the two. They occasionally have terrible rows, overheard by servants, as well as the parents. Evelyn has been known to emerge from her bedroom, crying, her hair a mess and insisting Claire has pulled it. On more than one occasion, she has appeared, with her dress ripped, in places it must have been difficult for her to reach. At their wits' end, Mr. and Mrs. Wainwright have asked me to examine their daughter with a view to determining the state of her mental health.'"

The professor folded over the sheet of paper.

"Utter nonsense," Evelyn said. "Claire is as real as you or I. Matthew told you. He has met her. Where did you get this from, anyway?"

"The letter is signed Edward Skelton."

"Skelton? Not Mr. Skelton, our neighbor?"

"The very same."

"But...how?"

It couldn't be true. None of it. "I need you to explain, Professor." Looking at Matthew, at the way he yet again avoided her eyes, Evelyn said, "You knew about this, didn't you? Is this why you came here? To spy on me? To try to trick me with this nonsense? What are you after? My money? You want to have me committed to an insane asylum and then, somehow, get hold of my money. This is all one gigantic confidence trick."

Matthew reached for her hand, but she pulled away. "Evelyn, please. I'm as confused by this as you are. Professor, what is this nonsense? Is Evelyn right? Is someone after her money?"

The professor rummaged in the box once more. "I can assure you this is no ruse to extort money from Miss Wainwright, although I can understand why it would seem like that to you. Mr. Skelton was quite a renowned psychiatrist in his day. It is, as you may know, a relatively new and misunderstood profession, but he has played his part on debunking a lot of nonsense. You have yourself played an unconscious role here." He nodded toward Evelyn, who bristled.

"Oh, have I really? And as for this ridiculous assertion that I invented Claire…" Words failed her, and she shook her head.

The professor calmly opened another sheet of paper. "These are notes from a series of sessions with you when you were fourteen."

Matthew stared, his lips slightly parted.

"But if I did go through these so-called sessions," Evelyn said, "why can't I remember any of them? As far as I am aware, the first time I met Mr. Skelton was in the lane outside here after we moved in."

"You don't remember, because Mr. Skelton put you in a state of deep hypnosis, as you will hear." Professor Mapplethorpe started to read. "'The patient, Evelyn Wainwright, appeared agitated and unwilling to cooperate at first. She insisted her sister was at home waiting for her and would be concerned if she did not return within the hour. As yet, I have made no progress in helping her to realize her sister is a myth created by her own imagination. After some persuasion, she did tell me she and Claire were writing stories together and that Claire had formed a strong affection for Branwell Brontë of the famous literary family. This had been the cause of some friction between them as Evelyn had tried to persuade her "sister" that Branwell couldn't possibly be visiting her as she claimed. She then refused to be questioned further, and I took the decision to induce a state of deep hypnosis in order to attempt to gain access to whatever trigger existed in her brain capable of causing such deeply held convictions. I fully realize my action in doing so may leave me open to question, but I have taken the precaution of securing her parents' written agreement to the procedure—'"

Evelyn sprang to her feet. "Stop. Please! I can't hear any more of this. I *won't*. What do you want from me?"

Matthew went to comfort her, but she shrugged him off and turned on him.

"As for you. You're the biggest traitor of them all. I suppose you're going to tell me I made up The Garden of Bewitchment and you went along with me. That it never really happened and I imagined it all."

"No, Evelyn. I'm not. And I haven't a clue what the professor is talking about when it comes to Claire. All I know is I am mixed up in your life because of that damned toy. The first time I met you, I recognized you, but I couldn't tell you at the time. Now I must."

"Recognized me? Where from?"

"All those years ago, in the attic of my uncle's house. You were one of the figures in the drawing room. Remember how you told me, when you found yourself in the doll's house, everything was made of cardboard? Even part of *you* when you touched your foot to the floor of the drawing room. Just for a second or two? And then again, at Monkton Hall. The figures in the dolls' house... We both saw them. One doll for each of us. Me, you, Mr. Skelton even... We are joined together in this in a way I don't understand, but, nevertheless, it's true."

Evelyn stared at him. It seemed every word served only to make things worse. Had she truly gone out of her mind? No. They were up to something. Trying to convince her she was mad. Well, they wouldn't succeed. She would find Claire. Whatever it took.

She wouldn't give Matthew the satisfaction of a reply, and, after a pause, he spoke. "You have distinctive eyes, Evelyn, and the drawing of the figures was so accurate. I never forgot those eyes, and I am looking at them now."

Was he flirting with her? Trying to win her round? She ignored him.

"Miss Wainwright," Professor Mapplethorpe said, "please understand, everybody has acted with the best of intentions. The rest of the information in this box goes on to describe many subsequent sessions between you and Mr. Skelton. Never once did you cooperate, and, in the end, he had to admit defeat, but, for your own protection, he made sure you wouldn't remember what had transpired in his consulting room. You will recall your parents were reluctant to let you leave home. The servants were sworn to secrecy – some more willingly than others, it has to be said. Promises, later fulfilled, of comfortable pensions helped with the more intransigent.

I don't believe the solicitor listed all the bequests at the reading of the will?"

Evelyn continued to stare straight ahead of her.

"Eventually, of course, the one thing your parents couldn't protect you from was their own mortality. They went along with your fantasies while they were alive. I understand from Mr. Skelton that this was an agreement between them. Left to your own devices, you seemed to grow much calmer. The relationship between you and 'Claire' seemed to evolve into a mainly harmonious one. Going out of the house proved problematical, I understand. People used to stare when you went along the street talking to yourself. You grew to dislike the unwarranted attention and to feel uncomfortable living in a large town, hence the move to Thornton Wensley, where, it so happened, Mr. Skelton lived. You gave him quite a shock the first time he saw you."

Matthew coughed. "I know you must feel deceived, Evelyn, but, I can see now, the professor is right. We have all been brought together not through a seemingly impossible series of coincidences but as a result of a carefully orchestrated plan."

Evelyn tensed. "You will forgive me if I find it very hard to swallow. Especially as my sanity has been called into question. In fact, you have, between you, declared me insane."

"But, Miss Wainwright," the professor said, "nothing could be further from the truth. You are most certainly not insane."

"Professor, if someone came to me and said they had been told they had imagined a sister for their entire lifetime, I should believe they were insane."

"Then you would be wrong. Very wrong."

"What would you call it then?"

"Certainly an illness of the mind. An illusion created by an overly active imagination, but insanity?" The professor shook his head. "Never. In all other respects you behave rationally and thoughtfully. You have not been a threat to yourself or anyone around you. With the possible exception of today…"

Evelyn fingered the scratches. He had suggested she had done this to herself. But she couldn't. She wouldn't. Would she?

Matthew cleared his throat. "I still don't understand how the woman I met who called herself Claire could not exist. Granted she looked identical to Evelyn, except a more untidy version perhaps, but I cannot believe she doesn't exist."

"That's because she does. Exist, I mean. In Evelyn's mind she is as real as you or I, and that is how she can present herself as an entirely different personality." The professor addressed himself to Evelyn. "You are categorically not insane, Miss Wainwright. However, I will reiterate. You do need professional help to come to terms with your...condition."

"You are splitting hairs, Professor."

"Evelyn, please," Matthew said. "This is getting us nowhere. Will you at least agree to see a psychiatrist, perhaps one recommended by Mr. Skelton? Then we will know the truth once and for all."

Evelyn looked from one to the other. Did she really have anything to lose? Claire existed. Of course she did. So if a psychiatrist told the professor and Matthew so, they would have to believe them and this nonsense could end right now.

"Very well," she said quietly, staring down at her hands. "But I will not consent to any...operations."

The professor nodded and stood, appearing anxious to leave. "I will arrange an appointment with someone of Mr. Skelton's choosing. It will probably be in Leeds."

"And why would my sister need a psychiatrist?" The voice came from the stairs.

Evelyn caught sight of her as she descended the final step. "Claire!" She dashed over to her. "Where have you been? What happened?" Evelyn gave a silent prayer of thanks. All trace of the beast had gone from her eyes, which now surveyed the astonished men.

"With Branwell. We had work to do. My, we do have some surprised faces here, don't we? Hello, Professor. Matthew, a pleasure to see you again."

"Claire!" he exclaimed and stared at the professor, whose face had blanched.

The two sisters stood, arms interlocked.

"What? Nothing to say, Professor?" Claire's voice held more than a trace of a sneer.

Professor Mapplethorpe blinked at her.

"Where have you been?" Matthew asked.

Claire released herself from her sister and took a few steps closer to the table. "Oh, here and there," she said with a slight wave of her hand. The other hand touched the book. "I see you have managed to keep it here. How useful. Oh, and the famous box. Made from the same combination of metals, with a heavy concentration of iron. They say iron repels the devil, but if that was the case, why would witches make cauldrons from it? No, the devil has plenty of uses for iron and every other metal. Some are forged in hell itself. Like this book." Claire tapped it, and the cover flew open. The pages skipped through until they stopped. She looked down at it. "Another new picture, I see. It's amazing how it does this, isn't it, Ev? Come and see."

Evelyn moved closer until she could see the illustration. She recoiled from it.

Claire laughed. "You should have believed," she said to the professor. "And so should you." She pointed at Evelyn. "My own sister. Blood of my blood. Flesh of my flesh. Bone of my bone." She moved around the table. "Except it's not quite like that, is it, sister?"

"I don't know what you mean." Suddenly fearful, Evelyn backed away as Claire's eyes filled with that other presence.

"You are not flesh, blood and bone, are you?"

"Of course I am."

Claire gave another dismissive wave of her hand. "And, as for you, dear Professor. You are most certainly not what you appear to be."

The professor stood firm. His gaze did not waver, although he must have known what was coming.

"Professor?" Matthew asked. "What is she talking about?"

"Look around you, Matthew," Claire said. "What do you see?"

"The drawing room. In your cottage."

Claire chuckled and turned to Evelyn. "Now it's your turn, Ev. What do you see?"

"What is this all about, Claire? You know perfectly well we are in our cottage."

"Are you sure? Look again. Both of you. The professor can see it already, can't you?"

He nodded slowly but said nothing.

The room was no longer there. She, Claire, Matthew and the professor were standing together in a graveyard in front of a headstone. Evelyn read the words carved on it.

Sacred to the memory of LAWRENCE MAPPLETHORPE born March 13th 1820, died April 30th 1885. A worthy academic and true friend.

Evelyn blinked a few times and closed her eyes. When she opened them, they were all back in the cottage.

"You're..." Matthew struggled to speak.

Claire finished this question for him. "Dead? Oh, yes, that's right, isn't it, Professor?"

The professor spoke quietly. "Yes."

"But that's impossible," Matthew said. "You're here, as alive as I am. My friend recommended you."

"You hadn't seen your friend in some time, had you?" The professor's voice became less distinct by the second and increasingly difficult to make out.

"Not for a long time, I must confess. We studied together."

"You hadn't seen him since those days. You merely wrote to him, and he sent you a letter back. He hasn't seen me in years either. He had no idea I was already cold in my grave."

"But Evelyn and I came to Leeds to consult you, and before that, I saw you on my own. "

The professor held up his hand. "Claire is right, Matthew. I am real to you and to Miss Wainwright. I am also real to Mr. Skelton, but anyone else will simply see a shadow at best, maybe a glimmer of light, but nothing more. As for your trips to see me in Leeds…" He let his words hang in the air. "I am only here because of this book—"

"And the key, Professor," Claire said. "Don't forget the key." She flipped open the box.

"Key?" Evelyn asked.

Claire rummaged under the papers and produced a small silver key. She held it up. "This key. You didn't suppose a pile of old medical notes would warrant such secrecy, did you?"

The professor looked at her, his face crestfallen. "They were never supposed to find it," he said. To Evelyn he seemed to be fading.

"But you must have known we would one day."

"Who are you, Claire?" Matthew asked. "I know who you are pretending to be, but who are you really?"

Claire ignored him. She returned to the book and turned the pages. The key glittered. She opened her fingers and let it fall, where it seemed to melt and become absorbed into the fabric of the book.

"It is done," she said.

"May God have mercy on you all." The professor's voice sounded far away. As Evelyn watched, he dissolved into shadow.

"Professor!" Matthew cried. "Professor!"

"He's gone," Claire said. "He could never succeed."

"Claire, you're my sister, but I feel as if I don't know you at all." Evelyn tried to reach for her, but she slipped out of reach.

"Oh, dear Evelyn. How little you understand. Even less than *him*." She nodded toward Matthew.

"Then help me understand." The façade had been stripped away. The woman standing there so calmly and with so much malevolence dripping from every word was not Claire. She had ceased to exist. An evil entity remained in her place.

"Very well," the creature said. "The book is sacred to the deity known as Dakraska, the Ancient One, who can manifest in many forms, including that of the Todeswurm. Dakraska lives in the halls of the deepest chasm. He appears to few but commands many. He is the creator, the destroyer, the grand manipulator. Long ago, meddling priests tried to bind him. They locked the most mystical parts of the book. Pages that could not be seen again until the key turned up. It was hidden in that box, but now I have put it back where it belongs."

The room began to darken. Evelyn shrank away from the stranger who had been her sister.

"None of this is real," Matthew said, moving closer to her. "Focus your mind on that, Evelyn. None of this is real."

Everything Evelyn had known – her entire world and life, past and present – had been called into question. And now Claire wasn't alone. Branwell had joined her. They stood together, smiling at her.

The book glowed with a golden light. It quickly turned to orange and red. Images appeared to dance off the pages. Words. Pictures. Evelyn saw her likeness weaving and writhing, her face contorted.

She could barely see across the room, and it seemed different. The wind howled, rain lashed down, soaking her instantly. Matthew tried to shield her but to no avail.

Up above a solitary curlew called.

Claire's laughter rang out, and Branwell began to change.

"Dakraska!" Claire cried.

Branwell's skin peeled from his face. Long strips of bloody flesh, soaked by the rain, dripped down his body. His scalp cracked open, and a thick, wormlike creature emerged, its mouth unhinged, revealing an abyss of black foulness. Even through the wind, Evelyn smelled the stench of death and putrefaction.

Weeds clung to Evelyn's legs, tried to climb up her, to drag her down into the muddy mire forming at her feet. She fought against them, ripping them off her. Matthew cried out in agony.

Dakraska discarded the last of Branwell's body. It shriveled and flaked into wet ash. The ground absorbed it instantly, and another weed grew, winding its tendrils upward, as if seeking a new host.

Matthew fell to the ground, choking as a tendril squeezed his throat closed. He put out his hand to Evelyn, his eyes bulging.

Finding strength from somewhere, Evelyn tore herself out of the clutches of the weeds binding her. She went to him and tugged desperately at the weed noose around his neck. It felt tough, rubbery.

Claire watched, a look of amusement on her face. The rain had not touched her, as if she was in some sort of protective cocoon.

Desperation filled Evelyn to the core. "Help him. For pity's sake. You can't do this to him. To me."

Claire said nothing. Dakraska weaved its way closer to Matthew and Evelyn. The overlapping scales were clearly visible, the translucent skin bubbled and spines stood up on its back.

"I will live," Claire said. "But you cannot."

"Why? Claire, why would you do this?"

Matthew fell limp at Evelyn's feet.

Claire sneered. "Your professor was right. You did create me, but I have a life of my own now. I don't need you. There can only be one of us, and it shall be me."

★   ★   ★

It seemed a veil had parted. The rain and wind died down. Matthew and Evelyn were off the moor and in a beautiful garden. The sun shone, birds of every hue fluttered and sang and purple butterflies darted from flower to flower. The scent of honeysuckle and jasmine mingled with roses, and a magnificent house awaited them.

Matthew stood beside Evelyn, apparently unharmed. She felt healed. No trace of the scratches, bruises, soaking wet clothes, strangling weeds.

Matthew took her arm. "Shall we go in?"

Evelyn had nowhere else to go. She knew now. Just as she knew that beyond the garden, in the wood, Dakraska waited. If she and Matthew tried to leave, it would kill them. At least Claire was nowhere to be seen.

The door opened for them, and they entered. "Which room?" Matthew asked.

The sound of the piano echoed through the hall.

"The drawing room."

Arm in arm, they crossed the threshold.

"Oh, Matthew. Look!" Evelyn stared down in dismay at her body, clothed for an instant in a flowing, yellow silk evening dress, only for it to change. No longer silk, just as she had become no longer flesh and blood, bone and sinew. She looked at Matthew. The same thing was happening to him. A short distance across the room, Mr. Skelton gazed sightlessly ahead.

The same as every figure in that room.

Made of cardboard.

Their expressions frozen in time.

EPILOGUE

2020

"Go and play upstairs, Lucy. I can't help it if it's raining." The exasperated mother unpacked shopping and put it away in unfamiliar cupboards.

"But it always rains here. Why couldn't we have gone to Spain for our holidays? Carrie's family *always* goes to Spain."

"Yes," said her father, "and Carrie's family have a Lexus and a six-bedroomed detached house. Now, do as your mother says. Go upstairs and play. There are some board games up there. Under your bed."

Lucy knew when she was beaten. She tightened her ponytail and ran up the stairs of the cottage. Thornton Wensley. Whoever came to Thornton Wensley for their holidays?

She fished out the small pile of games from under the bed and went through them, tossing aside Monopoly and Scrabble before coming across an unfamiliar one. It didn't look like a game at all. More like a toy you put together yourself.

'The Garden of Bewitchment,' she read. Sighing, she tossed that one aside as well. But…how strange. She couldn't have heard tiny cries coming from inside it, could she? As if she had hurt someone when she threw the toy away.

Curiosity got the better of her, and she lifted the lid. Such an amazing assortment of pieces. She took them out one by one, placing them randomly on the bed, until she came to the model of a house. She peered in through the windows, saw a woman seated at a piano and an audience listening to her performance. By the door, a couple stood, their arms linked. The cardboard woman wore a sumptuous yellow dress. Something glittered at the bottom of the box. She picked it up and held it, feeling an unfamiliar surge of energy.

Lucy put the house and the jewel down and picked up the folded board. She opened it up and began to assemble the garden.

In her toy cupboard, a strange book slowly turned its pages and began a new chapter.

ACKNOWLEDGMENTS

Julia Kavan, my friend and fellow writer, read an earlier draft and I am indebted to her for steering me on the right course, as always.

Don D'Auria was, as always, a pleasure to work with as well as everyone at Flame Tree Press who work so hard for us all.

The Brontës, without whom this story wouldn't exist. I just hope they will forgive me! Of the places mentioned in this story, Haworth is, of course, real although I have changed the names of the various hostelries. Of the other locations mentioned, Sugden Heath and Thornton Wensley are products of my imagination, borne of my youth growing up in Halifax in the West Riding of Yorkshire amid the remnants of the 'dark, satanic mills' and the wild, majestic moorland where curlews cried overhead and wind whipped through the heather…

And you, for reading this. Thank you for your support. It means such a lot to me. I hope to entertain you for many more years to come.

FLAME TREE PRESS
FICTION WITHOUT FRONTIERS
Award-Winning Authors & Original Voices

Flame Tree Press is the trade fiction imprint of Flame Tree Publishing, focusing on excellent writing in horror and the supernatural, crime and mystery, science fiction and fantasy. Our aim is to explore beyond the boundaries of the everyday, with tales from both award-winning authors and original voices.

•

Other titles available by Catherine Cavendish:
The Haunting of Henderson Close

Other horror titles available include:
Snowball by Gregory Bastianelli
Thirteen Days by Sunset Beach by Ramsey Campbell
Think Yourself Lucky by Ramsey Campbell
The Hungry Moon by Ramsey Campbell
The Influence by Ramsey Campbell
The House by the Cemetery by John Everson
The Devil's Equinox by John Everson
Hellrider by JG Faherty
The Toy Thief by D.W. Gillespie
One By One by D.W. Gillespie
Black Wings by Megan Hart
The Playing Card Killer by Russell James
The Siren and the Specter by Jonathan Janz
The Sorrows by Jonathan Janz
Castle of Sorrows by Jonathan Janz
The Dark Game by Jonathan Janz
House of Skin by Jonathan Janz
Will Haunt You by Brian Kirk
We Are Monsters by Brian Kirk
Hearthstone Cottage by Frazer Lee
Those Who Came Before by J.H. Moncrieff
Stoker's Wilde by Steven Hopstaken & Melissa Prusi
Creature by Hunter Shea
Ghost Mine by Hunter Shea
Slash by Hunter Shea
The Mouth of the Dark by Tim Waggoner
They Kill by Tim Waggoner

•

Join our mailing list for free short stories, new release details, news about our authors and special promotions:

flametreepress.com